MY
DETECTIVE

OTHER BOOKS BY
JEFFREY FLEISHMAN

Promised Virgins: A Novel of Jihad

Shadow Man

MY
DETECTIVE

Jeffrey Fleishman

**BLACK
STONE**
PUBLISHING

Printed in the United States of America

First edition: 2019
ISBN 978-1-9825-1729-8
Fiction / Mystery & Detective / General

1 3 5 7 9 10 8 6 4 2

CIP data for this book is available from the Library of Congress

Blackstone Publishing
31 Mistletoe Rd.
Ashland, OR 97520

www.BlackstonePublishing.com

For Aaron, Hannah, Barbra, and Ryan

CHAPTER 1

I sneak up from behind, yank his chin, lift the knife. So fast. The blade tugs at first but slides across the throat. His shoulders go slack; his chest softens. His feet do a puppet dance, but I thought there'd be more fight in this wiry rattle of a man. I lower the blade. He falls. Wobbly, slow, spastic. Facedown, blood spreading from his throat like a blown scarf. Knock-kneed, pigeon-toed. One arm stretched like a swimmer's, the other like a hinge. I kneel and wipe the blade on his jacket. I sheath it and look around. A thin wind and a whirl of papers. The sidewalk on this stretch of homeless territory is empty except for two shadows more than a block away. They can't see me beneath the broken streetlight outside the Chaplin Hotel. I'm black as a crow's wing: Lycra tights, long-sleeved running top, ski mask, gloves.

I put my ear to his mouth—silence—and brush back his hair. His profile hardens against the concrete. The conceit he brimmed with in life slithers away. It is splendid and strangely sacred, and I think that in the last beat, in the final act, he becomes almost human again—a sad, vulnerable creature succumbing to eternity. What power in this moment. What joy. I am in no hurry. I am strong. Deliberate. Precise as an equation. None of me will be found. I rise, glimpse the ragged corner, and slip the knife into my waistband.

I walk toward the neon, pulling off my mask and gloves, gliding up Main, turning left toward Spring, anonymous among downtown revelers, as if strolling home from a late workout at Planet Fitness. Voices, footsteps, music. I'm shaking a little but not so anyone can see. My pulse surges, my brain like ice. I breathe in and think that a killing, like a cathedral or a bridge in the Balkans, can be marveled at for the intricacy of its design. I walk for a while and veer off Spring back into the darkness, heading past tents and vagabond murmurs to my garage, rented from a peculiar man with a lisp who prefers burner phones and cash, where my Beemer waits and my strapless Herve Leger hangs on the wall.

The air cools.

I'd prepared for months, slicing with knives through rump roasts and working out on weights and treadmills, banging and heaving a punching bag. My trainer, Javier, a bulked Nicaraguan illegal who raps about Latina brides and car fins on the eastside, wiped sweat from my face last week and told me, "Dylan, you hit like you wanna hurt the world."

If he only knew.

My six-foot frame—my Croatian father taught me to embrace it—is imposing. "For a girl." That's what they'd say when I was a kid: "You're tall for a girl." Why the qualifier? Statistically speaking, it was accurate, but it bothered me until I realized that those who fit differently into the world were held to a crueler light. What a shame. But back in my tennis days, I moved with the grace and wonder of a prayer; my forehands flashed like comets. I am still a cry of nature. Michael Gallagher was so speckish and puny in my grasp. My only flaw is the chipped fingernail in my glove. Careless. It could have ripped through the leather and left a clue. Note to self: a killer can afford no vanity.

I arrive at the garage and close the door. I slip out of my clothes and toss them in a drum. I douse them with lighter fluid and strike a match. I stand naked before the flame, watching it rise. The smoke stings at first; the scent foul. But after a moment, the fabrics glow in crystalline embers and vanish to ash. The fire makes shadows on the wall. It seems ancient, erotic, to be alone and naked against the flicker and the brick, as if in a purification or some longed-for reckoning. I close my eyes. How lovely. The warmth. I wash my face, neck, breasts, arms, and hands. I pour alcohol over the knife, clean and wrap it in a towel, and slide it behind a loose cinder block that I push back into place. The fire dies. I step into my dress and hear sirens in the distance. My detective—he doesn't yet know he's my detective, my secret crush—will soon be heading toward what I've left for him. I put on my heels, start the car, and smile like a naughty cat.

Suddenly, though, I cry. I grip the wheel and cry.

CHAPTER 2

"Perfect cut."

"Ear to ear."

"Watch the blood."

"Witnesses?"

"Not likely. Canvassing now. You got here fast, Detective."

"I live downtown."

"No commute? Nice."

I snap on gloves and bend down. Death moves fast through the body. Skin cools; tissue retracts; clothes seem to grow. I reach into the guy's pocket for a wallet.

"Rules out robbery," says the uniform, a young, scrubbed guy named P. Hanson. "Who is he?"

I open it. Bundle of cash, rows of credit cards. All high grade.

"Shine the light here. Michael J. Gallagher. DOB 1980."

"Expensive haircut. What's he do?"

"I'm looking."

I finger deeper into the wallet.

"Business card says he's an architect. License says he lives in Coldwater Canyon. Have somebody run it."

The uniform turns away to make the call. I keep my eye on him and quickly reach into Michael J. Gallagher's jacket: change, stick of gum, museum ticket, and a wedding ring, which I slip into my pocket. It's a secret thing I do, like collecting souvenir spoons from states traveled through, before a body is bagged. I take a piece from the fallen—not in any weird, fetishistic way, but to know them, never to forget the moment I saw them lying oddly shaped and gone forever.

"What's he doing down here, you think?" says P. Hanson, stepping back toward me.

"Looking at the buildings. Meeting a friend. Lost."

"Hooker, more likely. We chased most of them out, but a few still run rooms in this place. Kinky shit."

"Know your territory, huh?"

"Dangerous vibe down here, Detective. Primal. A lot of guys are into that kind of thing. Sex, degradation, being bad—all sorts of wacky shit. Twisted fantasies. No question. You got one?" P. Hanson laughs, but I'm not in the mood. "The Hotel Cecil is a couple of blocks up," he says. "Some nutjob serial killer holed up there in the eighties. They made a movie or some shit about it. A song too. It'll all be boutique soon. The Renaissance is coming, Detective. Whole city's changing. Gangbangers gone, clearing out the homeless. Start-up geeks and trust-fund babies now. LA's hip, man."

"I thought Pittsburgh was hip."

"Fuck Pittsburgh."

"You should run a tour bus. You've got an interesting way of looking at things."

"I'm more of a poet."

He smiles and starts reciting Kafkaesque verse about cockroaches and candy wrappers. I can't tell whether he's being a wiseass, or really thinks he's a poet. No trace of joke or irony lifts off him. At least he didn't say he was an actor or a yogi. You get all kinds in the department these days. I wave my hand and cut P. Hanson off. Why can't cops just be cops? The white-suit guys arrive. Swabbers and collectors, a photographer, more uniforms, fire guys, ambulance guys—all kinds of guys clocking overtime. The machinery of the crime scene unit unfolds under pop-up lights like a little army gathered around doom. I'm still warm from the scotch I left sitting on the bar at the Little Easy. The buzz is fading, though, slow, like when day fizzes into night. A small crowd peers in from the edges, mostly young, pierced, tattooed women in ripped shirts and black boots, floating in marijuana haze toward some club or that Mexican place over on Olive Street.

"Hey," yells a doped-up crazy leaning on a construction fence across the street, "is this for real or are you filming something? I can never tell. Like last time I was down here, Mark Harmon was running around with a gun and gobbed up in makeup. Another time, it was like Ice Cube. Or maybe it was Snoop. Who can tell anymore? It's megaconfusing shit going on."

The moon is full.

"It's the wrath," comes another voice, from under a pile of blankets in the darkness. "Pestilence upon the land. Anyone seen my dog?"

My phone rings.

"Hey, Carver, Ortiz here. Ran that name you just sent. The stiff is apparently some rich schmuck architect. Big political donor. Friends in the mayor's office. Proceed with caution."

Click.

Ortiz, my boss. Short bursts of useful information, then silence. I step to the corner and look heavenward. I pat myself for a cigarette and remember I quit. I'd love another pour from barman Lenny, though. I'm looking at a long night. Planes bound for LAX loop and glitter in winds high above the San Gabriels. Cranes rise in the west, and to the south, a gray-black hangs over the 110 beyond Hawthorne and Compton. Neighborhoods reach into one another and stretch through canyons toward the ocean, on and on, like the flash and tremor of a dream, and somewhere deep in the earth, a fault slips into a brokenness waiting to rise, nobody knows when.

My mind drifts lately. I don't know why. Could be age, but I'm not so old. I take a breath, close my eyes and open them. Flashes scatter before me, a city of ghosts bright as paper lanterns, all demanding justice so they can go on their way. To be requited. That's what they want. A piece of truth to prove they were more than atoms and bone, voices and capillaries. I wonder if these flashes are digressions, unwanted fleeting asides, but a man cannot help what he sees. I close and open my eyes again. They're gone. I light a match, shake it out, and toss it to the ground—a quit-smoking ritual I picked up from a cop in Vice. I stare into the night, listening and watching shadows, wondering what infinitesimal trace will lead me to the doer.

"Hey, Detective!" yells P. Hanson. "Here's the la-a-ady he was seeing shortly before, you know …"

A woman in a kimono steps forward.

"I need a lawyer?"

"You do it?"

"'Course I didn't do it. He was a regular."

"Let's go upstairs and talk."

I follow her over the tile floor into a foyer, past a streaked mirror and a little front desk where, in better times, a night manger would have been perched with a liverwurst sandwich, a beer, and a racing form. The hooker leads me into an old sliding-gate elevator. It rattles to the third floor, where the woman—early thirties, red hair (a wig, but a good one), expert mascara, but not much else as far as makeup—waves me through the door to 305, a small perfume-scented room with a scarf over a lampshade, and dozens of charcoal sketches pinned to the walls. All of them nudes of her.

"Name?"

"Amber."

I grin.

"I know, right? But it's true, my parents actually named me Amber."

I pull out my notebook and pencil, glance at the walls.

"He did those," she says, "all of 'em. They're me. He liked sitting here drinking martinis and drawing me naked before we screwed, and after we screwed. He said I was more supple after."

"He saw you in a lot of ways."

"Tell me about it. It's like I'm facing all these different mirrors. I guess artists do that. He was an architect too, or something." She points to one of the drawings. "This is my favorite. It's me, but the inside me, you know, like that part you see but nobody else does. He gave me some bullshit about seeing my soul, but he saw *something*. Plus, look, he gave me perfect breasts in this one, which to be honest, I do have great breasts, but seeing them drawn like that, well, you know, they're just pretty."

She lights a cigarette and, unlike most whores, is not itching for my departure.

"What was he into?"

"Straight up, mostly. Not kinky, but he could get rough. He was kinda nerdy, but he had a meanness. A weird kid's meanness, you know? He was mostly good to me, though. Talked about himself a lot. One time, he brought this other guy to watch. The guy just sat there in a suit, vaping and drinking from a flask. Big, handsome guy. Like that dude out of *Mad Men*. Never saw him before or since."

"What else can you tell me about Mr. *Mad Men*? Did he have a name?"

"Not that I heard. He had blondish hair, I think. Like I said, a big guy. Kind of classy. That kind of look about him. But his hat was pulled low, and besides, I was compromised, if you know what I mean."

We both pause, let the thought seep in.

"How long had you been seeing Gallagher?"

"Two years, maybe a little longer."

"You live here?"

"No. He rented it. I think we were the only two who used it. He had a key. I had a key. He said he liked it down here. Said it felt real."

"You don't seem too broken up."

She offers me a cigarette. I wave it away.

"I liked Michael. I did. We had good times. Look at this room. It's what we created. 'An every-now-and-then home'—that's what he used to say." She swallows and turns away. "I'm sad he's gone. In shock, maybe. A kinda hollow feeling. But it's business, right? He wasn't inviting me to the opera or anything. I wasn't going to be Mrs. Architect planning charity balls at the Peninsula. Play it where it falls. My dad used to say that."

"He ever talk about anybody not liking him?"

"No."

"Did he seem upset or not himself?"

"He was chiller than usual. Relaxed."

"You have a lot of clients?"

"A few rich guys I mostly meet on the west side. But Michael liked it dirtier, I guess."

"You said he was mostly straight up."

"I mean the place, the scenery. You'd be surprised how much scenery has to do with things."

"So I'm told. Where you from?"

"South Pasadena."

"That's different scenery."

"I know, right? I run a second-hand dress shop. Vintage. Don't look at me like I'm making things up. It's hard running a shop. So much they don't tell you in community college. I took this course on entrepreneurship. It's fascinating how much goes into a business. Most people don't know. Really. This is my night job. I like sleeping with who I want when I want and getting paid for it."

I shake my head.

"How'd Gallagher find you?"

"Got a call one day."

"What'd he pay?"

"You the tax man?"

"Could be."

"Fifteen hundred a night."

She's putting on a brave face and talking beyond her depth. I can see she's upset and that when she gets home, she'll sit in her South Pasadena bathtub, run a washcloth over her face, and contemplate Gallagher's slit throat and the wad of cash in her vintage purse. Gallagher left this room about half an hour before the uniforms responded to a call of a man down on the sidewalk. He kissed her on the cheek and was gone, down the elevator to the sidewalk. I look around the room and out the window to the street. I tell her not to disappear. "We'll have more questions," I say. "Leave the charcoal drawings."

"Can I take this one, please? It's my favorite."

"It's a crime scene."

"Please. There's no crime on this paper."

She wants a piece of him. I understand. I nod.

She pulls the drawing of her "perfect" breasts from the wall and rolls it up. I head back to the street and catch the last glimpse of Gallagher's pale face before the zipper shuts.

I call Ortiz.

"Watcha got?"

"He was seeing a pricey hooker," I say. "He was a regular. She's clean. I'm heading up to Coldwater Canyon to check out the house. See who's there."

"High-end hooker, down there? Am I missing something?"

"I'll fill you in later."

"Anyway, the guy was divorced. Wife moved back to New York a couple or so years ago. No kids. What's it look like there?"

"Clean, deep cut. Done under a broken streetlight."

"Homeless wacko off his meds?"

"Too neat. Wallet wasn't taken, either."

I can hear Ortiz breathing, thinking.

"All right, go to his house see what's what. I'm tracking down names at his firm. Renowned architects. That's what the prick in the mayor's office tells me. *Renowned.* Says it real slow, like I don't understand. You know the type. A prick from his asshole to his eyeballs. Anyway, the renowned architects are doing that building near that Whole Foods over on Eighth, that weird-looking glass thing. Got a few other big projects in SoCal too. You got his phone?"

"Yeah, we caught a break on that. It had fingerprint ID. So …"

"You scanned the dead man's finger."

"And I scrolled."

"A lot of names and numbers?"

"Anybody who matters. Guy definitely had big-name friends."

"Shit."

I walk a few blocks to my car and drive west toward Coldwater Canyon, turning onto Mulholland and feeling lost like I always do up here. My headlights cut through dark, hypnotizing curves. Houses appear like small stars in the thicket; the scents of jacaranda and cottonwoods blow over me. You can feel the money in the seclusion, like a small heaven feeding off the land below, but there are stiffs here too: overdoses, suicides, drunken drownings in pools—the kinds of deaths that figure in battles over wills and possessions. I find Michael J. Gallagher's house—set back a ways, but no gate. Low-slung and angled, long windows, a roof of strange degrees, as if something landed from another planet. An odd silver, a glass jewel.

A small dog's claws clatter in the foyer; a Latina voice shoos it away. She opens the door. Doesn't know what's happened. She lets me in and hurries to her purse, hands me documents I don't want.

"Legal," says Maria Sanchez. "I very legal."

"I'm not here for that. I'm Detective Sam Carver."

I pass her papers back and give her the news. She wobbles a bit. Doesn't make a sound, steadying herself on a table beneath a mirror. She points me into the living room—three steps down, Iranian carpets, lived-in stately furniture, rich fabrics surrounded by abstract canvases on white walls and a long window looking out into the dark arroyo. She's from Colombia and has worked as Gallagher's cook and housekeeper for seven years. She sleeps here some nights in the last room down the far hall. Maria's in her early forties. A few threads of gray run through her long hair, but her face is barely lined, and she reminds me of a haunted, regal character in a John Rechy story.

"How could this happen to Mr. Michael?" she says, her fists tight in her lap, her eyes blinking. She doesn't know much. Gallagher worked long hours, and few people came to the house, except for an occasional office party. He spoke of no enemies and never seemed at odds. He drank wine and gin and listened to Celtic—that word comes out of her mouth funny—ballads and American blues. "Music always," she says. "I no see him much. He left notes. We sat by the pool every Wednesday morning and drank coffee. We talk about my chores and my home. About his place too. Ireland. His family came to here a long time ago. He told me about making buildings. One time, he spread drawings of buildings all over the pool deck." She takes a breath and relaxes her fists. "He stood over them. He said it was like what God felt when he imagined the world. I don't think a man should think like he knows God's mind. But I understood. Out of nothing, something comes."

"Your English is good."

"Not so good," she says, trying a half smile. "I take classes at the church. I teach to new people coming."

"Were you sleeping with him?"

She turns away and blushes. I open my notebook and write her name in pencil.

"No. Not like that," she says. "That is foolish for someone like me. You can't live in the life you clean. I did not know Mr. Michael that way. But people have other things."

"How well did you know his wife?"

"Miss Miranda. She gone more than two years ago. Never come back. I don't think. I never saw her again. They seemed happy and then they weren't. I don't know why. They were unhappy before she left. You know how people can be that way just being together."

"What did she do?"

"Miss Miranda was a lawyer. She worked for Disney."

"Did he have other women?"

"Not my business. He never bring anyone here."

We walk out by the pool. Still and quiet. I can feel Gallagher, see where he played God by the water. It must have been tempting to think so, to look out over the skyline and see a glimmer from your imagination rise in darkness. I stand a while longer. Suspended. Maria breathes beside me. "Sometimes," she says, "a mountain lion comes. Mr. Michael and I saw him one night. We shut off all lights in house. He walked along the pool. Quiet. He stopped and looked around. He looked lost, but I think he was waiting for another lion. None came. Mr. Michael put his arm around me. He never do that before. We stood for a long time, even after the lion go."

CHAPTER 3

My detective won't get much from the maid.

Sweet little Maria with her bus pass and her novenas.

It's cold in this curve. My Beemer's lights out, I'll wait and follow him back to town. My man: Detective Sam Carver. Don't you think it's a pretty name? Blunt but with an air of mystery, the way the last *r* rolls out and softly vanishes. I keep a picture of him from an old newspaper story. Black hair a few centimeters too long, trim waist, straight shoulders, and quick, dark eyes. Sharp profile and hands that move with a bird's grace; he's got that look some men have who know secrets that whisper around you like falling snow. I've never heard his voice, his sound. I wonder about it. Is it a rasp? A slight baritone? I'm sure it has gravity. You can just tell. I know him from afar. We have never met. That will change. But, to be honest, I do know him. I hacked him. Slid in on spyware. No firewalls. Laughable password: *Cop1*. I mean, c'mon. So much in a laptop. Diaries, pictures, bank statements, confessions, and dreams. We pretend it's all safe, locked in a cloud or sealed on a zip drive.

Have Snowden and the Russians taught us nothing about how easy it is to peek? Hacking is a hobby I picked up from Justin Ionelli, the guy (young man) who took my virginity (during the act, in a narrow bed in an attic room aglow with computers, he chanted "Dylan, Dylan, Dylan" in my ear as if summoning a Buddhist deity) when we were both underclassmen at Stanford. Justin was a noodge, but very smart in the parallel-universe kind of way. He spun code like spirals of DNA, floating it across screens and setting it to music. Beautiful. Really. He taught me how to manipulate twists of numbers and glimmers of letters, so that scrims fell away and the ether—that other dimension—shone with the hardness of pure light. "It is," Justin once said, his fingers tapping wildly, his boy-genius exuberance uncontainable, "like being a magician."

I like this new game I'm playing. There's a trace of smoke in my dress from my little barrel fire. Before the earlier, let us say, *incident*, I was at a Mahler concert at Disney Hall with Jacob, a movie producer who's crazy about me and conductor Gustavo Dudamel. The music was good but nowhere near as enticing as the flame afterward. I can still see the beauty of those embers and specks of Gallagher's blood vanishing into the air. Like a Mayan offering. This is my thinking: Architects, of which I am one, can get away with murder. We are precise, every line a purpose, every angle a need. We anticipate and correct. Did you ever navigate an easement? Untangle the subterranean? Well, then, you don't know. We aspire to perfection and delight in calculation. We defy gravity.

Yes, I will be good at this. One never thinks one will become a killer. We don't start out that way. Do we? There's a devilish epiphany to it, though. But the tears afterward troubled me. Perhaps I'm doubting myself, questioning my cause. If I were still in analysis, this would be many hours of chatter-babble with Dr.

Peterson, a pleasant pale-eyed man, but how could he pretend to know me? Anyone. I wonder what our session would sound like if I told him about Gallagher?

"You what?"

"Killed a man."

Gulp, startled twitch of his eyes, readjusting glasses, notepad slipping off knee.

"Dylan, this is such a setback. We were making progress. How?"

"With a knife."

"No. How in your mind?"

"Oh, that."

I wink.

Talk, talk, talk without absolution. I've stopped all that. Quit the meds too. I'm free, back to me, not a blurry composite courtesy of the pharmaceutical industry. Clarity is ascendant. I see like a raven. The side effect, though, is smoking. I smoke now. A small price. It's so peaceful out here, moonlight in the thicket. I crack the window and light up. The match strike, the smoke. I love the way it fills me.

I tilt the seat back and settle in. I play it over in my mind, the way Gallagher's body slipped from my embrace to the sidewalk. He deserved it. The why is not important now; I'll revisit the why and play out the rules of vengeance and forgiveness after it's all finished. I've done a lot of that already. I've considered every variable, like the grid of a fine building, every weight a counterweight, every angle a balance of beauty and purpose. There will be others. Bodies, I mean. Oh, yes. Did you know that soldiers who killed close up in battle carried inside them the face of the first one? But it faded over time and became ingrained in a mosaic of other faces until it was nothing special, just a prick of light, like a strange planet in the mind.

Why do I keep shaking? Little shivers run through me. Am I not as tough as I thought? I sound tough inside, the words going through my head, the fierceness I feel. But there are other things too, softer parts of me I thought were gone; they play and swirl like a river. Take a breath. Relax. I was careful to leave no clues. But one wonders, with DNA, microscopes, and infrared thingies. You could find a lot.

You can't find me.

What a night it's been. I keep the cigarette ember low. The air is cool, bracing; mist rolls in from the ocean. I turn on the radio. All those frequencies out there moving toward us, so much music and talk; those deep, calming voices of men at the lower end of the dial. Jazz DJs are the coolest. Every sentence a seduction. "Here's Miles from his blue period." You can hear it, right? The pause and purr and then that high, soft trumpet like a slender, slow arrow finding you in the dark. I blow smoke and feel a tingle. I don't think of the other thing I feel. I'll leave it alone and maybe it will slide away. I didn't expect it, but I should have. It's like a prickly-edged whisper.

Movement. I push my face to the windshield. My detective bends into that old Porsche of his, a battered thing from the late eighties, I think, but it fits him: lean, compact, a bit of rust. His taillights glow. He backs up slow, straightens, and heads down the canyon. I wait a moment, crush out my cigarette, and slide behind him. Too early for him to suspect anything. I'm just a girl on a milk run in the middle of the night, still in my concert dress. "Oh, Officer, if you could just give me a warning." How many times has that worked? Legs slightly open, a flash of silk, the dashboard light, the scent of leather, the glimpse of possibility. Men are so easily disarmed. My glove box overflows with warnings.

My detective—he's not like the others, I'm sure—snakes along dim roads and finally hits the 101 in the fast lane. I trail a few cars behind in the middle. It's the in-between time that is the darkest, those early a.m. hours when the unreconciled ride. How fitting. My detective accelerates, skimming past the Hollywood Bowl and the Capitol Records building. I'd like to race him, my black hair flying like a piece of night. Monteverdi blaring. But that's too bold. One day, maybe. We clear Silver Lake. I pull farther back and follow him to Temple and on to his apartment on Hill in the old Metro Station, a restored 1920s Italianate building that sits catty-corner to the Biltmore and the aesthetic tragedy of Pershing Square.

I pass and blow him a kiss he doesn't see, turning left toward Disney Hall, which is the color of the moon. It absorbs what illuminates it. Frank Gehry knew what he was doing. I despise Frank, but I admire how his abstract ornament—some say it resembles a ship, but I think it looks like a Picasso face of sliced silver—beckons from over the city. I cruise into Angelino Heights, thinking about who I am, distilling myself into a single line: insomniac daughter of a madwoman and the kindest of fathers.

CHAPTER 4

The maid knew nothing. She handed me a rosary on the way out the door. "Pray," she said. A crime scene unit is at the Coldwater Canyon house bagging Gallagher's laptop and things from his home office, medicine cabinets, and whatever else strikes them. Ortiz has left a message: "Hey, Carver, the mayor's office keeps crawling up my ass. Jesus. We gotta get somewhere on this quick. Know I'm stating the obvious, but you know these kinds of cases. Everyone sticking their fingers in. Never hear from them when a mother in Compton catches a stray. Fucking rich, huh. Why aren't we rich? You ever think about that? Give enough money and someone will care about your sorry ass. Call me. Oh, and destroy this message. And, oh, the *Times* called. What's that chick's name again? The pain-in-the-ass one. I referred her to PA, but you know how that goes."

I pour a drink and look over Hill Street. Four a.m. Esmeralda sleeps against the old Hotel Clark in a clump of bags, suitcases, boxes, and scarves. She's a little black Sisyphus, probably weighs no more than ninety pounds, pushing her belongings every day up and down the sidewalk. The Clark's been closed for years, gates locked, graffiti on the door, piss in the corners. The city's been trying to clean up the street as part of the Renaissance—a word spoken these days without a trace of smirk—and a lot of the homeless have moved on. But Esmeralda stays, peeking up from beneath her tarp. I watch her from up here on many nights as drunken couples from Perch stumble past her and make out in the Clark's doorway until an Uber comes.

I sit at the piano, an ancient upright I bought years ago from a junk man in Watts. The keys are the color of tea and the pedals are slack. I've been playing since I was a boy, taught by Miss Holloway, who smelled of cigarettes and bourbon and once performed in orchestras in Pittsburgh and St. Louis. She was funny and sly and loved Art Tatum, Jimi Hendrix, the B side of *Abbey Road*, and Bob Dylan's "Boots of Spanish Leather." "Turn the great noise around you into music, Sam." She said that all the time. I'm not very good, but when I can't sleep, I close my eyes and play soft, mostly standards and a few of my own compositions, which I've never written down. I like the way the keys feel beneath my fingers, the sounds that rise, the notes, restless souls meandering through the night. I know myself when I play. Who I am and the quiet that runs through me. Not as engaged as I should be, my mother used to say. She'd push me to parties and sleepovers, but I never really fit—at least, back then—into the lives of others. I wasn't weird, just solitary. I did have a moment of notoriety when Sarah Cullen, the reigning queen of the popular kids, kissed me in the hall and said with tenth-grade thespian aplomb: "Sam, take me for a pizza. I must get away from these children." We ate two slices each at Sal's and returned before sixth period, with Sarah whispering to me, "You said twenty-three words the whole time. I counted. This may not work as I had hoped." I leaned in and kissed her. "That," she said, patting my cheek and disappearing into Algebra, "must have taken courage."

I like the night, the stillness, the conniving characters in old movies and the things that come unexpected. I saw a coyote when I was playing about a year ago. He flashed in the window on the empty street, a bit of magic against the buildings. They do that. Just appear. Like Sofía Vergara walking the Palisades, or Maria's lion roaming in the canyon. Making you wonder whether it's a dream or real. I play a little more, press an F major, and stand. I boil water and go down and check on Esmeralda with a cup of tea and a bottle of whiskey.

"Why you waking me up? Go bother your own mother. Standing there like a ghost. Creepy, is what it is. Go home. Go to sleep. It's the devil's hour."

"I told you, my mother's ill in Boston."

"Dying?"

"No. Her mind."

"Well, I can't be your mother. I'm too busy."

"It's cold tonight."

"Cold don't know me. You took me outta my dream. A good dream, I think it was." She crinkles the tarp back, and her bony black face, bordered by a yellow scarf, looks up. "What are you holding?"

"Whiskey or tea?"

"Mmmmm. How about ten dollars?"

"Nope."

"Then pour some whiskey into the tea. A little more. Good."

I hand her the mug. She sips, and I sit beside her.

"You out here this late means you can't sleep. Means you got a body. So you come bug Esmeralda. Some Jesus guy was out here early trying to drag me to a shelter. Why does someone always want to put a roof over my head? I got my setup. Just want to be left alone. You're not so bad, I guess. But you need a life, a girl or something. Pour a little more whiskey. Who's the dead guy?"

"Some architect from Coldwater Canyon."

"Heard about it. Chaplin Hotel over on Main, right? Throat slit."

"How'd you know?"

"Street, man. Full of whispers. You know that. They rob him?"

"Nope."

"Mmmmm."

Esmeralda's sane tonight. On bad nights, she's a jumble of words and thoughts in the wind. Rails and cries and speaks in tongues. I wonder what she sees at those moments, the invisible self she screams at, like bees inside her, making her run zigzag and crazy. She's good tonight. She hands me the mug and pulls up the tarp. "I'm going to sleep." I sit for a while. Nothing moving. I close my eyes and lean back on the wall and look across the street to my building and my lighted window, alone against the darkened others. Two skateboarders pass. The sound of a siren approaches from the east, grows louder, and fades in the west. A bus filled with Latino faces passes. Dawn is not far off, but the twilight, helped by the whiskey and Esmeralda's breathing, is calm and cool, the air clean. Most people don't know how cold it can get in LA. The sky can press down gray and make you think of Cleveland or Berlin.

I slip a ten under Esmeralda's tarp and head around the corner to the Little Easy. It's way after hours, but I know Lenny—rag in hand, bow tie askew, dirty shirt, the scent of Old Spice—will be counting receipts and sitting in front of the expensive stuff near a painting of a man who looks like Napoleon.

"It's almost breakfast, Sam. Have a quick one and be on your way."

"I missed you."

Lenny smiles and pours a Johnnie Walker.

"Caught a bad one last night, huh?"

"Slice job. Dead architect."

"Don't get many of those, I suppose."

Lenny's a transplant from New York. Came out in the seventies to surf and stayed. Not a surprisingly original story, but Lenny got into dope trafficking, hiding white bags from Colombia in surfboards. He'd pick them up in Mexico and drive a few miles every day, surfing his way up the coast in no particular hurry to drop the stash off at an address in Toluca Lake. Ingenious, really. But a jilted girlfriend—a cokehead with a runny nose and a heart of vengeance—talked into a phone and Lenny was done. He did some time, got out, worked as a carpenter and a stagehand for a while, gave surf lessons. One of his students was the daughter of the guy who once owned the Little Easy. That's how things happen.

"What do you know about drones?" he says.

"We kill people with them in Yemen and Pakistan. Amazon delivers packages with them."

"Cop surveillance too, right?"

"Trade secret, Lenny." I wink, and he nods.

"Guy came in the other day," he says, "sat right over there. Ordered a Dewar's. Gentlemanly type. Said he landed at LAX a few hours earlier at dusk. In town for a convention. He told me he looked out the window of the plane and saw dozens of small drones buzzing like insects below in the pink-dark sky. Like *Blade Runner* or something. 'A smooth chaos of crisscrossing things.' That's what he said. Direct quote. Makes you wonder, doesn't it? What's up there looking down. Who's watching us? Who's driving those things?"

Lenny leans back, stands, crosses his arms, looks at me for an answer.

"You can buy drones in Target, Lenny. They're all over."

"It just makes you wonder. Drink up. I gotta close."

I set the glass down. Lenny leads me to the door.

"Get some sleep, Sam."

He locks the door behind me. A street-sweeper passes; the sky flickers. Soon, it will be light. I'll sleep for a couple of hours, shower, call Ortiz, check with the coroner, and head to Gallagher's office of *renowned* architects. The bronze doors to my building swing open to a foyer of marble and mosaic that, early last century, led to the tracks of the subway, remnants of which lie beneath in scents of oil and dust. I went down there once and roamed with a flashlight between the girders and into the tunnels, thinking of the workers' lights in the darkness, pounding away stone and earth beneath a city still young.

The security guard at the front desk nods; the sound system jangles with an eighties loop. Dog walkers stir in the half-light. My key clicks in the door and echoes down the hall. I follow the sound to bed and dream of my father running through a mist in a sweatshirt and punching the air.

CHAPTER 5

His father was a boxer.

A rough man with a broken hand and a quick temper.

It's all in my detective's laptop, the one I hacked. When I can't sleep, like now, I open the files and read about my detective. He's a bit of a diarist, my man. A letter writer and keeper of emails. To me, it's a map, words and folders leading here and there, and sometimes I don't want to look. I feel as if I'm stealing things I shouldn't. But I read on. I have to know him, what breaks and makes him strong, his fantasies and fears.

I like the glow of a laptop in the dark. It's cozy, blankets around me, dawn creeping up the streets to my home, a Victorian I bought after a streak of luck in the stock market and began renovating years ago. I live alone in this big place. I like it that way, wandering rooms, running fingers over banisters, contemplating tile and the arc of stained glass above the front door. The quiet. The way it enfolds. I've thought about having a child on my own. It takes so much to raise a life, intricacies I do not have but would like to. I could learn. I'd like to feel life come out of me. That's how it is when I draw. Buildings come out of me. That's different, I know. Miraculous yet different. My detective would make a good father. He knows what it is to have a scar and understand what put it there. What it leaves behind.

I slide the laptop aside and go to the window. A few headlights, the moan of a bus, men speaking Spanish, hurrying down the hill. The city spreads before me. I feel like Princess Daenerys Targaryen with her dragons in *Game of Thrones*. I don't usually like shows like that, but c'mon, fire and ice and treachery in a war for seven kingdoms? I'm in. I can almost touch the buildings in my own pop-up kingdom. Have you ever considered the precision of a line, how it thins and widens, cuts and curls, how it starts from a dot and lifts into porticoes and towers? Into cities that inspire and outlast us. They are what we leave to others, the semblances of ages that one day, when we are long gone, gather like ruins beneath the feet of those we never knew, and rise again.

I cry when I draw.

I pour fresh coffee and check the *Los Angeles Times* web page to read about Gallagher. Can you imagine, little ol' me, the angel of death? I scroll. No story yet. So much other news, though. Ethan Hawke has a new movie. Bitcoin is trading high. The Great Barrier Reef is dying. The warming ocean is turning rainbow colors of coral to ash. Amazing how sensitive it is. How finely calibrated. Just a degree or two of change in temperature, and nature's intricate architecture is in danger.

Light fills the house. I stare at a vase to an iris on a long stem, cut from my neighbor's garden a few nights ago, a delicate souvenir of illicit urge. No one knows what I do in my insomnia, flitting across dark yards and sidewalks. I am quite the petty thief.

Flower, toy, hose, hubcap. My detective's a bit of a heister too. He lifts things from crime scenes: bracelet, ripped cloth, dollar bill, license, bottle cap, eyeglasses, Bible, lock of hair, and, once, a tooth. Possessions of vics. I wonder what he took from Gallagher. He keeps them in an inlaid box under the leather chair in his living room, opening it from time to time, running fingers over his strange treasure. It reminds me of an archaeologist brushing away sand from a pharaoh's image, or a lepidopterist pinning butterflies inside a glass case. Some are from crimes solved, others not. I think it odd, but we all have our rituals and relics. Things only the darkness knows. He doesn't judge. Those of the innocent lie beside those of the guilty. Wife, skip-roper, gangbanger, priest, bride, barkeep, accountant, bus driver, and on and on. The dead. He writes a short paragraph about each: where they were found, what time, the position of the body, light and scent, and all else he sees on the small stage inside the yellow tape. "I don't want them forgotten," he wrote. "Each piece a part of someone who held a place in the world."

There is much sadness in his laptop.

I love Sundays. The stillness and the way the day lingers at its start and later, sometime after three, races toward dusk. Jacob, my relentless producer, called and left three messages.

"Dylan, pick up."

"Please, Dylan, let's talk. I missed you last night."

"Hey, let's go to a screening this week. You love screenings. New Tom Ford movie. Jake Gyllenhaal and Amy Adams. Some kind of psycho-thriller. What do you think? Call me."

He's hurt that I didn't go out to dinner after the Mahler concert with him and his Belgium banker and Milan set designer. Three men, cigars, and wine, chattering about prostates and how the world has changed; twinges of nostalgia, a round of brandies. You can just hear them. I had to tend to Gallagher last night, and I'm not in the mood for Jacob today. Note to self: I don't want any more Jacobs. Although, in his way he is sweet and considerate. In doses. But I don't want that kind of life. I have money, not as much as Jacob, certainly not, but more than most women on their own, which gives me, as my accountant, Sven, would say, *options*. They don't like us to have options, men. It bothers them—not like it did years ago, but you can see traces of betrayal on their faces when a woman pulls out her platinum card and opinions. Why is that? Are we not an elevated species? Hillary found out, but really, she was not the right woman for this time. Maybe it was the pantsuit. That seems trite, I know, but it said something, didn't it? It masculinized the feminine, made her, despite expert makeup and hair just right, a cross between us and them. You can't do that with pussy-grabbers about. I should put Trump on my list. Wouldn't that be something? *Sssshhh.* No, no, no. Homeland Security might swoop in like those monkeys from *The Wizard of Oz*, my favorite movie as a child. My mother and I watched it once a year before Easter. She'd put her arm around me and we'd sit in the dark in our pretend ruby slippers, singing "We're Off to See the Wizard" and going quiet when the sky said, "Surrender Dorothy." My mother was a great pretender. I would press against her warmth and close my eyes until the broom and the wicked witch flew away.

"My baby, Dylan," she'd say, "my sweet little girl. Don't let them get you."

"Who, Mommy?"

"The bad ones."

"Where are the bad ones?"

"Everywhere."

I don't want to think about that now.

I'll sit at the window and draw. I've been working on a sketch for a classical-and-glass design for a new library in Carmel. Light will fill the stacks, and old stones will conjure the Greeks. It's in the early stages, but I see it in my mind. My partner, John Hillerman, likes the idea. John's been good to me through so much. We have a way of seeing things so that each complements the other. He hired me after I got my master's at Pratt, and for a while I thought we'd have a fling, but we agreed that it could spoil how we collaborate; our blueprints and ideas are sacred to us. Besides, John loves his wife, Isabella, a gallerist and a volunteer at the women's shelter, someone you'd never want to hurt. Her Brazilian accent soothes, and she moves like an embracing force, a woman who knows that beauty is a collection of things. Maybe it's her South American roots. The ease of slipping into one's own skin. I like the light that comes off her.

"Dylan, Dylan!" yelled Isabella, banging on my door years ago before dawn, just after I joined John's firm.

"What?" I said, wrapped in a robe, my hair a mess.

"We're going to the mountains. You must see the San Gabriels. I know a place."

"It's dark."

"The day is coming. Hurry."

I barely knew her, but she was the boss' wife. I dressed quickly, a bit miffed, and we packed into her car. She handed me a coffee, and we sped toward La Cañada and north into the mountains.

"They come like whales out of the darkness," she said.

"What?"

"The mountains. They swim around us."

She laughed and turned up an Astrud Gilberto CD. We parked and followed a trail along a stream. Light was beginning to break through the trees. We climbed a steep incline to a ridge trail. We walked the rim, cool rising from the Valley, blackbirds circling, tumbling, dancing above us. The sun was cresting, and Isabella grabbed my hand and led me through a bit of thicket to a rock overhang. We sat with our feet dangling. She waved an arm over the narrow valley.

"This is my California," she said. "Not the beach, though that is beautiful. But this. Isn't it lovely? Don't you think it's lovely? John won't get up this early. He can be a layabout on weekends, but I wanted you to see this. I think people need to know things about one another, right at the beginning. Sometimes, we wait too long to learn what we should know. Now you know about me. My favorite California place. What do you think?"

I almost cried. She was unafraid and full of life. An offering in the dawn. A woman, not much older than me, inviting me in. That was rare. I didn't know what to do. It was a few weeks before the bad things that would happen happened. But even back then, I was reticent—in the thrall of a new career, yes, but I kept to myself and my designs. Not with Isabella—at least, not on that morning. We sat for hours. She told me about her family's village in Brazil, and her first trip to America. "You hear so much about it," she said, "and then this thing in your head becomes real, and you think it's yours." I told her about my mother, how it felt growing up tall, awkward, and lanky, like a bird too big for its wings. She laughed at that and told me all girls felt funny about something. She said women understood perfection better than men and, because of that, realized how far we all were from it.

"I never liked my nose," she said, turning to profile. "Look."

"It's a good nose."

"I don't think it fits. I could have had it fixed when I was twelve. I'm Brazilian, after all. But it's who I am."

"I like it."

"I like that you're tall."

She touched my hand.

"Dylan?"

"Yes."

"Be happy."

I don't mean to canonize Isabella, but some people are more blessed than the rest of us. It's hard knowing them; you can never be the thing you see they are, although perhaps, once, you weren't so far from it. A few months after our trip to the mountains, Isabella held me on the night when I thought I no longer belonged in the world. She stroked my hair and sang softly in my ear; she wiped my eyes and let me sleep in her arms. How long ago that seems. But how close too.

Yes, I'll draw for a few hours and then off to the Grove to browse and look for a blazer for my detective. He wears the same one from Macy's all the time. He doesn't buy much with his credit cards, my detective. His laptop file marked "bills" is sparse. On that salary, okay, I get it (although the overtime adds up), but still, it's important to have something in your closet that makes you feel rich. I should get him a Hugo Boss from Nordstrom's. Send it anonymously in a box with a bow. Would I be that brazen? I like to think so. I need to go by that sports shop and pick up black running tights, black top, gloves, and black running shoes; fold them in my bag, bring them home, lay them out on the bed in the guest room, in the shape of another me. Or maybe something different: a tight dress and

Salvatore Ferragamo heels. Waiting for that night when I kill again. Oh, yes. But not yet. My detective needs to get a little deeper into Gallagher before I deliver him another. This is my game. How smart is he? I have to be patient, which, I must say, is not a top-ten quality of mine.

CHAPTER 6

"You look like shit, Carver."

Coroner Lester Bryant is dressed in fresh whites, gloves snug. He stands beneath a light hanging over Gallagher's pale-bluish flesh. The morgue is quiet. Lester nods and waves me toward him. He's tall and thin, used to play basketball at La Salle before med school and a forensics career dicing stiffs and assigning causes of death—thousands over the years. He testifies at trials with the air of an unimpeachable uncle. Lester keeps a flute in the morgue and sometimes, mostly at night, sits on a stool and plays for the dead.

"Long night," I say.

"Not for this guy."

"What do you think?"

"I think a lot of stuff, but with this particular stiff, it seems he died from that big, smooth, even gash in his neck. Nothing else on him. No bruises or cuts. Kept himself nicely manicured. Look at those nails. That's a man who paid attention to detail. Lot of good it did him. Small guy too. Five-seven. Hundred and thirty-eight pounds. Scant muscle. Spindly. What'd you find at the scene?"

"Not much. Doesn't look like a robbery."

"Clean slice. Almost professional. Definitely a quality blade. He bled out in seconds," says Lester, reaching for tweezers and bending toward the gash. "I hear the mayor's office is paying attention. Big architect, huh?"

"Yeah."

"You'll be catching shit from all directions. Ortiz must be in a state. He's agitated when it's normal. Drinks way too much coffee."

"He's called a few times."

"You're calm, Carver. That's what I like about you. You've always been so calm, or are you just tired every time you roll in here?"

"I get excited."

"When?"

"Disneyland," I say, winking.

"Okay, sure, smart-ass. But when else?"

"When I catch a doer. Swim in the ocean, eat a breakfast burrito on the beach."

"Riveting. You should put that on a Tinder profile. Isn't that it, Tinder or Kinder or some shit like that?"

"I don't use them."

"Resistant to social media? You gotta embrace the now, man. You could be one swipe away from a goddess."

"Or a psycho."

Lester and I smile. He puts the tweezers down and sips coffee over Gallagher. A Chet Baker–like trumpet solo drifts up from a small Bose speaker. Other stiffs—a black guy, a Latina, an old white man with a missing arm, a young woman with a messed-up face—lie naked on slabs. Rows of cuts and traumas, bullet wounds and shattered bones. A few, like the black guy, lie there without a mark. But I have never seen one at peace here. The body is a land of sin and violation. It yields much. When I was starting as a detective, I'd come here and sit with them for hours. I thought they had something to tell me. A whisper between us. An understanding that I would close the final pages for them. Find who put them here and gather their silent shrieks for truth. You can hear them if you listen. My father taught me that. His was the first dead body I saw on a slab, in St. Catherine's Hospital in Newport, Rhode Island. He was beaten to death in an alley not far from the old wharf. His bruised and swollen face seemed too large and strangely colored for the rest of him. I was used to his damaged face; he boxed throughout New England, but the man lying on the slab was hurt more. It was him, though. Small demon tattoo; tight, compact muscles; bent fingers; big feet. So white he was under the light, as if scoured. Except his face. Most of his teeth had been knocked out, and I had imagined how he must have fought hard before he went down. My father was a battler, a man who inflicted and invited pain. I envied and despised him for that. He'd yank me out of bed at night and shadowbox around me like a phantom against moonlit walls. "Boom, boom, boom," he'd say. "Boom, boom, boom." Sometimes, he'd hit me. A glancing blow to the jaw, a jab to the gut—never enough to knock me down or make me cry, but just to let me know how cruelty was part of life. He said something like that once as we jogged along Cliff Walk with the ocean spread before us. My father came from old money, but he never fit into it. He started boxing when he was young, dropped out of Princeton and drifted back north. He married my mother, a schoolteacher. They lived in a small apartment off Malbone Road. When my grandfather, who called my father a "ruffian" and a "disappointment," died, he left my father one million dollars. The other four children received twenty million each. The rest was spread to trusts and charities. The big family home was sold, the possessions auctioned. My mother said the whole affair was a "great dismantling of what had been."

"Did you like him?" I asked her when I was a boy.

"Who?"

"Granddad. The rich one."

"No. He never looked at me. Isn't that strange? Never once. When someone doesn't look into your eyes, they can't know you and you can't like them."

"He didn't like Dad, either."

"Your father's a tough man to like."

"I don't"—I almost swallowed the words, but they came— "like him sometimes."

"We don't always like what we love. Do you love him?"

"I think I do. He scares me."

"He'd never hurt you. You know that. I would never let that happen."

"He read me a story last night."

"What kind of story?"

"It was about a sparrow and a statue and it made me sad at the end."

My mother insisted that my father's inheritance be kept for my college and future, and we lived a sparse life in a rich town, my father spending hours at the gym and occasionally working fishing boats, and my mother earning her master's in literature and rising to charter school principal. A man of quick edges and gazing silences, my father lived half in this world, half someplace else. He left me mostly to Mom. But he taught me how to box. I was good at it, but I never liked it, except how the world outside the ring went quiet. "That's the church of it," he told me once. "That silence in your head makes you sacred." He could say things like that, things that made Mom laugh and cry and sit on his lap in the kitchen and stroke his hair, patch his cuts, and whisper to him until morning. He died when I was eleven. They never found his killers. They let them sail away. How could that be? I've kept a lace from one of his boxing gloves. It is stiff and dry with sweat and blood.

A match strike, a wisp.

"What are you burning today, Lester?"

"Lavender."

"Can't really hide it, though."

"Nah, it stays in the nose."

"I heard you and your wife split."

"We did, but we're back," he says, peering into Gallagher's open throat. "Routine is a powerful thing. More durable than love. We started a ballroom dance class. My wife says dancing will help us understand each other's subtleties. We've been together thirty years, Carver. I know her subtleties and not-so-subtleties. What are you going to do? You gotta try, right?"

"I guess."

"Tinder aside, you have anybody?"

"Not at the moment."

"Find someone, Carver. Go to the zoo. Catch a movie. You still living in the old Metro building?"

"A few years," I say, looking down at Gallagher. "Hey, when tox comes back, let me know this guy's blood alcohol. He was a gin man and kept a hooker."

"That probably deadened the pain." Lester winks.

"I gotta go," I say. "Have to talk to one of his partners."

Lester turns back to Gallagher. I head out the door into Sunday morning sun. She blindsides me.

"Hey, Carver."

"No comment."

I slide on sunglasses and keep walking toward my car.

"C'mon, Carver. Slow down. What's the story? Rich, politically connected dead architect on a downtown sidewalk. Give me something. Off the record. We've got a short piece up on the web and an obit coming but not much on what happened."

"Call Public Affairs."

"You're not very pleasant when you're like this, Carver. Just a few sentences."

"You been following me?"

"In your dreams. Murder happens Saturday night, detective shows up at medical examiner's office Sunday morning. Pretty standard. I waited for you."

"You look like you've been up all night."

"Check the mirror yourself. Sleep much? Got a little gray in your stubble too, Carver. Getting old. It happens. What are you, thirty-eight, thirty-nine? Must be closing in on that midlife magic number."

Susan Chandler fires words more than speaks them. Blond hair, blue eyes, skirt, ankle boots, and denim jacket—she is a looker, the late-born daughter of hippies turned California real estate speculators, but a pain in the ass, a relentless interrogator and a top-notch writer. Her stories get the streets—compassionate but never sentimental. She's got a magpie's eye for detail, and the eloquence of a novelist. I don't tell her this. She's the kind of woman who would hold a compliment against you, parse through it, and see it as an attempt to manipulate her. She's been at the *Los Angeles Times* for a few years, bitching about editors, story play, and the shrinking fortunes of her business.

"I didn't think you guys were still publishing. All those layoffs, and that funny name your new owners gave the company. 'Schlonk,' is it?"

"'Tronc,'" she says. "That's the corporate name. Bunch of Chicago assholes thought it up. We're still the *Los Angeles Times*."

"Mmmm. What's a tronc, anyway?"

"Hell if I know."

We both laugh. She's doing her job; I'm doing mine.

"Can you give me anything?"

"Okay, listen. I'll tell you a few things. You know the stiff's name, what he does—did. Politically connected, et cetera. Doesn't look like a robbery. Had his wallet and cash."

"How much cash?"

"A thousand bucks."

"What was he doing down there at that time? Not really an architect's part of town."

"I'll tell you a few things. Background. You can't use it yet. Promise?"

"How can I promise if I don't know?"

"Okay, screw you, then."

"Carver, why do we always do this dance? You know you can trust me."

"You burned me once."

"You still hanging on to that? That was unavoidable. Police mix up evidence, and the wrong guy goes to jail. C'mon, Carver. That story had to be told. Besides, I never named you as the source."

"People knew."

"People thought they knew. You survived," she says, holding up an empty page in her notebook. "Can we get to present day? Why was Mr. Architect down there?"

"You never buy me a coffee. Ever notice that? I thought reporters took sources out to coffee."

"You want a latte, I'll buy you a latte."

"With caramel and whip cream. A grande."

"You're messing with me. And you're doing that quit-again smoker's thing."

"What?"

"Patting your pockets for a cigarette."

"I'm not."

"Are."

I cut her a glance.

"I don't like you most days."

"Mutual."

"Here's what we know," I say. "Guy was seeing a hooker downtown. He kept an apartment. I'm not telling you where. You figure it out. His throat was slit. Clean. Almost perfect. We don't have much else. But as I said, it's not a robbery, and likely not some homeless guy off his meds, although not ruling that out. Could have been something freakish like that. A crazy Captain America wannabe popping up in the night."

"There's passion in a slit throat, Carver. Someone who knew him."

"What I'm thinking."

"Okay, thanks."

"Don't use the slit throat or the hooker yet. You can say it was a stabbing. Technically, that's accurate. Let me get a little more ahead on this. Deal?"

"You still want a latte? I'll buy you a scone too."

"Rain check."

She turns to go and then looks up at me in the sunlight, hair blowing around her like gold.

"Carver, remember that night in your car? You think …"

"Let's not go there now."

I walk away, knowing she'll keep her promise not to use everything I told her. Some women are built right inside and out. I head over to Gallagher's offices near Seventh and Flower. I park outside, past stirring homeless guys and hipsters—I do hate that name, but what else are they?—strolling toward Whole Foods for Naked Juice, coffee, artisanal bread, and inflated Brie and Beaufort. I pass a bearded one in pants tight as pea pods, untucked blue shirt, a hashtag tattoo on his neck, and a Sinatra hat. The city is sprouting these guys. The alleged Renaissance is full of rangy men with stud earrings and lovely Asian girlfriends—a few of them, anyway. Hipsters make me feel as if I'm a beat off the rhythm and missing essentials. That's bullshit, I know; they don't have a fucking clue. But there is that sense of separation and the weight of age. I'm not even that old, but the young can make you feel hieroglyphic with their vapes, multiple playlists, tattoos, and coconut milk. I buzz Kimmel, Brady, and Gallagher Associates and take the elevator to the thirtieth floor. The door opens, and the city unwinds from the San Gabriels to the ocean. Clear, no smog. Magical.

Arthur Kimmel walks toward me in an open-collar white shirt, jeans, dark blazer, black loafers. Silver-haired, manicured, a Rolex snaking his wrist. He shakes my hand. He smells of cologne and coffee breath. One of those seventysomething guys who swim at five a.m. and flirt with women at parties, like a creature out of Updike or Cheever, a throwback with a year-round tan and too-bright veneers. He leads me to his office. Modern. Steel. Sparse. Rolled and unrolled drawings lie on a big desk, a few Macs aglow, one with the cosmos, the other with a shining tower in a place that looks like Dubai or Doha. We sit in rigid chairs of Swedish design; I think so, anyway. Kimmel crosses his legs and wipes his eyes with a handkerchief. A woman brings coffee and picks up a valise.

"You can go now, Mary. Thank you."

Kimmel sips his coffee, folds his kerchief away. Mary disappears. I open my notebook, flick through pages.

"This is all so tragic," he says. "Michael was such a fine architect. A good man too. To die like that. Alone on a sidewalk. In that part of town."

"You know a little of what happened."

"A friend from the mayor's office called last night, or I guess it must have been early morning. It was still dark. I was quite alarmed. You know, getting a call like that. Startled out of sleep. They said his throat was slit, but nothing was taken. What does that mean, Detective?"

"We don't know yet. Was Gallagher okay lately? Was he worried about anything? Mention anything that troubled him?"

"You mean did he have any enemies? Of course he did. Architects are a backbiting bunch, and with all that's going in the city, all the contracts, well, things have gotten testy. Yes, quite testy. Michael was a bit of an egotist, but what's wrong with that? I suppose he rubbed some of his colleagues the wrong way. But architects don't kill people." He looks away and back at me for verification. "I'm sorry to be terse. I'm hurt by this. I brought Michael into the firm. We were close because of that. He was brilliant in a way. A real modernist in how he saw the city—not just LA, but the concept of the city. Renewal and decay in timeless cycles."

Kimmel nods to the window.

"Look at it all down there," he says. "The cranes, the holes. Half finished. No one ever cared about downtown. That's changing, Detective. This city never had a center of balance. You can see that from up here. A strange garden. What's happening now will alter that. LA will have gravity. The question is, what will it look like? I wonder if we have the capacity to realize something bold and great. So much politics, so much intrusion into the creative. Michael and I talked about this a lot." He points to the new Wilshire Grand. "Our tallest new child. Korean money, but the design is something out of Doha. What does it say about who we are? It's not beautiful and it's not a horror. It's something in between."

"It's sleek. Like a crystal sail in the wind. It seems very much of today. But I'm no architect."

"Yes," says Kimmel, lifting a finger to his lip, pausing for a moment. "It's ironic, Detective, sitting way up here and staring down, thinking we have some control. I learned early in my career that an architect is less an artist and more an errand boy. That may be too harsh, I suppose. But so much time is spent haggling over materials, negotiating with contractors, acquiescing to the money. Endless regulations. It's not just earthquakes anymore. It's global warming. Tsunamis. It all must be considered. The building you start off with in your head, this very pure thing, becomes something else. Visions become shared. Compromised. I imagine it's what a director feels when a studio cuts twenty minutes from his film. Michael always fought that. He was young and brash, a bit of Ayn Rand in him. But his aesthetic was thoroughly modern. He saw what the future could be. It takes courage to be that way."

Kimmel wipes his eyes. He swallows. Weary.

"I'm sorry, Detective, I'm babbling."

I give him a few seconds to collect himself.

"How well did you know his wife?"

"Miranda? Hell of a lawyer. A damn fine cook too. She and Michael drifted apart. Couples do that, right, Detective? Nothing really lasts. I've had three wives. Buildings last—well, I suppose not forever, but longer than love." He leans in and looks at me. "Surely, you don't think Miranda is involved. They had a bitter split. But she would never do this. It's been too long. She left three years ago. New York."

"You say a bitter split."

"Something happened. Michael described it as a 'quiet, intense explosion.' He never told me about it. I didn't pry. But as I say, that 'explosion' came after what I had sensed was a longtime diminution of what once was. 'The brokenness of joy.' My second wife used that phrase in our divorce hearing. Women can be quite poetic when the goods are being divvied up. You certainly must know this. Human nature, I mean. That's your business. The flaws in us." He takes a deep breath. "I did see Miranda before she left. We went to dinner. She didn't let on why, either, but she seemed relieved. A weight lifted kind of thing. No, I don't think Miranda's involved."

Kimmel fills a lot of space with words. He doesn't want quiet. He'd sit here all day, skipping through thoughts, using Gallagher's death for his own introspection. Selfish but natural. Gallagher meant something to him. Old master, young protégé. Men like Kimmel need someone to carry on. They don't know that when they're gone, so are their conceits and the worlds they imagined.

Kimmel wipes his eyes and walks to the window. He stands with his back to me. I rise and look past him and out the glass.

Kimmel said he felt like an errand boy, but one could pretend to be untouchable up here, the horizon stretching to the sea, the world gnawing silently thirty floors below.

"How active was Michael politically? The mayor's office has taken a particular interest in the case."

"My firm gives a lot of money to a lot of politicians and parties," says Kimmel, turning toward me. "You have to. Cost of business. Nothing new in that, as I'm sure you know, Detective."

"Anyone else Michael was close to? Someone who might have insight."

"His best friend was Paul Jamieson over at McKinley, Jamieson, and Burns. We're collegial competitors. Odd but true. Paul and Michael ran around a lot. At one time, they talked about starting their own firm. There was a third friend. Michael brought him to an office party once. I can't remember his name. He was a few years older—an architect too. I suppose we're an incestuous bunch."

CHAPTER 7

Sleepless night.

Monday morning. I'm late.

I drink a quick espresso and slip on a V-neck white T and a pair of jeans. My hair's a mess. I twist it into a ponytail. No matter, it'll be an office day. Maybe lunch with John, but otherwise quiet except for my nine a.m. conference call to Chicago to discuss an art gallery John and I are designing. I pop a bagel into the toaster, unfold my laptop, and scroll.

He floats up the screen like a smiling, unrepentant ghost. Michael J. Gallagher leads the *Los Angeles Times* home page. The story's shorter than I would have imagined: a few pictures of the dead architect, one with his ex-wife on a rented yacht in Belize, and several buildings his firm designed—soulless deconstructionist abstractions that these days are called "brave" and "bold." Two *b* words I hate. It's jarring to see, though. I'm the only one who knows. The keeper of secrets, the hearer of his final breath. *Ahhhhhhhhh.* Or was it *erghhhhh*? Or just *nnnnnnnnnn*? He's a pixelated image now. He'll slip further down the screen, and soon he'll be gone. Resurrected every now and then by a keystroke, a stumbled-upon artifact, a mystery drifting in ether. I did that. The story says Gallagher was stabbed—whoa, understatement—and makes other allusions to the crime, but nothing solid. My detective doesn't have much in the way of clues. They'll trickle out, I suppose. They always do. But not this time. I bite into the bagel and check the clock. Lipstick, tweezers, liner, a quick pee.

I hop in the car and cross over the 101, take a left on Temple, past barred windows and into downtown. Beyoncé seethes about betrayal; Chrissie Hynde kicks ass; Amy Winehouse is a squall of lust. I click to a Joni Mitchell tune from way before my time. Too airy. Blondie? Almost. Drive music is tricky. I settle for the in-your-face voice of Courtney Love. Whatever happened to her? Where do the rabid ones go? I feel as if someone is watching me. *I'm a suspect.* I know that's not true, but Gallagher is in my head. I can feel him dying against me. I would do it again, yes, I would, but I am rattled, like a house of restless spirits. Not the serious kind they lock you up for, but the insistent ones, hovering, taunting, judging. I can almost hear them slipping through songs. Smug.

I crack the window and light a cigarette. It fills me. I blow the smoke and spirits away. I feel the car around me, shiny and fast. Sing Courtney. "I want to be the girl with the most cake." Love that line. I'm singing. I'm crying. A storm inside. I wonder whether anyone's looking. Probably not. Who cares, anyway? This is downtown LA. Crazy is normal. I sit at the light. A homeless guy with a dripping dirty rag approaches. I wave him off, but he steps closer and knocks on the window.

"Clean?"

"No, thank you."

"C'mon, honey, they're dirty. A woman needs clean windows. Why you crying? Too pretty to cry."

"Here."

I hand him a dollar. He looks at it.

"Can't hardly do anything with that," he says.

I hand him a five. He leans down, his face almost touching mine. He is frenetic, his eyes serene, as if two voices are pulling at him.

"I see all," he says. "All the world when no one's looking. I see you."

He laughs and slaps his rag on my hood. He steps back, spins in a slow dance with an imaginary partner. The light changes and I speed away. I glimpse him in the rearview, twirling his rag, pointing toward me and mouthing, *I see you.*

The wacko shit that ends up here—misplaced molecules and shopping-cart clairvoyants. I've just had my LA moment for the day—an unnerving truth whispered by a lunatic with opioid eyes, dog tags, and untied shoes. It's a pity what they come to, the lost ones, but they see things the rest of us can't, like animals that sense an earthquake coming. I wipe my eyes, click off Courtney, and focus in silence. I checked my detective's laptop last night. He created a Gallagher folder. Jottings of what he's picked up so far. He's quite the riffer. I can see him working it out—the mechanics, morality, and mystery, like Raymond Chandler (everyone who moves to LA encounters Chandler at least once) meets the Tibetan Book of the Dead. He's got folders on every murder case he's handled. Dozens of them. I've read only a few, but they would make a great Netflix or Hulu series. Note to self: We Angelenos think the little things we pick up, the tidbits we hear, should be scripted and put on a screen. It is annoying, but it's how the city works. Everything real can be dreamed again, only better—which, when you think about it, is the splendid lie of our time.

My detective has talked to Kimmel. He knows about Jamieson. He's planning to go to the funeral. Should I go? I'm an architect. A lot of us will be there, black-draped and mourning a fallen genius. One of *us*. I can hear them now, prattling through pretend sobs, discussing contracts and will-you-hire-me looks between shovels of dirt. Kimmel will be there, of course, a bereaved father figure from an opera. Jamieson too, no doubt, the grieving friend. The other one too, maybe, but we'll get to him later—no sense in dragging another name forward before it's time. We must stay with the plan. Cops look for suspects at funerals. Any crime novel reader knows that. Don't they? It would be enticing, though. I could fake a tear or two. Look mildly distraught in a shame-of-the-world kind of way. Added bonus: I could see my detective again in the flesh—which, I must say, I have been fantasizing about. Better not. Too risky. Every face a clue. It's working out, though, much as I expected.

Ohhh, my detective. I didn't even know he existed until two years ago, when the *Times* ran a profile on him after he solved the killing of a producer's assistant director in a labyrinthine—newspaper's word, not mine—scandal involving a studio exec, a hooker, an illegal from Guatemala, a bit of coke, adultery, a bag of money, a shih tzu, and a house in the Caymans. The body was folded into a dumpster downtown—my detective's territory. He traced the money, ran down leads, caught a few breaks, and came across an incriminating email involving the dog and the hooker. Annapurna Pictures bought the rights for a movie, but problems with financing and incoherent screenplays delayed shooting;

there were murmurs in the trades about another *Ishtar*. The *Times* printed a portrait of my man standing inside the Bradbury Building. I thought how beautiful they both were: the terra-cotta and brick, of course, with the intricate iron railings and ceiling of light, as if you'd wandered into an old European train station; and my detective for his face, angled and lonesome, black hair, rumpled, and his caravan eyes, which, I must say, looked right at me—not hard or distant, but as if he recognized me from some sweet past life. Oh, yes. I knew then he would be my detective, my man. You might say it got the ball rolling. The story said he was a cop who worked mostly alone. His boss, Manuel Ortiz, described him as "kind of different, you know, like one of those painter guys who wanders around and sees stuff that fits into other stuff and becomes a picture." I could tell that the woman who wrote it, Susan Chandler, had a crush on him, though she hid it cleverly in her pretty sentences. She didn't fool me. She liked my detective, and I felt jealous sitting in my house, my detective looking back at me on my laptop, with Susan Chandler's words all around him. Tingle. Envy. The story said he came from an Old East family. His father was a murdered boxer whose killers were never found. A few sailors from a Russian-type country merchant vessel were suspects. But they disappeared across the sea at first light, and nothing happened. The case stayed in a folder, as so many do. My detective's mother was a principal (loves Virginia Woolf and Jeanette Winterson, his files say) who schooled him in the finer ways. He took piano lessons as a boy and went to Berkeley to study literature but switched to criminology in his sophomore year, graduated, spent nine months in Europe, and ended up as a detective at the same LAPD that gave us Rodney King, race riots, and O. J.'s wild Bronco ride. I could tell by reading the story that my detective didn't like the attention. His quotes were sparse and reluctant. He came off well, though. A man who deserved the notoriety he didn't want. Rare in this town.

"Dylan," says John, hurrying into my office. "Did you hear the news about Michael Gallagher?"

"I read it this morning. Terrible."

John follows me and sits at my drafting desk by the window.

"What was he doing down there at night? I just saw him last week. He was eating lunch at Water Grill with a couple of political types."

"It's a shame," I say.

"You never liked his work."

"You, either."

"True. He was a bit pompous," says John.

"A bit?"

"Okay, grandiosely so. Like his designs. He was one of us, though—an architect, I mean."

"He wasn't one of me. But yes, it's tragic. I thought crime was going down."

"You think it was a robbery?"

"Who knows?" I say, pointing to my phone.

"Oh, yeah, the conference call," says John. "Let's get Chicago on the line."

Throughout the call, which lasts fifteen minutes, John is somewhere else, thinking about Gallagher and the cruel randomness of the world. John is an internalizer. In another life, he might have been a philosopher or a missionary. Gallagher will bother him all day. He'll parse it and talk about it and set it to some kind of meaning so that even if it doesn't make sense, it does. He runs a hand through his blond hair, which these days is longer than usual—Isabella likes it that way—giving him the air of a patrician wild man, although John is anything but patrician. He's from Oakland, the son of a seamstress and a tailor. He has delicate, tapered hands and, like Isabella, a quiet grace, which I found seductive when he first hired me.

That was years ago. I was so unknowing, so ready to redraw the skyline. I often think of the self who arrived here, innocent, unaware—mature, yes, but naive enough to believe my father's words that great things awaited. That is the wish of all parents, I suppose, but when it came from my father, who never lied to me and was there when my mother drifted from us into those hidden-mind places she went, I took it as holy. He was the soother of my tantrums and fears, the one who told me, when I was ten and much taller than fourteen-year-olds, that our family came to America before the Second World War, from a town called Split along the Croatian coast. "We are a tall people," he'd say, laughing. "One day, Dylan, you will hang a star." He loved that expression. "You will hang a star." My father cast the longest shadow in our neighborhood, but it's hard growing up tall as a girl. You're special but in ways you don't anticipate or want. Sometimes, you try to shrink and pull your bones into themselves, to compress, like a sparrow.

My father celebrated my height and kept telling me to push my shoulders back. "Every soul unique," he'd say. "Be who you are, Dylan. Rise and be tall." I did, for the most part. What must I have sounded like when I first landed in LA with my theories on modernism and the suburban metropolis? But the world moves in its own way. Moments are ascribed to us; things happen not of our choosing. But that is of little matter. We know only that afterward we are different. What once existed slips to a place we can't find anymore, like a voice in the wind, or a dream set on fire.

"Those were the details we needed," says John as the call goes quiet. "Wonder why it took them so long."

"You know Mort. He's scattered, a million things in his head."

"Thanks for pressing him. I'd like to finish this thing by the end of the year."

"Agreed."

"You know, I wonder, do you think Gallagher was on drugs?"

"Why would you say that?"

"Just trying to figure out why he'd be down there. At night."

"A lot's changed over there, John. It's not bad like it was. It's not even that far away from here. What, six or eight blocks?"

"Yes, but at night."

John purses his lips, shakes his head, and leaves my office. I exhale.

Tragic. I actually called Gallagher's death "tragic." To feign sorrow. I suppose it's what we killers do. It's like acting. I order lunch at my desk and close the door. It's quiet, the light soft, snug in our little firm tucked in a courtyard most people don't know about, just beyond the Biltmore. The designs for the Carmel library are spread before me. I eat my feta, spinach, and walnut salad and sip a pinot grigio. I want to be alone for a while. I hear John's muffled voice on the phone down the hall, probably talking to Isabella, laying out his thoughts on Gallagher and why we end up the way we do. I could tell him a lot. I won't. I cork the pinot and slide it back into my little fridge. Time to work, to imagine lines filling into form and shape.

I'll stay in here all day. It is the best place to be. I look at the framed photograph on my desk, of me playing tennis at Stanford. So tanned and quick and strong, the look on my face, the fierceness of my eyes locking on the ball, the breath, the racket back, the biceps fine and long. My frame supple as a reed; my father somewhere in the stands. He taught me when I was little— hours and hours of hitting balls, morning and dusk, like pearls on endless strands. When we finished, we'd go to a diner. He would order a beer and I'd get a milkshake and we'd sit against the big window, telling stories, laughing, watching the night fall. Where did that girl go? I think we all must ask that of ourselves. Our interior voice stays the same, but over time, it echoes differently, as if blended with a voice not intuitively our own yet part of us, a voice that has taken on burdens that the voice we started with, our birth voice, cannot endure. Does that make sense? I am no different. But I would love to be her again, to feel the way she felt before she knew the things she shouldn't. That's ridiculous, I know, but even bad people—and I'm not saying I am one— had something once, maybe a light that was taken the moment it burned brightest.

CHAPTER 8

"Jesus, lot of people."

"You checking up on me?"

"Look to your right."

"Mayor looks shiny. That a new suit? I never did get the appeal. He's plastic to me. Never trusted the eyes. Kind of shifty, don't you think, in that I'll-*say*-this-but-really-*do*-that kind of way?"

"Keep your voice down and don't be a wiseass," says Ortiz, looking me over. "You could have dressed a little better, Carver."

"This is dark," I say, pointing to my jacket. "Funeral attire. Polished shoes too."

"Stacked deck today. Police chief, commissioners. Bunch of brass. Reporters. I saw that chick from the *Times* again. Christ, she's pushy. You talk to her? These architects carry serious weight. Who would have thought, right? It's the money, man."

"And aesthetics."

"Yeah, that too," says Ortiz, rolling his eyes. "Building a whole new Rome, and shit. Need these guys, I guess."

"Hitler wanted to rebuild Berlin to look like ancient Athens."

"Screw Hitler. Who's this friend of Gallagher's? This Jamieson guy?"

I nod left.

"The big blond guy with the sunglasses."

"You talk to him yet?"

"I will after."

"Kimmel said he was close to Gallagher, right?"

"Best friends. You want to hold my hand on this?"

Ortiz gives me his best fuck-you glance.

"No. But I think you might need a partner for this one."

"I work alone."

"Yea, but a lot of pressure on this case."

"Let me work it like I do. I'm better that way. Haven't let you down yet. Besides, *you're* my partner."

"I'm your boss. I got a whole section to run."

"Which makes you the ideal partner." I smile.

"All right, I'll be over by the mayor, but we're not done talking about this partner thing," says Ortiz, tamping his black mustache the way he does when he's distracted by a moment of reflection. "Forest Lawn's a peaceful goddamn place, huh? Bucolic. Brochure says 'bucolic.' I should be planted up here. Nice chapel, good view of the city. Cost my whole pension probably. There's movie people up here. Michael Jackson's in some mausoleum. Remember that case? Christ. How's Gallagher doing it?"

"Cremation."

"The urn. Probably go that way myself. Tidy and cheap. You ever think about it? The end?"

Ortiz slips toward the mayor's entourage. The crowd follows a curl of incense into the chapel. The altar is crowded with lilies in glass vases. A priest in green and gold vestments raises his hands. A big red book opens, and the death mass begins. The readings are brisk. Stories of prophets and disciples, dust and paradise. Redemption has become a cheap word, but it is all we have, I guess—a bit of succor for the corrupt soul. Death came so fast to Gallagher that he didn't have time to atone. I don't know what his sins were, except maybe the hooker, but is that enough to keep a man out of heaven? He had marks on his soul, though. We all do. Venial and mortal, glowing in the recesses.

The priest swings incense over Gallagher's bronze urn, and the scent reminds me of when I was a boy on Sundays in St. Mary's, sitting with my mother and sometimes my father, studying the stained glass and wondering about the weight of the cross and how a man is lifted into the clouds. It is a wondrous story. The sky opening, the tomb, the shroud pushed aside. Perfect story for a cop. The priest's voice fades. He closes his red book. The altar boys flutter, and the architects file out of the chapel and into the sunlight. They look like the feathers on a crow's wing stretching through the grass. The mayor shakes a few hands and scurries away.

"Tragic day, Detective," says Arthur Kimmel, wiping his eyes and folding his handkerchief into his breast pocket. He looks back to the chapel doors and then to me. "If there's anything you need, let me know. Do you have any leads you can talk about? Are you close to knowing who did this? I talked to the mayor and he assured me you're doing everything you can."

"We are. I'm here to talk to Paul Jamieson. I'm hoping he might have insight that could be useful."

Kimmel looks over grass and hills of stones and symmetrical rows.

"There's Paul over there. Let me introduce you."

He hurries forward.

"Paul, this is Detective Sam Carver. He wants to speak with you about Michael. I'll leave you two."

Kimmel wanders away. Jamieson and I walk through mourners to the side of the chapel. Men pat him on the back. A woman holding a lily hugs him. He's about six-two, blond, and packed, with the fading lines of a flanker. His eyes are green, his face smooth as if shaved by a barber. His is the air of a man who lets others tend to the lesser things. He is accustomed, I can tell, to praise and to people humming like bees about him. But the boy in him—I can see him just behind the eyes—is not quite sure what to do with Gallagher's death, as if it were a sacrilege against men so brazen and sure of themselves.

"I saw Michael two days before he died," Jamieson says in a voice higher than the rest of him suggests. "We had a burger in Los Feliz and drove to Perch for a few drinks. We were supposed to play tennis Sunday, but …"

He wipes his eyes and slides on sunglasses.

"Was there anything bothering him? Anything different?"

"Not that I could tell. He was himself. He was planning on buying a new car and he had convinced me to take another surfing lesson with him. He wasn't very good, but he was determined. Neither of us are natives. We'd lived here long enough, though, that Michael said it was a sin we hadn't learned how to surf. He called someone in Venice, and we decided to start next month."

"You look like a surfer. Where you from?"

"Back east. Port Jefferson, Long Island."

"I grew up in Newport."

"No shit. An LA detective from Rhode Island. Not many of you, I'd guess."

"I'm it."

Jamieson rubs his hand over the chapel's stone wall.

"Feel this. Old World." I reach for the wall; he presses his face closer to the cuts and chisel marks. "Why do we want this stone, this style, Detective?" he says, turning to me as if I am someone to be taught. "These buildings hold the past up for us. I suppose they fit the quaint notion of religion, don't you think? God, at least the Christian one, was enshrined in architecture the moment the medieval touched the Renaissance. It fits, though, doesn't it? A kind of permanence that reminds us of our imperfections and how temporary we are. Here, at least. Among the stained glass and the dead."

He pulls his hand away and wipes another tear.

"It doesn't have to be about the past, though, does it? People like the Europe of cathedrals and palaces. Those gargoyles and gilded halls. I love them too. They inspire, but I don't want to imitate them. Why rebuild what once was, Detective? You can't anyway. There are no stonecutters anymore. The earth has changed. Cities grow and evolve. Our notions of beauty change. Don't you think? We must build from the materials and genius at hand. To take the now and coax into tomorrow. That sounds pompous, I suppose. But I've been thinking a lot about this since Michael died. We talked often about this." He takes a breath. "Michael loved Disney Hall. Its curves and angles and stainless steel skin. A building as vital to its time as the Pantheon was to ancient Rome. Michael called it a 'great silver dream.'"

Jamieson puts his hand back on the chapel wall.

"In its day, this design was modern, Detective, but now it's dead."

He pulls his hand away and wipes another tear.

I pull out my notebook, see the way he reacts to it, and slide it back into my pocket.

"Arthur tells me it wasn't robbery," he says. "His wallet wasn't taken. Was it some homeless nut?"

"Not likely."

"I can't imagine who, then. I've been trying. Michael could be a hard-ass. He was vain. He understood how big his talent was, and he wasn't shy about it. That naturally turned a lot of people off. But he was respected. I can't imagine anyone wanting to kill him. He was rarely disturbed by anything, not that I noticed anyway. The only time I saw him not his confident self was a year or so ago. His computer had been hacked. His laptop at home, not his work one. I suppose he kept some work on it—we all do—but not important projects. He felt quite violated. As anyone would."

"Did he have any idea who might have done it? A competing firm?"

"No."

"Were files stolen? How did he know?"

"An alert from his firewall. He didn't know if anything had been taken or if it was a malware infection or something else. He destroyed the computer. Smashed it with a hammer and threw it in the ocean. That's what he told me."

"Any idea what could have been on it that somebody would have wanted?"

"No. I mean, how would I know?"

"You two were close."

Jamieson doesn't answer. He's told me something he wishes he hadn't. I let it pass.

"How well did you know Miranda?"

"The three of us were close. Have you seen Miranda? She's

quite lovely in a waifish way. She's like a fairy. You would not have put her and Michael together. That's nothing against Michael, but Miranda is a woman easily noticed. She loved him, though. You could tell that over time. She was fascinated by him. Michael could be poetic when he talked about architecture, what it means, how it defines us and yet is in a constant state of metamorphosis. He never seemed to arrive at what he wanted to be."

"He was young."

"Incredibly impatient."

"Why did they split?"

"I don't know, Detective. You'll have to ask Miranda."

"He must have told you something."

"Things like that he kept to himself. Michael was very compartmentalized."

His answer is terse, but again I note it and let it pass.

"So you don't think …"

"No, Detective. Not a chance Miranda could have had anything to do with this. She doesn't need the money, and vengeance is not her style."

"Why do you say 'vengeance'?"

"A word I associate with hurt, I suppose."

"So she was hurt?"

"They both were."

"But you sound as if it may have been Michael's doing."

"I don't know anything about that, Detective."

"Have you spoken to her?"

"No. Arthur called her and gave her the news."

Jamieson runs a hand through his hair. He feels for his tie, brushes his jacket sleeve. He looks right, left, anywhere but at me. I can't see what's in his eyes. His sunglasses reflect only me. He takes a breath and apologizes for not knowing more and being out of sorts. "You can understand, I suppose," he says.

"Yes," I say. He likes the word "suppose"; it hangs like an affectation, a sound of both condescension and wonder. I stand in silence, keeping him in my gravity. Pauses are good, let the moments linger between questions. I pat my pocket but remember I don't smoke anymore. Jamieson wants to slip away, but he won't. We watch the passing faces of mourners, mostly men, their small, whispered huddles filling the air like the hum of insects. The priest, vestments slung over his arm, walks down the hill, a black figure growing smaller against the gravestones.

"Arthur tells me you and Michael were close to another man—an architect too."

"We ran around for a while with Stephen Jensen. The three of us met years ago at Cornell and ended up out here. Michael and I joined firms. Stephen went out on his own. He's a few years older than us. Late to college. His office is in Santa Monica. I haven't seen him in a few years, except at parties now and then. We went our separate ways, I suppose. Michael and I stayed close, but Stephen had other aspirations and interests."

"He's not here today?"

"No. As I said, I haven't seen him in a while. He may be out of the country. He travels a lot."

"Did you guys have a falling out?"

"No. Nothing like that. Men change, I suppose."

"Not a lot, in my experience."

Two birds flicker in the sky. I shake Jamieson's hand.

"Thank you. If I need anything else, I'll be in touch."

"Whatever I can do to help. Michael was dear to me."

He turns.

"Oh, one more thing," I say. "Did you know about Gallagher's hooker friend downtown? The one he kept a room with at the Chaplin Hotel? He had just left her when he was killed."

Jamieson's cheeks flush. He swallows, takes a soft breath, and, after a moment, regains composure.

"No, Detective, I didn't know about her. I find that rather surprising."

"True, nonetheless," I say. "The woman said he once brought a man with him. Big, handsome blond guy, like you. Had a *Mad Men* look to him, she said."

"Wasn't me. Not my style. This is LA, Detective; lot of Mad Men out here. I must get going."

"Must have been someone else. We'll figure it out. Thanks."

He walks away and joins Kimmel. The mourners are gone. The two men walk side by side down the hill. The last streak of incense fades. I'm alone at the chapel. I run my hand over the chiseled stone, remembering the months I spent backpacking across Europe—my mother insisted—after graduating from Berkeley. One morning, just after dawn, I awoke on a hilltop above Assisi. A river of cloud ran below me over the valley, obscuring all except the top of the basilica, which pricked the blue sky and seemed to float between two worlds. I stood there until the cloud burned away and the line between heaven and earth disappeared in the clearing of a new day. It was an astonishing moment. I felt alone but not abandoned, and tears came to my eyes—not from a holy revelation, but from my capacity to imagine myself in the world.

The groundskeeper closes the chapel door. The sun skims west. I head down the hill and call Ortiz and tell him I'm flying to New York to talk to Miranda.

CHAPTER 9

I've been going through my man's files.

We're a lot alike.

Our thoughts, how we wonder about things, and our melancholy, which gives us comfort. It's an old word, "melancholy." But it is how my detective and I see the world. Through bruises. We are not morose. That is a different word. We hear what others do not. He came to it earlier than I did.

The files on his father—a novel's worth in length—are visitations on a man he never really knew, a boxer in the twilight, fascinating and frightening, a man who left a boy half-formed. The damage fathers can do, forcing boys to stand over the body of the man who gave them life but no sense of how to live it. Thank God for his mother. She rescued and healed him and set him right, and she is loved, though her passages are short. But it is the father he writes about to pick apart the mystery of self. My realization of self came much later and, I would say—and I do think I can be trusted on this—in a quicker, more shattering way.

But we are the same, and now we are in this game together—my game. I hold the instructions, the rules, the hourglass, and the pieces. Oh, yes.

He's onto Jamieson. That prick. Although, I must say, I admire Jamieson's aesthetics, his sense of style and meaning, much more than Gallagher's. Jamieson understands classicism. His buildings possess a flourish, often just a nod, to what came before. A hint of Greek, a twist of art deco, Beaux-Arts. It gives his work modern sensibility and the air of permanence, as if architecture is not inevitable decay, but reincarnation through different forms. Not easy. But still, he's a prick. He so desires invincibility that he doesn't see the cracks, the clay feet (to borrow a Greek analogy) that can destroy him. I do. He told my detective about Gallagher's computer. The hacking. *Oh, my. I'm blushing. It was me.* Gallagher's laptop was tougher to crack than my detective's. He had a formidable firewall and a cryptic password that read something like this: "pq@z#%oo&bilbao." Yikes. Gallagher called a friend who knew a computer geek. They went about trying to find the hacker. No luck. They lost my scent at every turn. I slid like a phantom back into the ether. This is a very critical time in my game. My detective's off to New York. Miranda could tell him a lot. She knows what was on the computer. Oh, yes. She discovered it quite by chance, and she flew away years ago in a mist of bank accounts and tears. Jamieson knows what was on the computer too. Gallagher had sent him and Stephen Jensen a few incriminating files, like boys exchanging Pokémons or baseball cards or whatever it is little boys do. It was Gallagher's conceit and Nietzsche-like vanity that led to his undoing. Smug, pale, wiry, and small, he couldn't help himself. He once wrote to Jamieson in an email:

I feel the rest of them don't see things the way we do. They are uninspiring men. Their visions are gone, if they had them at all. Gehry and a few others are still good and capable. But not most. How do you build a Renaissance with mediocrity? I don't know. I suppose great architects like us have had to contend with lesser talents throughout history. Maybe LA is too fragmented. No center of gravity. By the way, we really should learn to surf. I think it would help us see an integral part of what we need to know about man and his place in nature, which—I'm sure you will agree—is the aesthetic of this place. I bought a board and a wet suit. Did I tell you I'm looking at a new Porsche?????

What an asshole Gallagher was; I'm glad he'll never again see a pretty crack of dusk rise in the west. That is my thought when Jacob and I stop at a light. I promised myself I'd stop seeing Jacob, but he called, and I thought, well, it might be good for a few hours to think about something other than the game. I could never love Jacob, but I do like him—at times, anyway. He soothes me. He's driving us down Wilshire to the screening of a new Tom Ford movie, which Jacob didn't produce. But like all producers, he is curious about what his brethren—his word, not mine—are up to. Producers are very much like architects. I'm wearing black jeans, a matching tank, and a waist blazer. The outfit is a bit of a disappointment to Jacob, who prefers short skirts and bare legs, but I'm not in a slinky mood.

"You're not listening to me."

"Sorry, a bit preoccupied." (Hello, understatement.)

"Well, I was saying the Chinese are becoming a real problem. In film, I mean."

"Mmmmm."

"That's a huge market, right? Two billion–plus people. But the party, the Communist party, keeps a tight lid. *A very tight lid.*" He raises his eyebrows for effect. "But they can't stop it. They'll eventually succumb to Twitter, Facebook, all of it. I mean, how can you not? It's inevitable. The Chinese want control. They're trying to cramp us. Limited theater runs. Restrictions on stories. Do you know we can't have Chinese bad guys in a script? Their censors won't allow it. I heard they asked Lionsgate to make one bad guy a monk from Tibet. I mean, how can you make a monk a bad guy?" He sighs. "The Chinese want to inflate their own film industry and shrink our piece of the market. Puts them in control, you know?"

Another light. Bach plays light on Jacob's speakers.

"I read about it the other day in the *Times,*" I say. "What globalization will do to Hollywood. Marvel and superhero comic book stuff—that's what Hollywood is offering the world. That's not much, Jacob. I'm sorry, but it's not much. Will the X-Men be our legacy?" Now I'm suddenly pissed. "It's what sells, though. Right? That crap won't sell forever. It's money. Why are you surprised the Chinese want some of it? Two billion people can make a lot of movies. Besides, we need Beijing to handle North Korea."

Jacob slips out of his comfort zone.

"Who said anything about North Korea? I'm talking about Hollywood."

"It's all connected. The bigger picture. Nukes. Films. The price of cars."

"Screw the bigger picture. I make movies."

He glances over at me and smiles—a plea for a topic change. Another light. A homeless man with a shopping cart crosses the street, his plastics rattling in the breeze. Jacob's eyes follow him.

Jacob is manicured and combed. He's kept his dark, curly hair, and despite his paunch (which appears smaller tonight), he's attractive, though not handsome, in the way rich men—he's in his fifties—are when they have acquired what they think might get them to the finish line. Jacob wants more. I do like that about him: his restless, insatiable need for the deal. The light turns green. He pats me on the knee.

"It's good to be with you again, Dylan."

"I'm glad you called. I needed to get out."

"I'm anxious to see this film."

"Isn't Tom Ford a fashion designer?"

"Yup. I think this is his second movie."

"So, if nothing else, it will be pretty to look at."

"You sound like a critic." He laughs, patting me on the knee again, happy to be far away from North Korea and other global nuisances. We park and slip into a small screening room. No one recognizable. Most of the crowd looks like film bloggers and friends of gaffers, but Jacob, who likes to spot a star or two, seems content, leaning back as the lights go down and offering me a gumdrop.

Fat women—no, obese women—fill the screen, dancing naked and holding sparklers, their flesh pale, mottled, swaying. They are lipsticked and unashamed, inviting almost, wearing red, white, and blue hats as if the Fourth of July had descended on a surreal land of misshapen elephants. And I think, how can this be? How can they dance so honest and happy in their ugliness? Who taught them that? One dancer changes into another, a chorus of fat ladies mocking the lines of beauty. How false it is, how great a facade. We're all beautiful, right? But maybe, inside, we're ugly and dancing with sparklers, or maybe the notions of beauty have changed, or maybe nothing is as it appears and all is a trick of the mind. Or maybe they are new symbols of America. Excess until it becomes disfigured and sad. It is always women, though, isn't? Whose skin they want? Our flesh sold, bartered, and displayed. We surrender too easily. That is their game against us. As the fat dancing women fade, the camera finds Amy Adams, nose sharp as cut glass, dressed crisp and fine, an art dealer of wealth and style, a lady of the canyons. Her skin so pale. But the fat ladies dance out of sight, silently swaying. You can feel their girth. The rest of the movie, I must say, is not too good, overlapping stories of a kidnapping, rape—Hollywood loves a good rape—and a doomed romance. A bit pretentious, as art-house things can be. The lights come up, and the bloggers text and scurry out, comparing notes as if they had just witnessed something of great importance but don't know why that is so or how they feel about it. It's all very nebulous. Not for Jacob.

"Excellent," he says. "Wasn't it just excellent? The lovers, the crime. The loss of things you never get back. The hurt. What'd you think?"

"I thought it odd that a guy would mail his ex-girlfriend a novel about rape and torture. Who does that? And why does the movie want us to feel more sympathy for the man who can't stop the rape than for the victims? As if his failure as a man could be compared to the pain and death of the women. Jesus. It's fucked up—pardon my French."

"Mmmmm. You may have a point."

"Of course I have a point. Hollywood does this all the time," I say, taking a breath and calming. "Did you like the dancing fat ladies?"

"Ooooh, what a way to start a picture, huh? A metaphor, I suppose. I wanted to close my eyes but couldn't. Then it all seemed kind of normal. They bother you?"

"Yes, they did. But I'll admit they intrigued me."

"That's a good word."

"It's a very LA word. Everyone out here is intrigued."

"True," says Jacob, sensing my peeve at the current state of Hollywood and wanting again to shift subjects. "What shall we do? Late dinner? Drink?"

Jacob turns right on Wilshire. The night is cool; the hills glimmer. One could feel content, sitting in Jacob's leather seat, watching his hands on the wheel, the hermetic quiet of the car, the faint music, safe from the world beyond the windshield. I don't feel that way, but I'm sure people do. Jacob pats my knee. Says nothing. He's just there, lit by oncoming headlights.

We haven't slept together since the night we first met, after a John Adams symphony at the Phil. Letting him into me was a mistake. I went to the bathroom afterward and cried while he slept. It was at his house. I had no room of my own. I stared at myself in the mirror, touched my face, my breasts, wondered whether they felt the same to Jacob, to any man. The bathroom lighting was soft, and I glowed—my tallness, tapered lines, flat belly, blue eyes, the way my black hair fell to my shoulders. A woman of my height can intimidate. You can see it in men's eyes. They want, but inside their desire is a curl of doubt, like when Odysseus approached the Sirens. I leaned closer to the mirror. Was I beautiful? No. But not as far away as many. I stood there for a while. Running my fingers over myself. Into myself. Deciphering. The body absorbs what the mind cannot believe. It whispers to us; oh, yes, if you listen the body will speak. It is mostly honest, but like the mind, it can play tricks too. I left the bathroom and wiped my eyes and slid back into bed with Jacob, studying him in the dark, his profile (he's an inch shorter than I) sharpening with the dawn. He awoke and kissed me and I pretended it was all okay and we lay in sheets imported from Argentina or was it India and I listened as Jacob smoked and talked about wanting to get Kenneth Branagh to direct a film that would star Annette Bening and Kristen Stewart; the script was in its third rewrite but almost ready and the financing was falling into place and Jacob could see the stars aligning in the strange, hopeful math that is a producer's life.

"You know," Jacob says as we cross La Brea, "there's a new place that opened in Koreatown. Jonathan Gold raves about it. It's one of those out-of-the-way places he tends to find—you know, a kind of hole-in-the-wall. Want to try it?"

"Not tonight. I'm a bit tired and have an early day tomorrow."

"Another time, maybe."

Jacob sighs and turns the music up. He looks over at me and winks. Harry Nilsson's voice rises. The soundtrack to *Midnight Cowboy*, Jacob's favorite, the movie that changed his life. He can't help himself. He tells me again the story of his revelation. Jacob can be cute when he's enthused. But I can't indulge him, or we'll drive around LA until the sun comes up, while he exhausts me with his cinematic catalogue. Besides, I want to get away from him, back to my Victorian in Angelino Heights, to the quiet wood and empty rooms. I have boxes that must be filled.

"I had never seen anything like it before," he says. "So raw and real. Hoffman and Voight. The cruelness of New York. The tenderness misfits can find in one another. That's what life is, don't you think? Giving and collecting grace. It came off the screen at me. That's what I wanted to do. Isn't that how you told me you felt about architecture? That little church you saw."

"You know the story."

"Remind me."

Oh, God. His cuteness has turned insufferable.

"A summer road trip," I say. "I was eight or nine. My father loved to drive with no destination in mind. My mother didn't come. We stopped in a town in western New Mexico. I don't remember the name. We parked at a whitewashed church designed in the mission style. It was small. Not remarkable, but to me it was perfect. That shape and those simple lines rising from the dirt. My father was a contractor. He used to take me to his work sites and teach me to draw. To imagine something out of nothing. We sat on the car hood that day. The sun went down behind the church. People came. A man opened the church and they went inside and lit candles. It was a holy day, I think. My father put his arm around me and I thought, I would like to design such a place."

"Why didn't your mother go on that trip? You never say much about her."

"She floated in and out. My father called her 'the butterfly.' I loved that he gave her that name. He was such a protector. She was manic. Darkness and light. I'm sure you know the condition."

"Euphoria and despair."

"In extremes. She'd fill the house with music and sing and paint and dance with me around the living room. She could be magic. Very childlike. Every experience the first. Then she'd crash and close the door and lock herself away. For days. In her room. My father tending to her and wiping away my tears about Mommy. He was a strong, loving man. He checked her into a few institutions, and she would be better for a while and she'd come home. She never came back the same. Something gets taken, you know? A kind of vacancy. She was like that. Different. Medicated. 'They've stolen the stars from my sky,' she'd say. She'd wander through rooms. She left the stove on one day and burned our house down. I was ten or eleven. My father and I had gone to play tennis, and when we got home, she was standing in the front yard in her nightgown. The flames were wild behind her. She ran to us and we all held one another like it was normal, like you could burn down a house and it would be okay. She was like that. Beautiful like that. I feel those highs sometimes. The lows too. Not like hers. Hers hit the stratosphere and the abyss."

"Do you have a therapist? I know a few good ones. Yogis, too."

"I'm sure you do, Jacob. I was seeing someone. I'm better now. Much better. I run and exercise. I meditate. I shouldn't have told you. You'll think I'm nuts."

I want out of this conversation. But he pulls over and stops. He leans toward me and pats my cheeks with a handkerchief. He takes my tears, the ones I didn't feel coming. If I were in love with him, this would be the moment that would make it last. The tender revelation of imperfection. We are drawn to flaws by a vanity that we alone can fix them. That is love, isn't it? The delusion that we, as my father thought with my mother, can mend the broken parts. You cannot. I glance at Jacob so he knows this. So clever and smooth he thinks he is. He's detected weakness, and there's smug compassion in his eyes. That's unfair. I am the false one. Deceitful. I would like him to know I wasn't always so. I could tell him everything. No. It's time to clip this, get back on the road and into the falling night. He leans closer, thinking he's connected to a piece of me in a moment he's captured. No, Jacob, no. I cannot give what you want.

"What happened to your mother?" he whispers, looking, he thinks, dead into me.

"I don't want to talk anymore, Jacob," I answer, my voice curt.

The desired effect. He retracts his handkerchief. Shakes his head, puts a palm to my face as if he understood. But how can he? Slink back into your seat, Jacob. You don't get my mother; you don't get my life, my history. We sit in silence. The outside noises return. He eases into traffic. After a few blocks, we stop at a light. Our tender storm has passed. He turns up the volume on the radio. "A Famous Myth," sung by the Groop, plays from the soundtrack, and Jacob, who seems quite pleased with himself, explains the music and mood that made *Midnight Cowboy*.

"C'mon," says Jacob, in full cheery mode. God. Was he not living in the same moment as I? "We're almost at Koreatown. Let's stop at that place."

"Not tonight. Please."

"Okay, but one night soon."

He is persistent. I guess that's how movies get made. He wants to go back to our first night. He wants me and he thinks he's found a way in. There's so much he'll never know. I look out the window. Jacob cuts north to Third Street, and we drift through Larchmont and down toward Rampart, where Our Lady of Guadalupe is spray-painted on bodega walls, and Korean children play borrowed violins in open windows. I watch as we roll past. There's a lot to be done. What's started can't be left unfinished. My game must begin again.

CHAPTER 10

The taxi drops me at a walk-up north of Houston Street in the Village. I hurry through the rain and inhale New York: asphalt, flowers, bread, coffee, sewage, salt, and the bite of winter. I haven't been here in years. I buzz. "Detective Sam Carver." A voice comes back: "Elevator, fourth floor." I am delivered to a loft of wood floors, high beams, industrial windows, a stainless steel kitchen, a bed against a brick wall, and black-and-white photographs, all of New York, spread over the expanse. A Pollock-style painting, as if a rabid portal to another world, hangs between two windows.

"It's not him. It's an original by a lesser-known. But I do like it. The photographs are mine. My new hobby."

Miranda Gallagher walks toward me, as slight as the "fairy" Jamieson told me she was. Ginger hair pulled back in a ponytail. Her face—you can tell she was a freckled child—is bone white and austere. The hand she offers is small but strong, and her green eyes stay on mine as if coming across an old friend and wondering where all the years went. Her smile is a flash. It softens her. She leads me across the apartment—must be two thousand square feet—to a corner of Afghan rugs, a couch, and scattered chairs that has the air of a Moroccan salon. She lights up a joint and extends the match to a candle. Not the Disney lawyer I had imagined.

"It's been raining for days," she says. "How's LA?"

"Cloudless."

"As ever. You want some?"

She offers me the joint. I decline.

"I'm on duty."

"You're three thousand miles away from the office. I don't think anyone will know. Besides, this is just an informal talk, right?"

The scent is sweet. She takes a hit, blows smoke. She looks at me and out to the rain.

"I've been trying to mourn him, but I can't," she says. "Maybe it's shock. The news went through me when Arthur called, but I've been away a long time and it seems like Michael is still just on the other coast. We hadn't talked in more than two years. I suppose you've heard it ended badly or abruptly or however Arthur may have put it. Arthur's a good man—a bit pompous, as I'm sure you've gathered— but he's not always succinct, except of course in his architecture."

She takes another hit.

"That's why I wanted to talk to you," I say.

"I didn't hate him, and I didn't kill him, so let's get that settled. I'm a lawyer, as you know."

"Disney."

"Back there, yes. I've opened a small office here. Venture capital clients mostly. Michael and I made good investments over the years. I don't worry about money. I hope that doesn't sound pretentious. It's not meant to. I'm just letting you know."

"When did you last see him?"

"The day I left. We spoke once on the phone after that, mostly about financial things."

"He never came to New York?"

"If he did, he didn't call me."

"I thought you might be at the funeral."

"Why would you ever think that? Is that common in your work, for the ex to show up and weep over the coffin?"

"It happens."

"How sad."

"Why did you and Michael split?"

She walks to the kitchen. Things clatter and hiss, and she returns with a pot of tea, a French press of coffee, croissants, and jam. She puts the tray down, stands at the window, tracing squiggles of rain on the glass. She turns back toward me, tamps out her joint, and sits down. She holds the silence for a while, and I gather she's a good trial lawyer, in control, every movement compact and purposeful. Juries like that.

"I was in love with Michael, and for a long time, he loved me. We had a good life, Detective. We each had plenty of space. Our careers fulfilled us. Michael, as I'm sure you've been told, had quite an ego, but he was a man in search of perfect buildings. Elusive, impossible, I know. But I admired that. I loved that, actually." She sipped tea and gestured for me to have something. "I don't know how love dies, Detective, but it does. You don't notice at first, and then one day, it's not there."

I pull out my notebook and thumb through pages.

"Arthur said there was a turning point. He said Michael told him there was a 'quiet, intense explosion.'"

She winced.

"What does that mean?" she says, mouthing the words to

herself: *quiet … intense … explosion.* "I don't know what that means, Detective. It sounds quite self-contradictory. How can an explosion be quiet? Is it a riddle? Arthur loves riddles. Michael and I did have a few fights, but by then it was over anyway. Just noise, really. The spirit had even gone out of those fights at the end."

I sit back and look around. She sips.

"Did he have an affair? Did you? Forgive me, but I'm just trying to figure it out."

"No one had an affair," she says, looking at me, not blinking. "I really don't have anything else to say. Michael and I fell out of love. Maybe it was ugly in the end. Failure makes people angry and ugly. Maybe pots were thrown. But that's our business. That's personal."

I sip my coffee. I reach for a croissant, spread apricot jam on it. She pours herself more tea.

"Did you know Paul Jamieson well?"

"He was Michael's closest friend. He was at the house a lot. I liked him to a point. Everything about Paul was seduction. I even think he tried to seduce *me.* It was just his way. He and Michael go back to Cornell, you know. And Stephen Jensen. Stephen was much quieter. He filled the room less than Michael and Paul, if you know what I mean. Somewhere along the line, years before I left, Stephen went his own way too. I don't know why. Michael and Paul could be suffocating presences. It was always about them, their ideas, their jokes, their very certain views of the world. Don't even mention architecture. They'd go on for hours about the obscurest thing. Gargoyles and plinths. Postmodern and Wright's organic designs. Los Angeles is a strange mingling of so much. 'Like the Bible,' Michael used to say."

"Paul mentioned Michael's laptop had been hacked."

"Oh, that. Yes, I remember. He was frantic. In a rage. He knew it had been hacked, but he didn't know what had been taken, if anything. It drove him crazy. At first, he thought it was someone trying to steal his designs. *A great architectural conspiracy.* The firms are intense in LA now. All the buildings and contracts. Billions. But Michael didn't keep much company work on that laptop. It was his personal one. Maybe he was laying out a grand scheme for a new city, like Albert Speer. Do you know him?"

"Hitler's architect."

"Yes. There's a passage in his diaries—Michael read them many times—of Speer being flown back to Berlin after the Nuremberg trials. He was going to prison at Spandau. He looked out of the plane and saw old women scavenging for wood in the Tiergarten. He saw miles of smoke and bombed streets. Rubble. His dream destroyed. The Olympus he was going to build for Hitler came to ash. Imagine that, Detective: all you could have had, gone. Vanished."

"He lived a long time in prison, as I recall."

"Writing memoirs, gardening, and feeding mice."

She stops and looks around the room and up to the rafters.

"What must that be like, Detective, to be alone in a small cell with your failure?"

"Some endure. Some go crazy."

"I'd go nuts."

She nods toward the tray. "Have another croissant, Detective. You must be hungry. I get them at a bakery around the corner, run by a French-Lebanese. They're very good."

"They are," I say, taking a bite. "What did Michael do with the computer?"

"Smashed it with a hammer and threw it in the ocean. That's what he told me anyway."

"With everything on it?"

"I don't know what he did with the files. But as I said, it really unnerved him. I told him it could have been random. Some malware or troll. But he wouldn't have it. He thought it personal."

"I guess, in a way, it is. What kind of things do you think he kept on it? Did he have a grand city? Something else?"

"I wouldn't begin to know. What's in someone's soul, you might as well ask."

"Did he have enemi—"

"Of course he had enemies. Who doesn't? But someone who would kill him? I don't think so."

Tears shine in her eyes. She wipes them. She knows more than she's saying. The ex always does. She masks it well, but there's hurt in her sentences, as if she's holding her breath, leaving an empty space at some betrayal, an unexpected transgression from a man she thought she knew. Enough to quit a job and move here, taking pictures and pulling joints from a small box of inlaid mother-of-pearl. The rain beats hard against the windows. We stand and look out. The street is slick, umbrellas bob, clouds roll in low from the south. A city in the rain feels ancient—the mist and the half-light, the sounds of voices hurrying.

"This building used to be a machine shop," she says. "Before that, way before, it was a factory where immigrants sewed. I have a picture of it somewhere. Rows of women and spindles. Italians, Hungarians, Greeks, Germans. It must have been quite a time back then in the city. Would you like more coffee, Detective?"

"No, thank you."

"It's odd how we end up, isn't it? The curves and crooked lines we take."

"There are few straight lines."

"In architecture but not in life. Michael taught me that."

"I think you're not telling me something."

"I don't know what that would be, Detective," she says, with a deep, unwavering stare. She's good. "But the laptop does seem intriguing, doesn't it?"

She lights the joint again.

"When did you start smoking?"

"In LA. I don't do it much. But every now and then, like when an ex-husband dies, I like feeling a little fuzzy."

"Medicinal."

"Yes, that's the word."

I turn and look at her.

"If you think of anything else," I say.

"Of course," she says. "I'm sorry you had to come all this way. I don't imagine I was much help. I did love him, you know. Once. Do you think he felt any pain? The way he died, I mean?"

"I don't think so. It happened fast."

"People want to know that, don't they? If someone felt pain. Is that compassion or curiosity?"

"It's human nature."

"Yes, it must be."

I head to the door; she floats to the kitchen. The elevator rattles down and I slip past the mailman and down the steps. I'm out in the rain. She looks down from her window and waves. Disappears. I walk to the corner, buy an umbrella and a *New York Times* from an African wearing a scarf and a Yankees cap. Trump. Russians. Women's marches planned across the country. It's nearly dusk. Candles burn in restaurant windows. The sounds of taxi tires rise and fade. Footsteps. Faces. So long since I've been here.

When I returned from Europe after college, I lived in New York for a few months, holing up with a musician friend from Berkeley who had a band. I played piano on Radiohead and Pearl Jam covers, drifting from club to club in the East Village and across the river to Brooklyn. It was my "wild time," as my mother said. I still smile at the conspiring way she said "wild," as if it were something not of me, a gift she wanted me to taste. I understood why.

My father's death was hard to escape. It became, as my childhood went by, almost mythical—a memory of another world that left me with the outlines of a man. He boxed; he ran; he worked fishing boats; he died. The rest of him I filled in with a boy's imaginings: trips to the beach, throwing a baseball, teaching me to drive, giving me a favorite book so I could know things that couldn't be said, telling me about girls, which, in my mind, made us both blush. My mother wanted me freed of that. "You cannot remake him," she said. "Let him be the way he was, and let him go." But some things won't let go, and others we refuse to release.

Still, it was a good time back then in New York. I was understanding things: how the world fit together and how its pieces moved; the knowledge, even in its naïveté, that a young man accumulates on the way to what he is to become; those moments that lodge deep, as time and people slide by. It snowed a lot, and I lived my days in museums, a happy vagrant, learning shortcut alleys and smoking Camels on fire escapes.

The band broke up, and I moved in with a punk-rock singer who wore a Blondie haircut and diaper-pin earrings. She talked about the genesis of sin and how the spiritual ecstasy of St. Augustine—"a blister of transcendence" was how she put it—turned sex into something evil. "It all goes to him," she'd say, waving *The Confessions* while we strolled through the village. "Adam and Eve were just a weird little story until he came along. He condemned our natural desires, that little monk, who—and this is the killer—had his own mistresses and perversions. He went whoring in Carthage; don't think otherwise. Stay away from anyone who repents, is my advice." I said, "He was searching for grace." She replied, "Why does grace always have to be against impulse?" She'd go on for hours, not just about St. Augustine but about any headline, book, or magazine article that defied her sense of the world. She said to me once, "You're the quiet kind, which is good, but … Jesus, start yapping a little every now and then." One day, she announced she was taking her band, the Lies, out on tour. She broke up with me a few weeks later, writing on a postcard from Ohio, "I don't think it's working."

I walk north, listening to rain rattle and thinking how different New York is from Los Angeles, how much older and deeper, the lives that passed through here in the century before, the ships from Europe sailing toward the towering light of a promised world—not like scrambling over a fence with scrub and desert ahead of you. I call Ortiz.

"She knows."

"Ex always does. You think she did it?"

"No. But she knows. Something was on his laptop. It was hacked."

"We got it in evidence."

"Not that one."

"Which one?"

"The one in the ocean."

A famous Ortiz pause. I can see him biting his lip, fingering his mustache.

"Shit."

"Yeah."

"What about this Stephen Jensen character?"

"I'll talk to him when I get back. How's the mayor?"

"Little quieter since the funeral. Story's died down a bit. But that chick from the *Times* keeps calling. Jesus, I don't like her. Carver, we need an arrest."

"I know. Listen, though; since I'm here I'm going to take the train to Boston to see my mother. Just a day. I'll go up tomorrow and be back in LA on Sunday."

"Jesus," he says. Another long pause. "Okay, but it's not the best time. I'll cover for you for a day. But get your ass back here. This is what I mean when I talk about getting you a partner." Another pause. "You haven't seen your mom in a while. How is she?"

"The same, I think."

I pocket the phone and keep walking. I meander all night, past headlights and ghosts leading me to Grand Central Station, where I board an early train north as the sky clears over Greenwich and the ocean breaks on dark rocks along the coast. I sip a coffee and feel rumpled. My feet are wet. One change of clothes in the backpack. But I know this terrain. Sun shines on the window. The seat next to me is empty, and I don't know why but I feel rich and warm. I settle back and pull out a book of poems by Raymond Carver. I read one about a man standing on a bluff and looking over the ocean on a cold, clear morning. His thoughts fall away, and he loses himself. He tries to hold the moment; to stay suspended from intrusions of all he is and all he must do, but a flock of birds rises and leads him home. It's one of the few poems I've nearly memorized. I've brought the book on this journey to my mother, who, many years ago, handed it to me and said, "There's some in here you'll particularly enjoy. You'll see your father." I took the book from her and read the poems over and over. She was right. He was there in the black lines, imperfect and carrying bits of shame.

The train glides into South Station. The doors hiss open. I walk a dozen or so blocks and hail a cab to a brick row house with the green door and bronze knocker I remember from my childhood. My aunt Maggie hugs me and leads me to the kitchen, her favorite room, cluttered and unchanged for decades. She opens two beers and slides me a glass and a sandwich.

"Tuna still your favorite?"

"You know it is."

"How long can you stay this time?"

"Just the night. How is she?"

Maggie takes a long sip and purses her lips. She pauses for a second, closes her eyes, puts down the glass.

"I think we may be losing her, Sam. She fades a little every day. Her eyes are more unsure. They jitter. When she looks at me, sometimes, I think she sees a stranger. She has good days too. Had one last week. She talked a lot and read and cursed at something in the *Globe*. She talked about you and your father and how she loved being young in Newport, although I never knew why, with your father being the way he was. Let's not get into that. Anyway, Sam, she's getting worse."

"How are you doing?"

"It never changes with me. I'm good. Still strong. My left eye's a little fuzzy. Cataracts, maybe. I like being with her."

"I feel …"

"Don't say it. You say it too much. I want to care for her. She's my sister. I have no one else."

I wink at her.

"You could have had that guy—what was his name? The professor."

Maggie smiles and sips, lets the mood lighten.

"Jesus, him. It's been years. I think he's dead. Boating accident in China, someplace over there. I read it in the *Globe*. So many come and go, don't they, Sam? Suppose we all do. You have anybody out there in LA? Any starlets?"

"No."

"Two peas, huh?"

Maggie pours the last of the beer into her glass.

"How's the money?"

"There's still money from your father's inheritance," she says. "We're good, and with what you send, no problems. We're flush, as they say."

She sips and looks around the kitchen. Her hair is gray and long, but in a way that fits her, falling around her, bringing out the color of her blue eyes. Five years older than my mother, she went gray early, and now the rest of her has caught up. Maggie was a traveler and a hippie for a while, marched against nuclear power, Reagan, domestic violence, and Iraq. Twice. When I was a child, her hands intrigued me; long and smooth, they moved like white fish in a current. They are like that still, only a bit spotted, the veins raised. Her beer is almost finished. She likes to let the last swallow sit for a while. My dad did too. And so do I.

"You want to go up?"

"Yes."

"Her naps are longer now, the medication. But she should be waking."

I follow Maggie up the stairs, past family pictures, my favorite being my mother, father, and me on a small sailboat, white chop of sea, wind in our hair, faces tan, the horizon hard and blue. Maggie opens the door. My mother sits in a chair looking out the window, books around her, charcoal drawings on a sketch pad.

"They say," Maggie whispers, "drawing is good therapy. Keeps the mind alert."

My mother turns, and for a moment her eyes don't register. She leans forward and studies me.

"It's Sam," says Maggie.

My mother sits back and puts a hand to her mouth.

"Sam," she says. "My Sam?"

"Yes, Mom."

She stands and walks to me. She touches my face.

"Your father's out somewhere. I've been waiting, but I don't know where he is. Have you seen him, Sam?"

I hug her and kiss her on the forehead.

"Dad died a long time ago."

Her lips quiver; she shakes her head.

"I don't think so, Sam. He was here yesterday."

"Sam's come to visit for a day," says Maggie.

My mother looks around, uncertain. She lifts the sketch pad. Pencil strokes and scratches, eraser smudges. I can't make out what the drawings are. They seem marks left by sporadic winds.

"I've been trying to draw a bird outside the window. A little sparrow, but he won't sit still. He flies around, and I can't get him right. See? Look. His wings aren't right. He's so small. I don't think sparrows live long, Sam. I'll have to ask your father when he comes back. But he doesn't usually know about such things. He's a boxer. Did you ever see him fight?"

"Yes, Mom."

"He's beautiful. The way he moves, I mean. Even all cut and bloody, he is beautiful."

"He's gone, Mom."

"Yes, he's gone out somewhere. We should wait here."

She sits down with the sketch pad and looks out the window.

"See, the sparrow's back now." Her pencil moves in a jagged line. "Oh, he's gone again. He never stays on the branch long."

She quiets. I sit beside her. Maggie leans against the bed. The afternoon light is thinning. I feel a cold sliver through the window. The radiator kicks on, heavy with clatter, and then calms, warmth spreading over the room. The early white of the moon appears. Lights are coming on in houses, and I hear distant and approaching voices lifting off the sidewalk as I did when I was a child. They seemed full of mystery back then. We sit for a long while in silence. I put my hand on my mother's and kiss her on the cheek. She turns and smiles, but I can tell she doesn't know me. I am a shadow in the dying afternoon light. I tell her about the books we read together, the plays we went to (to New York on the train, after my father died) and about the short stories she wrote that were published in New England journals and later put into a book. She nods her head but doesn't remember. She presses her face to the windowpane.

"Is the sparrow there? It's getting dark. I can't see him."

"No, Mom, he's gone."

"Maybe tomorrow."

I help her up and we go to the kitchen with Maggie. We eat a dinner of vegetable soup, cheese, and shepherd's bread. My mother is frail, bundled in a sweater. She wears slippers, and glasses dangle from a chain around her neck. Her silver-gray hair floats around her. She speaks of my father, certain he's just gone to the store or out for a drink. "Sam's in LA now," says Maggie. My mother looks at her and at me. "That's far, isn't it? Is he Sam?" she says. "He's the one in LA?"

"Yes," says Maggie.

"Well, I hope you like it out there," says my mother. "Are there sparrows in LA?"

I go to the sink and look out the window. I brush back a tear. My father was a boxer, but my mother was grace, a boy's protector. Maggie comes behind me and rubs my shoulder. "Some days she remembers so much. When you call and talk to her on the phone, I can see recognition, as if she's trying to reach back and fit the voice to a face. It's your father who's always there, Sam. Like a ghost."

"For me too," I say.

I turn and look at Maggie, and she hugs me, and I feel like a boy.

I kiss my mother good night. Maggie takes her upstairs and changes her into a nightgown. I hear my mother yelling, a short, angry, confused burst, like a child's bedtime protest. She quiets. Maggie returns to the kitchen and makes tea; we eat pound cake with whipped cream.

"What should we do?"

"There's nothing to do, Sam. She gets angry sometimes. Smashes things. A few times, she's gotten very mean. She curses me. She called me an asshole, even worse. Can you imagine your mother speaking like that? I don't want her to hurt herself. She can get so frustrated. But we go on like this. I can care for her. It's not a burden. Those days when she remembers and I see a glimmer of her old self, that's all I need."

"Those days will be fewer."

"Yes, but she's my sister."

"I should move here."

"Don't be silly. We've talked about this. If I can't do it anymore, I'll let you know. But I can."

"I love you, Maggie."

She looks away and then back to me. This is our conversation, our ritual, whether I'm here or calling from LA. Maggie assuring me the way she did when I was a child and she stood with my mother and me at my father's grave, the three of us with flowers in the rain on the day after we buried him, when I demanded we go to the cemetery to make sure the dirt and new grass over his coffin had not washed away. I didn't want him to get wet, and I kept seeing him in my mind, alone beneath me in the narrow dark.

"So, what do you make of our new president?"

Maggie's face tightens; she shakes her head.

"Please, Sam, don't get me going. What have we done? Sometimes, I think we're in a skit, you know, a farce that will end and the lights will come up and it will be over."

"I don't think so."

"Let's not talk about that crude, rude man and his silly circus. Imagine. Our president talks like he's a thirteen-year-old boy with Tourette's. No, Sam, let's talk about anything else. How is it in LA? Must be ten years now."

"Twelve."

"Have you met anyone? I worry about you and the kind of work you do. I know you're good at it, but you must carry a lot home. It'd be nice to have someone there."

"I have girlfriends off and on. One of them said I was 'shut down' in my own space. I didn't share enough, or something like that. It's the work. Maybe it's me."

"You're getting sex, I hope."

She looks at me.

"Don't blush," she says. "A person needs sex."

"Yes, Maggie, I am."

"The right one will come. She's out there. Probably someone

you'd never even guess. That's the best kind, I think, the ones who come out of nowhere."

"You're a romantic."

"Some nights. What case you workin' on?"

"A well-known architect was killed downtown. Not much to go on yet."

"Shot?"

"Throat slit."

"Anything stolen?"

"No."

"Hmmmm."

"Still reading crime mysteries, huh?"

"When you started as a detective, I got into them. They give me a feel for what you do. I like the newer ones, but Chandler is still my favorite. That time. The way he saw it." She wipes the table with her hand. "Your mom and I always said—and I know you know this because we've talked about it—that you became a detective to solve your father's murder. Not that exactly, but you know what I mean. Armchair psychology, I know, but I think it's true. He drew you to that."

I shake my head and smile. Maggie likes to talk like this. She likes to go deep, and I imagine all the stories and revelations told in this quiet kitchen, some involving me and other people I have never met but know by name and reference because they've been stitched into Maggie's voice as she serves tea and cake.

"A murder's a story with an end, but you have to find the beginning," I say. "I like that. Going back and finding. I wish they'd done that with Dad. Remember how I felt then? Not having an answer. Mom and I would go to the police station in Newport. Every week, we checked. They said sailors from a Ukrainian freighter probably did it. They'd shipped out the next day. That was it. They didn't look anymore. They kept telling Mom and me they were doing everything they could. But my dad was dead, and I was a child with an unanswered why. There should be answers, you know, Maggie?"

She reaches over and brushes my hair back.

"He was a troubled man," she says. "All that boxing and running and working those boats when he did. I think he needed to feel and give pain. It was probably just a fight. He got loud in the bar with the wrong people and they killed him. Simple. But I think it's true. You always wanted there to be more to it. Sometimes things are as they are. Maybe that's what confounds you. Your father was like a storm, Sam. Always more questions than answers. What makes people like that? Your mother loved him, though. She did. She told me once, 'Maggie, in all that roughness there is quiet.' Did you ever see that quiet? I certainly never did. I don't think he really liked me. We had an understanding, though."

"He was calm just after dawn. He'd sit in the kitchen drinking coffee and listening to the radio. A station that played old music. Kept it real low, like company. He'd gather himself for the day, piece by piece till he was whole again. I feel like that sometimes. How to get through it all, you know. I never figured out how I felt about him. He was my father. I loved him. I think I did. But I didn't know him. He never let me get close, not like Mom. She got close."

Maggie clears the plates, kisses me on the forehead, and goes to bed. I sit for a while in the kitchen. I liked being alone here as a child when we'd visit. I was never scared of this house in the way children can be in the darkness with unfamiliar things. I drink a beer and listen to the creak of wood and the faint whistle of a radiator. My mother doesn't know me. A parent should never have to bury a child, but a child, even when he's a man, should not be forgotten. She waits by the window for my father and her sparrow. I turn off the light and walk up the stairs to the small bedroom at the end of the hall. I undress and slide into bed and pull the covers up. The air is the air of my boyhood: cool, bracing. The moon is in the window. Bright. I turn toward it and fade away.

CHAPTER 11

Hellooooo.

A little attention here, Mr. Detective.

We have a murder, you know. *A body. A mystery.* And you're in Boston holding your mother's hand while she draws sparrows. Okay, that's sad. And your father—yes, that legacy is unfortunate too. But we all have our burdens. (You don't want to get me started on my mother.) And what's with St. Maggie? (That old dope-smoking leftist has a whole folder in your laptop—pictures too.) Now, can we please get back to the matter at hand? My game. You are testing my empathy gene, and that gene is shrinking. I'm agitated, nerves on skin. Flying upward and back on a swing of loose chains. Do you know that feeling? I hide mine well. Most of the time. I've learned to tame it, but, you know, there are cracks. I should get back to playing tennis. Hit the ball. Focus. My father taught me, every day, hitting balls at the courts down the street. So often that it became instinct. I loved to watch my father smile, amazed at me, his daughter, tall and quick, hitting balls on the rise. It took me to Stanford, that game. But I outgrew it. One day, I woke up and felt as if part of me had left. It was hard to imagine. Does that make sense? I found architecture, different lines and grace. My mind is racing. Maybe I should go back on pharmaceuticals. A little lithium or Zyprexa might even me out. But the numbness would come. The blurry lack of sensation. I can't have that. I need all pixels flaming. Vibrant. Everything. All the senses. Who wants an unsweet orange? Am I right? I want a taste explosion. I need a cigarette. The strike of the match, the smoke. It fills me. Note to self: Am I making sense?

I'll have a present for you when you get back.

I'm marching past your building now with women carrying signs, holding balloons, yelling and singing, some dancing. The police are here, but nothing's dangerous, just a great trembling sound beneath the blue sky. Girls are here, so many little girls, holding mothers' hands in awe and wonder. I want that wonder. Where does it go? Why do they take it from us? One girl has a painted face and she is singing; another climbs into the arms of her mother. I want to hold the little girls and whisper things they should know. We are passing Grand Central Market, the great swell of us. Footsteps like horses in canyons. Helicopters skim above. It is beautiful to be alive. Can I put this moment in my heart? Keep it there. A woman next to me is crying, not sad but joyous, defiant. She's holding a sign with a lyric from Fiona Apple: "Keep your tiny hands off my underpants." I feel that I know this woman, that she is in part of me somewhere, in my woman genes, my spirit, myself, the XX that makes me different from the XY; she shares my chromosomes, a pool of my uniqueness. We are in front of City Hall now, the sea of us, and he is there, our new president Trump, defiled on posters and buttons. It is not rage we feel; rage destroys. No, we feel the collective, the spirit that won't be taken. But it is taken sometimes, and we must get it back. Oh, yes. In our own little ways, we must reclaim. I hadn't expected to be here, but I looked down from Angelino Heights and saw them filling the streets, their colors. My sisters drew me to them. The architecture of the crowd: moving lines, splendid patterns, like great buildings come to life. Marching. Still coming. I can't see beyond them. They are my horizon. They don't know what I have done. What I will do. I don't want them to. I want to be part of their purity; they seem so pure. I know they're not, that each of them, like me, has something—not as bad as mine, but something they carry, some mark they don't want their daughters to inherit. The loudspeakers boom. The speeches begin. A small woman in a head scarf. A black woman. An East Asian. A Buddhist in saffron. A Sikh. An angel with a pink umbrella; two topless lesbians with nipple rings and a sign, "This pussy grabs back"; a woman in chiffon; a transgender in satin; a Mona Lisa; a Susan B. Anthony; a homeless woman yelling scripture; Latina girls with Oreos and bandannas; a man in a gold cape; the president swinging in effigy like a bloated orange Ken doll. Others, too—so many others, holding microphones, telling stories. I feel my rushing pulse. Could I stay here in this moment? Could all else fall away? My buildings, my drawings, my designs? No. That's okay. It is enough to be in it now in this transitory joy. A woman hands me a sign: "My Mind, My Body, My Choice." Oh, would that it were so.

"This is America," says the woman who has handed me the sign. "I didn't think I'd come, but my daughters put me on the bus. They're here somewhere. Isn't it great? To do this, to fight back. I was too young for the sixties. I didn't know how I felt about the Iraq war. But I know how I feel about this."

I shake my head. She wipes her eyes. Transformed.

"I hope it doesn't die after today," she says. "This spirit. I don't think it will."

"It won't," I say. "Too much to lose."

She sways her arms and spins.

"I feel like a child, a girl," she says. "How do you feel?"

"Lifted."

"Yes, I know what you mean. *Lifted*—I like that. I was worried, you know, about things. Ever since the election. So ugly. All that anger. Those terrible things said. I don't feel that way now. This is part of the rescue, I think. All of us. I'm not religious, but it's a kind of religion. A bonding. My one daughter, Tara—she's a teacher—says it's a reawakening. As if we've all been asleep."

The woman hugs me. I feel her warmth, sweat, and joy. No woman's hugged me in so long, not since that night Isabella saved me. I feel odd being held in a crowd, so publicly. It doesn't matter, though. There is nothing odd here. I smell her herbal shampoo and perfume. Her spearmint breath. I hold my sign in one hand and her with the other. People passing might think we're mother and daughter. What a notion.

My mother is dead. She killed herself. My father and I never knew whether it was mistake or intent. We found pills scattered around her on the floor. She'd fallen into a low period after being so high. The light had drained. I had seen it often as a child, the desperation in her eyes to find a way back. I used to think she was a lost woman in a dark story and that I could save her. That my presence standing before her, willing her to be happy and join my father and me at dinner, was enough. That I could heal.

You believe that as a child: a moment of invincibility before life settles around you with its truths. For a long time, I pretended she wasn't dead and that I would receive a postcard from a distant place where she had found peace and where, one day, I would be invited. Where would it be? I guessed in the north—she loved the snow and was a fearless sledder. On winter vacations, she'd slide me between her legs as she held the ropes, and we teetered forward and then, as if in flight, swept down the hill in wind and laughter. My father called her "the butterfly." I think he was referring to her moods and how she would drift around us, disappear, and come back. A constant flickering in the house. I imagine her over a field, sun on her wings. I read her medical files the year I went to college. Parts of her, I recognized; other parts, the doctors didn't get right. But how could they? I saw some of me in those lines. Mother, daughter. Deformations and blessings handed down, mine nowhere near as extreme as hers, not as colorful or dark, more like trills than cymbal crashes. We are tricks to ourselves. I think this. I pretend this woman hugging me now, this stranger, is my mother. I close my eyes, and for a second, my mother and I are dancing in the dawn in our nightgowns. It is okay to feel this way among my sisters, this great tribe of women. I can see them through my tears.

The woman releases me and dances into the swarm. She waves and throws a kiss. The sun on my face. I look to the sky. I want to stand here and never go. I want to pull this sea around me, this noise, this joy, this echo of girlhood, gangly and clean.

They say it's snowing in Boston. Flurries. Not here. The winter moon and the sun share the same blue. Isn't that something? You'll be back soon from your mother's. The red-eye. I've been thinking. I have decided that at some point we should meet. Oh, yes. I want to be beside you. To see you up close. Maybe we could lie together. Just once. To feel each other, to see deep inside. I think we have that connection. Such an unromantic word, *connection.* Not pretty. But you know what I mean. I think we could. Just once. My plan will not allow more, though I wish it would. Perhaps we'll meet at that bar you like, the one where Lenny pours and talks too much, but still you like him. You like all the misfits—Esmeralda too, that homeless lady camped across from your window every night. Yes, I know her. She's in your files. I have entered your files. Well, not me exactly, but the unknown me who killed Gallagher. I am not even a suspect yet; no one is. You don't know my name. My existence. Isn't that magnificent? Because I know you so well. So many murders over the years have worn you down, though not in a bitter way. You still have faith in the world. Still want to rescue, to solve. I find that remarkable for someone like you. You are called when we have done our worst. It's hard, isn't it? Bodies on slabs. The cutting away for clues and truth. We'll all be there one day, won't we? Forensics and scalpels. That's what we come to. You like that place where the dead lie for the final offering. You sit among them. You say, in your file marked "The Sacred," that they whisper to you. They don't. It is your own voice. The dead are silent. When the last breath leaves, they evaporate in bits and specks. Why am I having dark thoughts? They find me even here in front of City Hall, among the women. The girls. I have my sign. My declaration, but still … I don't know; these dark things come and go. A woman onstage is singing with a guitar. She is a dot, but her voice is strong; it rolls over us, our huge beautiful crowd, and echoes through the buildings and rises toward the hills and the ocean. I breathe it all in.

I work my way out of the crowd and head back to the Heights.

It is dusk when I return. I pour a pinot and put on Chopin. I light a candle and a cigarette and sit in the almost night. I go over the plan once more. It's a tricky one. A masquerade, really. I have to become someone else, not just the outside but the inside too. It won't work otherwise. It's hard, you know, slipping into a pretend skin. But I've prepared. As I did with Gallagher. He was easy, though. I was a force from behind, knife flashing in the dark. He was so small and wiry, anyway. A punk. I felt so strong that night. All my weightlifting and hitting the heavy bag paid off. He went down quite easily. Jamieson will be different. You'll see what I mean, of course. You'll probably get the call shortly after you land. (Have you noticed I'm calling you "you" instead of "my detective"? I suppose we're intimate now.) Anyway, you'll find him.

My coming-home present to you.

CHAPTER 12

He sits naked in a chair, a pale blue ribbon tied in a bow around his neck. He's wearing finely drawn black eyeliner and purple lipstick. His skin is powdered. His feet point straight ahead. His back is rigid. He seems a statue—a strange one, with a knife wound to the heart, and the index finger missing from its left hand. Cut clean. Eyes open, twenty-seven floors up, as if he's looking out over the top of Disney Hall to the San Gabriels. A wineglass sits on the table. Why just one? An empty bottle of Shiraz from a vineyard in Paso Robles. A pair of women's underpants. Lace and pale blue, the color of the bow, laid out like a wing below the wine bottle. He's posed as if waiting for a show to begin. A slight grin. It can't be—must be the way the powder and the lipstick meet. I bend down and examine a speck of red on the neck bow. I slide on latex gloves and lift the bow a bit with my pen and see a prick on the skin. From a needle, most likely. His blond hair is combed. A scent of cologne. A rose tattoo on his shoulder. Small. I step back.

"You know this guy, Detective?" says a uniform, a Latina with short-cropped hair.

"Paul Jamieson. He was a friend of the architect killed over on Main."

"This guy an architect too?"

"Yes. He was."

"Bad month for architects." She scribbles in a notepad. The crime scene unit spreads through the apartment. Cameras flash. Stuff is bagged. The underpants tweezered into plastic. The bottle. The wineglass. Jamieson, undisturbed by it all.

"Guy's packed."

"What?"

"Strong. Look at those arms and pecs. Lot of his kind at my gym. Must have been caught by surprise."

"Judging by the fact that he's sitting naked with a bow around his neck, I'd say so. Or drugged. You work out a lot?"

"Training for an Iron Woman."

"No kidding. Remind me not to piss you off."

She closes her notebook, smiles, and nods. Most uniforms wait for instructions. She's a beat ahead of me.

"I'm going to knock on some doors."

"Last night would be my guess," I say.

"Yeah, he still looks close enough to life. Lipstick, eyeliner. Some kink going on. What is it with guys?"

"What are you thinking?" I say, glancing at her badge. "What's your first name, Hernandez?"

"Lily."

"Okay, Lily."

"Doer's definitely a woman. No man could put on lipstick and eyeliner like that. That's a woman's touch. Expert. The perfume's

Estée Lauder. My sister works at Macy's. Brings cosmetics and shit home all the time. Why he's coated in powder, I don't know. That's Kabuki shit. Maybe the doer put it on when he was alive, letting him know he was going to be a ghost soon. The rest is all a woman's work, or maybe a gay makeup artist from the Valley. It's too neat. Like looking in a mirror."

"Estée Lauder?"

"Couldn't you smell it?"

"Maybe the stiff did it himself, playing dress-up. A fantasy."

"Nothing else in this place suggests that. The doer came and left with the makeup."

"Made him pretty, then killed him?"

"Like I said, Detective, kinky shit."

"Hooker?"

"Hate. This is planned. Hate plans. Hookers don't hate."

"What about the finger?"

"Token. Souvenir. Diversion."

"You're pretty good at this, Lily Hernandez. Go shake loose a neighbor."

Hernandez drifts out and knocks on the door across the hall. I wander through the apartment—two bedrooms, maybe twelve hundred square feet, lightly furnished with expensive, sleek taste. Fine carpets. Turkish in blues, cumin, and eggplant. A few paintings from the Old World, but this is not a full-time home. Must be his downtown place. Celebs and the rich are buying apartments to be close to the Renaissance. A lot of good grooming on Bunker Hill and around the lofts on Spring going down toward the Eastern building and the Ace Hotel. Rooftop pit fires, Belvedere bottles, and women coming and going in Escalades. How things change. Every dead body tells a new story about the city. Gallagher liked it here too, but in the seedier heart of downtown. Jamieson preferred his dirt clean, I guess, twenty-seven floors up, immaculate, windows so clear they seem not to be there. The bed's not slept in; the shower's dry, the sink too. Nothing out of place. No scent or faint trace of another. Who was she? Or was it a she? The underpants don't look lived in. Displayed like a taunt. But who knows? Lipstick. Mascara. A bow. The emasculation of a man—even the way his legs are slightly parted, his penis lonely, exposed. That's taking something from a man. This isn't like Gallagher. It's performance art. To set it all exactly as she wanted. Sly and meticulous. I'm thinking she (or whoever) made Jamieson suffer to take in the full perversion of her design. The whole thing has the staged air of a *Vanity Fair* cover and will probably pop up on YouTube one day.

"Hey, Detective," says Hernandez, "can't find the finger. They're getting ready to bag him. You need anything more?"

"No. What about the neighbors?"

"One lady saw nothing. No one else is home."

"We have the lobby and elevator videos. See what you can get from building security."

"You look beat."

"Just got in from Boston."

Jamieson was uptight at Gallagher's funeral. My questions about Gallagher's hacked laptop agitated him. He knew more than he said. Miranda too. She all but told me the secret was on the laptop. If that's true, what I need to know is at the bottom of the ocean. What's on Jamieson's laptop? There's not one here; must be somewhere in his other home or his office. I walk back to the living room. A zipper whines. A crinkle. Another architect bagged.

"Where's his wallet?"

Hernandez nods toward the counter.

I check the driver's license: 1980. Same age as Gallagher. The address is in the Hills above Sunset. The wallet—caramel leather—holds eighteen hundred dollars and a black-and-white picture of a girl. *Sadie*. Written on the back: 1984–1997. Credit cards, a few business cards, and a folded newspaper clipping of a runner, hair flying and racing toward a finish line. "Paul Jamieson Wins 440: On Way to Nationals." He looked the part: handsome, well cut, his young face pushing toward victory, eyes alight. He kept that moment, hidden beneath his credit cards with dead Sadie. Sister? Cousin? First love? It's amazing, the things that mark us. Maybe Jamieson pulled the clipping out every chance he could, but my sense is, he didn't and this was a piece of him he kept private. He and Gallagher were successful and vain, men I'm sure I would not have liked, except for their conceit in the belief that they mattered. That would have amused me. Their buildings were the measure of who they wanted to be in the world. Their reflections. They sought no smaller definitions. Yet Jamieson did. In the slender recess of his wallet. I liked that it was there. I slide the clipping into my pocket. Mine now.

"Where's his phone?"

"Didn't find one," says Lily Hernandez, who I'm starting to like. Direct, looking right at me.

"You always want to be a cop?"

"My dad and his dad came before me."

"Where you from?"

"Boyle Heights."

"I'm thinking the doer took the phone."

"No one forgets a phone."

"Easy enough to trace the records."

She walks to the window, trim even with her gun-and-leather cop bulk. The sun catches her badge.

"Pretty up here, isn't it?" she says. "Wonder what he was thinking looking at the view. It was night if he was killed when we think, so it was black, the lights of the city shining up."

"I always wonder about the final thought. The last image a vic has. What did you think? See? Or was there anything at all. Maybe the brain shuts off, you know, slips off the grid and goes dark."

"Could be. You're sitting there drinking your wine, looking at the lights. Thinking about tomorrow. That's what I'd be doing. Sitting by this window watching all the little things below. Thinking I must be doing okay sitting way up here."

"You Catholic?"

"Raised but not practicing."

"How many miles you run a day?"

"Ten," says Lily Hernandez.

"You swim too, right? Bike? Isn't that how it works?"

"I swim a couple miles in the ocean on the weekends unless I'm pulling OT."

"I need to get in better shape," I say.

"You look all right. Tired, like I said, but all right."

"I'm going to start running again. I used to run and lift. Not like you, but enough."

"Thing about working out is, you can't talk about it. Just gotta do it, Detective. Show up and do it."

"Isn't that in an ad?"

"Maybe." She laughs. "But it's true."

"I'm thinking this," I say. "Jamieson's sitting there drinking his wine, and there's a girl doing a dance for him. She dances against the window like she's floating. He's drinking. She's dancing. He's letting it build. But she's letting it build too. Dancing around him. She knows how the night will end. He has no idea."

"Healthy imagination, Detective. Could be. Who is she?"

Hernandez's shoulder radio squawks.

"I gotta take off, Detective."

"Go ahead. Thanks for the good work. I'm going to go dig out my free weights one of these days."

She looks at me as if she's going to say something. I wait, hoping. But she smiles and disappears. My phone buzzes. I know who it is before I see the glow. Ortiz.

"Jesus, Carver. You leave town for two days and we got another fucking dead architect. The mayor's office is way up the chief's ass, which means—you guessed it—the chief's way up mine. Why is someone killing architects? Some kind of contract shit going on? Somebody not getting enough of the building pie? Someone doesn't like the designs? Would architects kill one another for that? If it is even an architect. I'm sending two people over to City Hall to check building contracts. Who's got what, et cetera, et cetera. You get over to his firm and then to the coroner's. We got a team up at his house."

"Make sure they get the computers."

Deep breath, exhale. Fingers to mustache. I can't see him, but I know.

"What are you thinking, Carver?"

"Obviously connected. But …"

"The 'but' is what we need. Press is going to eat this up. You can just see it. A new LA noir. They love that. Especially with everyone involved."

"Have you been reading again, Ortiz?"

"Read this."

He clicks off. I stop in the lobby and talk to the guard at the desk. He leads me to a small room in the back, with a bank of monitors. He rewinds the last twenty-four hours and then fast-forwards. The images on the screens move in blurs, faces and bodies, colliding into one another, rushing past, impressionistic—a day compressed into a montage, a disorienting and hypnotic moment. I feel like God on speed, my creations scattering before me. I'm tired. I need a long sleep. The guard stops at 10:07 p.m. The lobby is empty. The doors swing open. A figure appears. A woman in a fedora. Long coat, like a raincoat but not—flimsier, as if made of bees' wings or air. High heels. She walks past the desk, tilting her head so the guard, if he's looking, can't make her out. She stands at the elevators. They open. She tilts her head down. A guy with a dog gets off. She slips in. Alone. Pushes the button for Jamieson's floor with a gloved finger. The fedora hides her face. She reveals only a flash of chin. A bag over her shoulder. She gets off the elevator and walks down the hall, knocks on Jamieson's door. A hand reaches out. A crack of light. The door closes. I tell the guard to play it again. Slower. Zoomed in. The black-and-white footage gives her a ghostly grace.

"She knows," I say.

"What?"

"Where your cameras are. She hides her face, never looks toward a camera. Who was on your front desk last night?"

"See, that's the thing," says the guard. "That'd be Manny, and even though he's not supposed to, Manny goes outside for a cigarette a few minutes after ten every night."

"No one covers for him?"

The guard looks to the screens. Shrugs.

"No. Sorry. You think we have to mention that?"

He plays the video for me again. There she is. My doer. I press closer to the screen. She moves before me, slow, like a flicker.

CHAPTER 13

A brief appearance by me.

The game is back on.

Oh, yes. Did you like your present? I'm here in the café across the street. All the other cop people have left, but you're still inside. I know what you're doing. You're watching me. *Tingle.* Do you like my hat? My coat? Mysterious, right? No face. I like it that way. You can imagine. Men do. Who is your fantasy? I will be her. You can fill it in. But I know who she is. It's in your files. You love *Casablanca.* I am Ingrid. I'm sure you're thinking that. Like a little boy in a prepubescent dream. That's what I imagine, sitting here with my latte—I've decided I don't like soy, by the way—looking out the window. So fine the city is up here, almost too clean, don't you think? But I am comfortable and happy. Tired too, if I must be honest.

No one saw me last night except the guy coming out of the elevator, but I looked down and away and he was chattering some ridiculous thing to his dog, the way they do. There was another guy outside smoking after, but I was quick and gone. You'll get no descriptions from them or the cameras, as I'm sure you know by now. That's why you're still inside. Studying me frame by frame. It's our little movie. I was careful. Like with Gallagher, but this one's quite different, no? Gallagher was my first, and I wanted it done fast. But I thought Jamieson's end should linger. Just the two of us, he and I, suspended above the city, the lights hard and bright below. Kind of beautiful, actually.

I came in disguise. But before his last breath, while he was sitting harmless and stripped—doesn't it look like he's watching a movie?—I pulled off my wig and stood naked before him, a call girl turned into a remembered face. You should have seen him remember. Startled. Incredulous. The list goes on. He couldn't move by that time. Your coroner—what's his name? Oh, yes, Lester—will fill you in on the drug. An easily googled concoction. I sat with Jamieson by the window.

"Hi, Paul. What a surprise after all this time."

"Errrr, uggghh."

"You used to be more articulate. What's happened, Paul? Drug got your tongue? You sound like a caveman. Try again."

"Errrr, uggghh."

"Mmmmmm. You're drooling."

I leaned in, spoke his sins to him, watched his face realize there was no escape, no absolution, just my words in his ear. Hushed. Like raindrops and seduction. I laid out underpants, bow, knife (You've noticed he's missing a finger, but where is it?), powder, lipstick, mascara, and eyeliner on the table. He tried to move but couldn't. What must he have been thinking? We had drunk a bottle of wine by then, and I came from behind with my needle. A prick for a prick. You know, he never suspected. Thought I was a girl from the service he used. What is it about

Gallagher and Jamieson, the need to pay for it? I suppose, no strings, a transaction, and a way to do things you can't do with the women you take to plays and symphonies. I'll leave that to you. *Men.* I pressed my face to his. "You are my mask," I said. *Mask* had a special meaning between Jamieson and me. You might find out later, Detective, if things break your way. I drew lipstick on Jamieson. Never did I want a line to be so perfect. Purple, a few shades from magenta, dark and bold, an elegant, strange snail sleeping on his lips. I put lipstick on too, so he could see, like they do on girls' nights at the mall. I pretended I might kiss him. But didn't. Then the mascara and liner, each eyelash a pretty, curling stem. Black. I dusted him with powder. It took an hour, my creation of a demon. I held up a mirror so he could see, and it was then that I saw in his eyes how ashamed he was, sitting there motionless and naked, the city spread before him. And because he was an architect, I knew he saw the gaps in the night—the lightless, abandoned places he wanted to bring light to.

I whispered to him, "Other people, other buildings."

He knew what I meant. He would not leave his mark on Los Angeles, not in any magnificent way. He would not be mentioned in books not yet written. The Renaissance would have to do without Paul Jamieson. I sat beside him naked. An unattainable bounty.

"What's it like to be here now these many years later?"

"Errrr, uggghh."

"Yes, yes, Paul. I know. So hard to describe. But you look so pretty. Don't try to speak. Let's just sit here in the night and imagine. Look out there. So clear and hard. It's so lovely, isn't it? The beauty out there. It grabs my heart sometimes. What have you been designing lately? Don't speak. I suppose it really doesn't matter. Should we play some music? Opera, perhaps?"

He didn't answer. He couldn't; the drug had taken every muscle from him. I didn't want him to answer, anyway. It was my night, and I would fill in the blanks. Jamieson loved opera. The drama, the scales. I gave him an ending worthy of Puccini.

Don't you think?

So this is where we are, my darling detective. You'll learn more when Lester's scalpel gets to work. You like Lester, don't you? It's in your files. After all his years of seeing the worst that can be done to us, Lester is not a cynic. He's like you, holding a glimmer that we're not as bad as we appear. I want to believe that. I think I once did. But there's so many shades of me now. I've noticed. I wake up and don't know who I'm going to be. It comes in gradations, a slipping away, a shedding of skins. It's not all that odd, I guess. Given what I've done this past week. Two for two. Still, I keep a balance.

I've learned about myself over time, how I'm not like everyone, even before, way before this. It's not that bad. Not like my mother. She was bad. When she would veer from highs to lows in that circus of her mind, my father would bring me to the living room and put on Roberta Flack singing "Bridge over Troubled Water." Did you ever hear her sing it? It makes you feel all will be okay. That the world has prayers that can reach you. My father and I would sit and listen, smiling and sometimes crying with each other as my mother railed and broke things in other rooms.

"It will pass," he'd say. "She'll come back. She always does."

"What if she doesn't this time?" I'd say.

"Don't be scared, Dylan. You have me. I am here."

Those words. *I am here.* It's all a child wants. A promise. I still listen to that record. I played it a lot after that night years ago when I first met Jamieson and Gallagher. I was doing fine until then. I really was. But, well, what can I say? I smoke too. It calms me. By the way, did you like Jamieson's carpets? I know you like carpets. It's in your files. I especially liked the small Iranian one with the peacocks and foxes by the door.

Children are passing. A yellow bus. They must be on a field trip to the Museum of Contemporary Art. Chirping little voices, holding hands, two-by-two. Remember those days? Graham crackers and milk at recess, liking a boy (in your case, a girl) from a distance, glimpsing him with his book bag, a flash with the others into the afternoon toward home. Gone.

My latte's almost gone. I must get to the office. Designs, you know. A whole city needing shape, order, symmetry. It's delicate, the science and art of public space and function. To inspire yet be useful. That's the trick. To be beautiful with purpose. I've been thinking about that a lot lately. Architecture and life. I won't burden you with it now, but one day I'd like to talk with you about the city, the rise of steel, the shine of glass, the suppleness of a building that must give and sway, like a dancer, when the earth trembles. People should think more about what they live, work, pray, and fuck in. That's an indelicate word. Sorry, they sneak out sometimes.

You're still inside watching me. Looking for clues. No crime is perfect. That's not true. Perfect crimes are committed every day. Look into the eyes on the street; you'll see small and big offenses, ordinary and human, piles of infractions. It is who we are. Everyone a doer and a vic. Your terminology. No escape. Now I'm sad. I got myself sad. I don't want to be sad. My latte is finished. I'm leaving. I thought I might see you come out, but I must go.

Do you know I've never heard your voice? I passed you once at the symphony, brushed beside you, a touch barely felt; you didn't notice. You didn't see me in my black dress the night of poor Gallagher's demise. You smelled of witch hazel, scotch, and something else. But no voice. What is your sound, the pitch of you? Deep. Soft. High. A rasp maybe; you used to smoke, still sneak one sometimes. Yes, maybe a raspy little a growl. I would like that. It would be tender, though. It would soothe. I'll hear you one day. I'll listen to your words. To meet as strangers and speak, those first clumsy, beautiful syllables. I'm a kind of romantic. An idealist, really. I see things in my mind's eye so perfectly. Aahhhh. To live there. To fold into thought. Still, I must hear your voice. One day soon. Oh, yes. It's cool and windy on the sidewalk. I feel it blow through me, walking down Grand, my hair a whirl, the sadness leaving me, the resolve to finish. I must finish. It's so hard, though. Yes, I have doubts. But I lock them away. Look at me; a killer in the light. No one knows, not even you. But if you're as smart as I think, well, maybe, just maybe …

CHAPTER 14

Matthew McKinley at McKinley, Jamieson, and Burns isn't much help. He's in shock from the news. He'd tried to reach Jamieson all morning to go over plans for a hotel on Pico and then drive to Santa Monica for lunch at the Water Grill. McKinley is lean with white hair that billows like a cloud. Tapered blue shirt, red tie, and cuff links. Tailored pants and English shoes. He reminds me a little of Arthur Kimmel, Gallagher's partner, but Kimmel has more of a casual LA flair. McKinley is old school, prim as a newly minted dollar. He leads me into Jamieson's office. Scrolls, books, Macs, and a Caravaggio—not a real one but a fine reproduction of *The Cardsharps*. A shaft of light across cunning faces. It covers one wall.

"Do you like it, Detective? Paul had it painted by a local artist of little renown. Took him three months. He was a strange fellow. Moody, as artists can be. He'd come in every morning and leave after we all had left. Covered in paint. The whole office smelled of paint and turpentine and was littered with rags. But Paul insisted, and we indulged. He needed to be indulged. I don't suggest that in a negative way. You don't know what will inspire someone. With Paul, it was Caravaggio. Paul was a man between two worlds. He adored the art and architecture of the old Italians, but his projects spoke to his time and place. The best architects do that. They are mirrors. Why would anyone think Los Angeles should look like Rome or Paris?" McKinley trails off, then looks at me. "You don't think this painter could have had anything to do with it, do you, Detective? He was a scurrilous sort."

"We're looking into everything," I say.

McKinley leans against a drafting table. I think he might faint.

"I'm sorry," he says, loosening his tie. "How does one make sense of this?"

"How long have you worked together?"

"Paul became a partner five years ago, but he's worked here since shortly after he graduated from Cornell."

McKinley offers a few other details. Jamieson had no wife. He worked out a lot and boxed at Larry Clabon's gym, where Denzel and other movie stars hit speed bags and skip rope. He loved the opera. He partied on weekends and had a collection of girlfriends, including an actress with a small part in a Hulu series about transgenders, and a cellist from Spain who played with the Los Angeles Philharmonic. "And, of course," said McKinley, "he was thick as thieves with Gallagher. A shame what happened to him too. But he was a sneaky sort. Always plotting. Ferrety eyes. I never liked him. He had math but no art in him, if you know what I mean, Detective. His designs had some fine lines; some were even unique, but they didn't touch the eye or move the soul. A building must do that. Paul had that. I worried he was too close to Gallagher and might lose it."

"Do you know if Paul used an escort service?"

"Paul? Nooooo. Why would Paul need that? I just told you, women adored him."

McKinley's eyes fill with tears.

"This is so terrible. How are these related, Detective? Two friends, two architects."

"We don't know yet. There's a lot of competition for contracts in this city."

"I don't think we have an architect hit man running around erasing the competition. This is not the sanitation business in New Jersey."

"Like I said, we're looking at every angle."

"Yes, I understand. I'm sorry. That just seems far-fetched to me."

"Do you know Stephen Jensen?"

"Jensen. Jensen. Ahhh, yes, he's an architect in Santa Monica. Does homes mostly. Beautiful homes along the coast. You know, that's the thing about LA, Detective. Some of its best architecture is hidden behind bushes and hedgerows. In homes. Organic, as if the air conspired with the land. I always tell people that. To know LA, you have to know its homes." McKinley is drifting, wiping his eyes, speaking in tangents. "I'm sorry. But yes, Jensen's carved out quite a niche for himself over the years. You suspect him. A slender fellow. A quiet, unassuming sort, as I recall. A man you would not notice coming to or leaving a party."

"Was he close with Paul and Gallagher?"

"At one time, yes. But I have not seen Jensen around or heard Paul mention him in ages. What are you thinking, Detective, if I may ask?"

"Just looking at everything."

"You think Jensen did it … or could be next?"

McKinley is starting to annoy me. He's gone from demure

and broken to pointed and quizzical. They do that sometimes, feel they're characters in a mystery, a breath away from a killer. He doesn't have much else to offer, but I tell him I'll be back and that we'll need to look through Jamieson's Macs.

"Have your office computers ever been hacked?"

"Certainly not."

"What about Paul's personal laptop? He ever mention something like that happening?"

"Not to me."

"If you can think of anything," I say, handing him my card.

I take a few more notes and thank McKinley and head over to the coroner's office. The city feels fresh, clean almost—last bits of morning shade, unfinished buildings draped in meshings like ghosts. I hear workers' voices above me, their clatter and laughs, but I can't see them. My Porsche jerks—the clutch slave cylinder acting up—and I join the traffic, drifting beneath palms and murals: a five-story Anthony Quinn dancing on brick at the old Victor Clothing Company across from the Bradbury and, farther down Broadway, a skeleton in a sombrero, sipping from a beer bottle. I park in front of a big-windowed café and run in for a quick espresso, but espressos, despite the name, are seldom quick in America. Mine slides toward me half-warm and bitter, no foam. I mention this to the barista. She looks at me with a sneer and takes my four bucks.

"Morning, Lester," I say, stepping into the morgue. "Not too many bodies today."

"Violent crime is down, haven't you heard?"

"How about my guy?"

"The architect. Two in a week. That's trending, or something like that. A Twitter thing." Lester nods and points to a few bodies down. He's listening to a Gerry Mulligan–Stan Getz CD and burning mint-orange incense. He clicks on the light over Jamieson's naked corpse. Powdered skin, faint webs of veins, but the eyes still open, the face calm, lips smeared purple, the pale blue bow around his neck.

"You thinking kinky?" says Lester.

"You're quite perceptive."

"Ah, wise guy today, huh? I'll indulge. Mascara, lipstick, ribbon."

"There's a pinprick on the neck."

"A needle," says Lester. "But the stab to the heart killed him. You find the knife?"

"No."

"Clean plunge. That Gallagher guy, that other architect—he had a clean slice to the neck. Care, skill, you know."

"What are you thinking?"

"I haven't had my scalpel on him yet."

"Looks like it could have been a woman," I say. "Saw her on the building's video surveillance."

"Mmmmm. Well, then, here's my wild-ass guess until I do the science. This guy's strong, powerful. Look at his arms and shoulders. No woman took him down without a little help. She may have needled him with a paralyzing drug. Tranquilizer of some sort. You can get all kinds of stuff on the web. You ever notice that? How much crap you can buy just sitting around at home? Or maybe she knew a vet or a doctor. She zaps him with the needle. She probably slipped something into his drink so he'd be woozy by the time she injected him. Anyway, he can't move. The knife comes out. Clean cut on the finger too. You find it?"

"No."

"Who takes a finger?"

"A collector," I say, half smiling.

"Two dead architects but no pattern—that's what you're looking at. Somebody's messing with you."

We stand over the body.

"We come and go in mystery, don't we, Carver?"

"Womb to grave."

"And all the stuff between. Speaking of which, my wife and I went dancing the other night. She said we were in sync, the way we moved. It did feel like that. For a minute. We seemed to float. I have to branch out more. Try new things. A lot of stuff to do before the grave."

"Glad you're working it out," I say.

"Whatever. Dancing one night. The next, who knows?"

"I might start working out. Get back to running and lifting."

"That'd be good for you," says Lester. "You look like you could be a jock. Meet someone?"

"Can't a guy just work out?"

Lester looks at me, raises his eyebrows. He unties the blue ribbon. He slides it into a clear plastic bag and bends over and studies Jamieson's face. He snips an eyelash with scissors, puts it in a bag; swabs the eyeliner, puts it in a bag; swabs the lipstick, puts it in a bag; swabs the powder, puts it in a bag. Step by step, it accumulates, the tiny, intricate things that will fill a box marked "evidence."

"All right," says Lester, "let me get on with it. Call me or stop by later. I'll try to have something solid."

I nod goodbye and head to the door.

"Hey," he says, "turn that music up on the way out. It's lonely down here today."

Back in the car. *Buzz*. Ortiz.

"Crime scene guys got his lap at the house. Nice place in the hills off Sunset. You better get up there. Guys say a lot of paintings on the walls. Not abstract splatter, but real paintings, like the old guys from Europe. Anyway, get there. Chief's in a meeting with the commissioners. Turns out Paul Jamieson—and I quote from some douche bag in the mayor's office—was 'an important architect but not a big political donor like our Mr. Gallagher.' Which is good and bad, but it takes a little heat off. Not much, but a little."

"We still have two dead architects."

"This is what I'm saying, asshole. But one's not politically connected, so …"

"What about the Renaissance?"

"Yeah, I know, we don't want to spoil that. The heat is on, don't get me wrong."

"You seem confused."

"I'm full of clarity."

"You get my text about the video surveillance?"

"A woman, huh? Makes sense with Jamieson, the way you say he was all posed and made-up. But Gallagher took strength. Cut like that coming from behind. Not that women aren't strong—Jesus, you know, I gotta watch what I say or I'll get written up for being sexist or some shit. Sure, a woman could have done it, but it'd have to be a strong one. The one in the video look strong?"

"Couldn't tell. She looked lovely, though."

"What …?"

"Breezy coat and a fedora. Like from an old movie."

"You sleeping enough? We don't want wet dreams over murderers, Carver. Keep that shit to yourself and arrest somebody, lovely or not." I hear him breathing, know he's fingering the mustache. "That broad from the *Times* has been calling again. Important message to give you. What's that about?"

"'Broad.' What is this, the thirties? Have you been watching *LA Confidential* again?"

"I love that. Only one to get it right. But no. I'm just saying."

"She's been calling. I don't answer."

"Best way to handle a reporter."

"I'm driving to Santa Monica to see Stephen Jensen."

"The third Musketeer."

"He and Gallagher and Jamieson were close once, but then they split. Don't know why. Gallagher and Jamieson stayed tight, but Jensen went his own way."

"Okay, go there and swing by Jamieson's house on the way back."

"Yeah. One more thing. You know a uniform named Lily Hernandez? She was at the Jamieson scene. Smart cop. Strong too. She does Iron Woman competitions. Swims miles in the ocean. I don't need a partner. Don't want one, but if one day you forced one on me, maybe she …"

"Don't know her. Let me check. It'd take a while to bump a uniform up."

"Just mentioning it. That's all. For later. Not now. I'm on my own on this case."

The 10 is clogged. I get off at Culver City and take Washington to Lincoln. Salt and breeze. I park and stand and watch the ocean. Every wave a sound and roll from another time, white, green, glittering. A few surfers. Tourists. Russians. Iranians. A busload of Koreans. That dog with sunglasses and his wino owner, yoga classes, volleyballers, homeless, shopping carts, jugglers, a snake charmer, and a doom prophet, his long black hair down and wet, his tie-dye shirt drying on the sand like a banner in the sun. I point my face to the sky. Noises at the edges. I am warm and I could sleep. I could sleep for ages.

Jensen's office is at the top of an eight-story art deco between the Santa Monica Pier and the Palisades. Scattered papers and blueprints. A tall, slender black woman appears and draws back a curtain. Light fills the room. Half-finished drawings of houses hang on the walls; photographs of monks and skylines and deserts and savannas and rain forests; rocks in a glass case, hammered copper pots, a tin can from Kenya, a postcard from Amsterdam. The woman—she is black and swanlike—steps into an adjoining room and opens another curtain. More light. Two cracked Oxford blood-leather chairs, two Macs, a drafting table, a cuckoo clock, a small TV, muted and tuned to CNN, and a large photograph of a sunset on a tea plantation in a place I do not know.

"What house is yours?" says the woman.

"I don't have a house."

"Oh, I thought you were checking on a design. We've been busy. Chinese. Europeans. Everybody wants a house on the coast. There's only so much coast. People don't realize that. It is finite. I'm Wanita."

"Is Stephen here?"

"No. He's gone," she says. Her accent is African, curled vowels, floating consonants. "I think Montana. Fishing or hiking or climbing. I can't keep up with Stephen."

"Can you reach him?"

"He goes off the grid when he goes. Shuts his phone off and returns when he returns. Usually no more than two weeks."

"How long has he been gone?"

"Four or five days. He is, as my father would say, a spirit man. Can I give him a message?"

"I'm Detective Sam Carver. I need to ask him a few questions about Michael Gallagher."

Her face tightens. I reach for my notebook.

"It is a shame. I read about it in the *Times*. Stephen was quite shaken. He's a delicate person. His feelings, I mean."

"Was he close to him?"

"Once, yes, but not for years."

"How long have you been with Stephen?"

She nods, pours two coffees, and leads me to leather chairs by the window. We sit and look out to the blue, beyond the waves to the calmer water where freighters and sailboats move on the horizon. Her black skin shines in the light. Stephen, she says, was friends with Gallagher and Jamieson before she and Stephen met. He talked about them sometimes, pointed out their work when he would take her on "his meticulous architectural tours of Los Angeles. Hours and hours we would drive and each time was like seeing the city for the first time."

Jensen, Gallagher, and Jamieson were students together at Cornell, and one by one, Stephen said quite by chance, they arrived here. They stayed close, but there was a falling-out. When she asked why he didn't see them anymore, Jensen would shake his head and change the subject. "What happened, I don't know," she says, "but it hurt him. We saw them once at a conference in San Diego. Stephen nodded to them from across the room, and we quickly left. They lifted their glasses. They seemed like two brash schoolboys to me. Self-satisfied. Do you know the kind? Smug. Stephen is not like that." She and Jensen met in Ethiopia. He had traveled to Addis Ababa to meet her father, an architect and archaeologist, who took him to ruins and medieval churches in Aksum and Lalibela. Wanita was her father's assistant, and she accompanied them. She and Jensen fell in love, and he extended his visa and kept a journal and a sketchbook. After traveling back and forth for a year, they married. "All of this," she says, "happened after what happened with Michael and Paul."

"But you have no inkling of what broke up three friends? You must have sensed something."

"I didn't sense anything," she says, tightening her jaw and looking at me hard. "As I told you, Stephen never spoke of it."

"Paul Jamieson is dead," I say.

The news moves through her. A tear rises at the edge of her eye. She stands with her coffee and looks at the ocean.

"What has happened, Detective?"

"We don't know."

"When did Paul die? Was he killed?"

"Yes. We found him this morning. Most likely, he was killed last night."

"Stephen has been away. As I said, he left three, four days ago, after Michael was killed. I had never seen him so upset. The news came on the TV while he was working. He said he had to get away. He is a traveler, Detective. His comfort is the road."

She sips. "Oh, God." She sips again. "It's cold." She turns from the window, takes my cup, and pours fresh coffee.

"Should I be worried, Detective? He hasn't seen them in so long. Why this? What connection could he possibly have?"

"We don't know. We need to find out."

"I'll call him now," she says. She hits a button. I hear it ring. No answer. "Please give me your number, Detective. I'll leave it with Stephen. He will not answer. He never does on a trip. I will leave it on his voice mail, and maybe by chance he'll check it." She writes and hands me a number on paper. "This is Stephen's phone." I give her my card. She walks around the room, unrolls a blueprint on the drafting table. "He designs homes, Detective. Wonderful homes." She wipes her eyes. "I don't know how to feel. How should I feel? How do people feel in situations like this? Stephen may be in danger." She lifts her coffee, puts it down before drinking it. She picks up her phone and walks back to the window and stands for a while. She calls Jensen again and leaves a message. Urgent, stern. She turns and walks back toward me, smooths her husband's blueprint. "My father was a smart man, a man of history and a bit of a philosopher. I missed him for such a long time when I moved here with Stephen. He visited several times and died a few years ago. He loved wandering the ruins of my country and the traces left by Europeans. 'Listen,' he would say, 'they are here in the air all around you. Listen.' I remember that so clearly. The voices he said we could hear." She shakes her head. "I am sorry, Detective. I'm rambling. Why would you want to know about my father? I don't know what thought to have, how to feel. My father and his spirits came into my head. We are silly people, aren't we, Detective? Silly people with ghosts."

I close my notebook, slide my pencil away.

"How do you fit so much on such small pages?" she says.

The sun sets in my rearview. I exit the 10 at Robertson and head north of Sunset. I drive into the hills, thinking about Wanita and how her accent made me think of maps and books. Jensen's a suspect. Has to be. A falling-out with two dead men years ago and now off to Montana, or so Wanita says. If he's the doer, who's the woman in the video? Wanita was rattled. More scared that Jensen could be the next victim than of his being the killer. Gallagher's wife, Miranda, did not have that look on her face when she spoke of her dead husband. Hers was the stare of the betrayed. Wanita's was different; it came from love. A rare thing. What is the connection between Gallagher, Jamieson, and Jensen? What split them apart? What was on Gallagher's computer? I park, slip beneath yellow tape, past two uniforms and into Jamieson's house.

Three stories. Rising like a tree house. Windows open to a back courtyard of stone, ivy, bougainvillea, sage, and a small fountain with a statue, *The Rape of Proserpina*, glowing in moonlight. I remember seeing the original by Bernini years ago in Rome, on my European backpacking trip after college. A young Italian woman, Lucia, stood beside me as we admired it. "So much beauty in evil," she said. She sketched it quickly and handed me the page of Pluto carrying the terrified maiden to the underworld. We went for Campari in the gardens, listening to footsteps in gravel and a man playing a violin amid busts of soldiers and poets. She told me that God was the first sculptor, the original artist, and that at night, he whispered his secrets into the dreams of Bernini and Michelangelo. We talked for a while; I was amazed at how you could meet a stranger in a museum and hours would go by and you'd be lost in those hours, in no hurry to have them end or to carry on with what you had been doing. She took my hand and led me to her Vespa. We drove to a small flat in Trastevere. It was messy with paintings, jars of brushes, loaves of bread. The sounds of stirred pots and old men with newspapers drifted through the square and into the alley. We drank wine and made love until morning. She disappeared before dawn, leaving on her table a sketch of me sleeping. I folded it into my backpack and took a train to Florence.

I run my hand over Jamieson's statue. Smooth, cool, supple.

Pluto's fingers pressing into the maiden as if stone had become skin. Like the Caravaggio of the cardsharps in Jamieson's office, the statue is a fine reproduction but slightly off, as if the artist had wanted to pay homage but leave a part of himself in it too. I listen to the water and breathe in the night. A bikini top hangs on a nail in a tree. A telescope tilts skyward near a chair. I peek in. Cassiopeia fills my eye. I step over a half-finished bottle of vodka, a constellation map, a bag of peat, and a small garden trowel. I wander back inside. The crime scene guys are gone. A uniform sits at the kitchen counter.

"Nice place. Guy really liked art. Old stuff, though, huh? Stuff they showed us in school," he says.

"Reproductions."

"Pardon."

"Not originals."

"Yeah. Hey, Detective, I'm about ready to roll. Crime scene told me to let you know they took a couple of laptops and other things off his desk. They'll sweep them and let you know. Other than that, they bagged a few bottles from the medicine cabinet and took two wineglasses and a pair of bikini bottoms that were hanging from the fridge handle. Party for two, I guess."

The uniform nods and vanishes. I'm alone. I turn on a few lights, pull a bottle of scotch from the liquor cabinet. It's quiet. The traffic on Sunset doesn't reach this far—nothing but a dry breeze, scents of flowers and rich neighbors, all in for the night. It's strange even now, after so many years, being alone in a victim's house amid possessions arranged in a pattern that suited him. The line of a couch, angle of a chair. Every house is an intricate geography of things that don't speak, but in their own way, they tell stories. I take a few sips. I could sleep here amid his things, the ghosts he's left behind, framed photographs, books, blueprints, and a map of the world drawn before anyone knew of America. It is a good home. The lamps glow with an inviting, soft light, and the last music played was "Miserere," by Allegri, and "Baby, I Love You," by the Ramones.

McKinley was right about Jamieson. He lived between two worlds. I can see that here. The statue and reproductions spoke to something ancient in him, but the scattered drawings on his desk have the lines, angles, and curves of a man who saw forward. One design is of an apartment building. It looks like a horizontal stack of cards, protruding left and right at increments. Rows of windows shine between the cards, and the building appears uneven, yet it is magically delicate, as if it could be subsumed by air and light and then reappear again.

I polish my prints from the bottle and slide it back into the cabinet. I turn off the lights. The moon fills the windows and shines on the pool and *The Rape of Proserpina*. I close the front door, slip back under the yellow tape, and drive downtown.

CHAPTER 15

"You haven't been yourself, Dylan" says Isabella.

"Yes," says John. "You've been distracted."

My boss and his lovely wife are concerned. They think I'm unhinged. That may be too strong a word, but they, in their tender, elliptical way, in a dinner out at my favorite restaurant—the one Isabella introduced me to when I first arrived in Los Angeles—believe I need mending.

"Is this an intervention?" I say, laughing. "Get me out in public where I can't make a scene. Boo."

They smile uncomfortably. The candlelight is gauzy. An evening rain sweeps the street and disappears. Voices, the snap of a napkin, the rattle of silverware. It's good to be out. It's been a rough week. (Do I even register irony anymore?) I do feel out of sorts, a kind of unraveling. I must stay composed. Pull myself together. Am I biting my nails? Is my hair okay? My clothes are fine. Skirt, matching top, smart jacket, shaved legs, and I can see in the window that my face is right. I look good. I say that with humility, but I do. Yet still … two men down. A toll. I expected it to be hard.

There were moments when it felt almost glorious to be so powerful. A force. Oh, yes. That rush of things colliding in me, all of it sacred, animalistic. But hours later, when it fades, when the pulse slows, there are these things inside, images and thoughts, not loud but echoing. Maybe that's what John and Isabella see. Maybe what's inside slips out into the world if we're not careful. Breathe. Breathe. Slow the heart, allow no betrayal on the face. Smile. Notice things. An old man pulls a chair out for a lady. The waiter is handsome, buttoned up in his white shirt. Calm. Calm. Let the minutes tick; calm. I can do this.

"Do you still see that producer?" says Isabella. "What's his name?"

"Jacob. That's not a steady thing. Jacob's my diversion. My loyal, misbegotten terrier. He calls and takes me places I like, but no, Jacob is not a keeper. I do like his company, though, at times. He's like one of those white-noise machines when you can't sleep." I smile at the metaphor, but John and Isabella, I suppose, are not here for laughs. "We saw a movie the other night. *Nocturnal Animals*. Have you heard of it? It opened with fat ladies dancing naked with sparklers."

"How fat?"

"Obese. Like fleshy mountains."

"Why?"

"I never figured it out."

"Jacob's not your type," says John, steering us away from the sparkler ladies.

"What is my type?" I say, playing their game, sipping Shiraz in soft light. They are so good, John and Isabella, so pained and worried. I tell them they shouldn't be. My work has been fine; my designs never better. John said so the other day. If they only knew, but why should they? Even my detective doesn't know; he's getting close, though. Jensen is the key. What shall I do with him? I always knew he'd be the toughest one. The chink. Jensen and his African queen wife, Wanita. What's behind *her* regal mask? I'd like to know. I have seen them together. I have spied. Poor Jensen, not like the other two. He is ... I don't know how to say it, but Jensen is delicate, a man-boy almost. You can see it in his eyes, warm and fascinated, like beekeepers' eyes. He got mixed up in it. But still he made choices. Yes, he did. We are as accountable for our weaknesses as for our strengths. I wish it weren't so, that a measure of absolution could be given, but it can't. He made choices. *Choices. Choices. Choices.* The word ricochets. Maybe I'll discuss it with my detective. One day. But Jensen is the rub. That's why he's last. Isabella and John are looking at me.

"I'm fine, really," I say. "It's lovely of you to care. Maybe I've been a little distracted. There's so much to do. Some days, I'm full of energy; other days, overwhelmed. I'm sure you both feel that, from time to time. You have moods. The good days and the bad. Even you, Saint Isabella."

Why did I say that? That was mean. Unnecessary. She looks at me, hurt. I reach for her hand, whisper, "Sorry."

"Of course I do," says Isabella, recovering and determined to keep eyes on me. "It never stops at the shelter. Homeless women, abused women. They come every day. How to fix them? That's what I tell John at night. How to fix them? It's the world, isn't it? How far we've let things go. What we accept. The gallery is a headache too. Artist egos. Haggling over prices, and even a few small tragedies. The other day, a glass sculpture by a Korean artist—you've never heard of her, but one day she'll be big—tumbled off its pedestal and shattered across the floor."

"You have insurance?"

"Yes. But every work is irreplaceable. Like a life, you know. What is that word? Ah, yes, '*singular.*' Every piece exists only once. I called her, and she cried for hours. I felt terrible."

John touches his wife's shoulder. They look at one another, then at me.

"We're worried about you," says Isabella. "Is it like the time before?"

"No, no." I shake my head. Be calm. Be calm. "That was different."

I wanted to die back then. Took all those pills in two gulps and waited to vanish away from what Gallagher, Jamieson, and Jensen did to me. But John and Isabella found me and took me to the hospital. I told them on that long-ago night about my crazy, manic mother. I was never as bad as she. Nooo. She could be so present, though, when she was there. Full of life. A splendid, restless cartoon. Then, the next day, curled in bed, covers up, blinds drawn. I'm not like that. I've been good for years.

Isabella looks away and back. I think she might cry.

"We care about you," says John.

The handsome waiter appears. Thank God. The table quiets. Lamb. Trout. Something vegetarian for Isabella. More bread. Fresh pours. An anything-else smile. He's gone. I feel a tear coming, but I push it back. *Strong. Strong. Strong.* No cracks. But for a second, I think I'd like to cry in Isabella's arms. Her warm, giving arms, her breasts, the scent of her, the Brazilian saint that she is. She has healing powers, I'm sure. I could say it all in a flood of words. Confess. Over dinner. My last supper. But no. Jensen may be weak; I am not. They made me strong, those men. They miscalculated. But here sits Isabella in candlelight, drawing me to her. Her alluring foreign accent, her giving self, her black hair falling, the glint of earrings. I almost lean in; part of me wants to. No. I stay in my seat and swallow my weakness.

"I'll never forget that night," says Isabella. "You had just started working with John. We stopped by your house by chance. You were stripping wood floors and we wanted to help. You were unconscious. When we got back from the hospital, I held you on the couch until dawn."

"That's why we're worried," says John. "We don't know what happened before, so we don't know if it's happening again."

"It's not."

"But ..."

"But what?"

I'm silent. My eyes dart over them. My heart beats fast. I don't like this interrogation. These questions. Why am I holding the butter knife so tightly? I release it, take a sip of wine. Calm, calm. They are friends. Smile.

"Why did you stop seeing your therapist?" says Isabella, so gentle in cutting to the matter.

"I was cured." I laugh with perhaps a bit too much force. We are in need of levity, but I can see in their eyes, it's no time for humor. I have a flashing thought, Detective: Will you look at me one day the way they are looking at me now? Oh, dear, I hope not. But I was done with therapy and dissecting childhood and adolescence. My shrink had me on too many meds. I'm better now, despite what they might think. I see the world clearly. I admit to being a little distracted, out of sorts, as they say, but it will pass. It will pass very soon. Note to self: It will pass.

"All we want is to help."

"You are helping. This dinner, your friendship. You are the dearest people to me."

John reaches out and holds my hand. Isabella my other. I feel their warmth. But I can go no further. I can't tell them what led me here, what led me to that night years ago when they found me on the floor. It is a ghost, yes, a reappearing ghost. But she's mine.

Dessert comes. Isabella and I share a chocolate cake; John has ice cream and a brandy. It's good to be out. The hum of people. The charged air. The waiter glides along the bar. John looks up to the TV. Images but no sound. A picture of Jamieson appears with one of those cutouts like the dead-man graphics the TV uses for murder victims. John goes to the bar. The anchor speaks. The camera pans Jamieson's building, the outside of his firm, one of his designs. Gallagher's face pops up next to Jamieson's. They look like two boys in a yearbook: the pretty one; the wiry, deviant one. The police chief speaks from a podium. A shot to the skyline of Los Angeles. And back to the outside of Jamieson's building on Grand, the one where the deed was done, and dare I see, just beyond the yellow tape, you, my detective. A fleeting instant and you're gone. Euphoria. I needed to see you. To know you are on the case. And you are. You look tired, though. Could use a haircut. But it's you following clues. Back to the anchor. He purses his lips. We fade to weather.

John returns to the table, shaken.

"Paul Jamieson's been murdered," he says. "They found him naked in his apartment. A finger missing."

The finger is irrelevant. Really. It was a whim, just happened. A sudden impulse. Like picking at a scab. It must have been in my subconscious. God knows what's down there. But the news likes a missing finger. I can't blame them. It is a nice tidbit, a ghoulish touch for my mystery. John sits at the table. His ice cream is nearly melted. Isabella holds his hand. He finishes his brandy and looks back to the TV as if Jamieson will reappear.

"What's happening?" he says. "Two architects in less than a week. Something's connected."

"I didn't know them well," I say.

"They're looking for Stephen Jensen."

I think to myself with a sly inside smile, *Oh, where, oh, where can he be?*

CHAPTER 16

I get home and toss my shield and gun across the counter. I'll call Ortiz later. Another message from Susan Chandler at the *Times*. She's relentless, but I don't feel like talking to the fourth estate. I shower, pour a French press, and sit by the window in my leather chair, looking down Hill Street into the jewelry district. Nine p.m. Tired but restless. I go to the piano, try to play, but nothing comes. I pour scotch into the coffee and rifle through a pile of mail. Dentist. Credit card. Save a dog. Rescue a child. I turn on a lamp and read all the *New Yorker* cartoons. I think of my life as a cartoon, and what bit of satire or dry wit I could be reduced to. I put the magazine aside and sink back into the chair. It's good and worn; its soft cracks run like veins. The feel of the leather makes me feel rich in a way I can't explain. I found it years ago on a sidewalk outside a bankrupt lawyer's office. A uniform and I threw it in a cruiser.

I lift an inlaid box from beneath the chair and fish Jamieson's track victory news clipping out of my pocket. I drop it into the box next to Gallagher's wedding ring, and mementos from other vics over the years. I've collected something from every body I've come across. They're like mass cards to help me remember. The tooth from Jamal Lewis, eight years old, killed in a drive-by; a lock of hair from Ji Su Kim, shot in a market robbery, the doer whacked out on opioids; the St. Teresa medal of Andrea Torres, an illegal beaten to death and left in an alley off Broadway, her body never claimed; a quarter spilled from the pocket of Patrick Davis, a USC student carjacked two days from graduation. I run my fingers over them, hold them one by one up to the light. Pieces and artifacts of strangers, except for one: a lace from my father's boxing glove. Hard and stiff, faint with his blood, it was the first thing I put into the box. I think, at times, I should stop collecting. I can't. It's not so much compulsion as a need to record. But I do feel a bit like some meticulous night manager in a back office with a ledger. Each belonging tells of a mistake, a lead missed, evidence lost; those failings that make me less than omniscient and remind me how lonely it is to die in a place invisibly marked for you. Not to know it's coming, and then to be gone. I wonder where my place will be. When? It's better not knowing. I'm heading toward it, though; we all are. It could be years, could be tomorrow, but the place is there, waiting.

I close the box and turn to the window. Esmeralda is coming up Hill with two suitcases in tow, a clump of scarves around her neck, and a bright orange cap. She arranges herself in front of the Hotel Clark. Placing the two suitcases like walls, she slides between them, throws over a sheet of plastic, and disappears until she emerges seconds later like a flower peeking through dirt. That is her pose. I get dressed, pour a mug of tea, and head down to her.

"Here."

"What is it?"

"What is it always? Tea."

"A little scotch in there?"

"I'm out."

"What kind of man could be out of scotch? I'll tell you what kind. A sorry-ass one. A man who's lost his way and given up on things that matter. What day is it? Feels like night was just here; now it's back. Where you been?"

"Went to Boston to see my mother."

"You got a mother, huh? Still alive?"

"Not doing well. Remember, I told you her mind's going."

She looks at me as if I were an odd face in the mirror.

"What kind of tea is this?"

"Green," I say.

"Tastes more like hot water. You come down here giving me hot water pretending it's tea."

"It's tea."

"Hmmmmm. How about ten dollars?"

"I'm short this week."

"Short on cash and no scotch? What good are you?" She laughs, orange cap bobbing in the night. But quickly her eyes sharpen and her words get tight. "What's it like in that building you live in over there?"

"It's an old subway station. Built back in the nineteen-twenties."

"They got tracks inside?"

"Way underneath."

"Something about that building," she says, one eye squinting at me, her voice dropping. "I think that building's got monsters in it. Creatures. I watch it at night. I see them crawling out windows. Over walls. Seen one on the roof, dancing. You see 'em? Not always. Monsters don't show you always. But sometimes. At night, mostly. I see 'em. You a monster?" She turns her narrow face and looks at me. She has slipped to that other place. "Maybe you change into one. Go from man to monster. I see 'em. Up there. In your building."

"I'm …"

"I used to know Jesus songs. Forgot 'em all. What's that one, 'Quiet Night'?"

"'Silent Night.'"

"Yeah. That one. Bunches more. Forgot 'em all. Jesus keeps the monsters away. The mission priest said so."

"Maybe you should sing more."

"Tell me a story. A nice one. No monsters. You know what I do when I see them? Count. Close my eyes and count. One, two, three, four, five, five, six, eight, eleven … I keep counting and counting and counting, and when I open my eyes, they're gone. That's the trick with monsters. If you don't see them, they don't see you." She sips her tea, rubs her face, scratches her head, her cap going back and forth. She stills. "My daddy taught me that. Long ago. Dead. I see him sometimes over on San Pedro. At the shelter or outside that raggedy-assed tavern—you know the one. Where the dead go. We wave, but he's not the same. The dead aren't the same as us. They ain't got that thing inside. That white, shiny thing. What's it called? That thing that floats? I don't know. But the dead are here. Can't just ignore them." She starts to cry. She wipes her eyes and nose with a sleeve, opens her mouth in silent anguish, scratches her cheek. Shakes her head side to side, like a million nos. She stills again. "Tea's cold. You got any whiskey? How about ten dollars? Look." She nods toward my building. "I think I see one. Up there. See him? In that window. He's watching us." She pulls the plastic cover up to her nose. She closes her eyes. "One, two, three, four, five, six, eighteen, twenty-three, seven …"

I listen. She doesn't stop. Her eyes clench shut. I try to figure out the pattern of the numbers, the sequence she chooses. There is none. She doesn't know I'm beside her anymore. I stand and look at my building. Maybe there are monsters. I walk toward the corner. Two women, teetering from a night of cocktails at the Perch, run across the street in heels. Two men follow. I turn the corner and head toward the Little Easy.

"There he is," says Lenny, standing at the far end of the bar, loosening his bow tie. "Man of the hour."

"Why do you even bother with that thing?"

"Owner wants us to look presentable. You don't like my bow tie?"

"It never seems quite right. Perpetually crooked."

"Fuck it," he says, pulling it off and setting it on the bar.

"Quiet tonight."

"Oddly so."

He pours me a scotch and leans on the bar so he's face-to-face with me, the priest to my penitent.

"Another architect, huh?"

"Two down."

"In a week."

"I'm thinking it's over contracts, something, you know, professional."

"Why's that?"

"Seems the most natural to me. These guys are at the center of what's happening, the change. They're designing what we're going to look like. The new city. Lot of power in that. Lot of bad little nasty things, I bet."

He pulls back, taking his Old Spice scent with him.

"C'mon, Lenny. You'll have to do better than that."

"That's all I got. Is it true he was found naked, with a finger missing?"

I wink and sip.

"Damn."

"Let's talk about something else, Lenny."

His eyes narrow, hand to chin.

"Immigration. That's the hot topic," he says. "What do we do? We can't live without 'em. Whole damn economy would collapse. High-priced fruit. Unpicked vineyards. A national calamity. You know, California's, like, the fifth- or sixth-largest economy in the world. We're talking the whole goddamn planet. I think, if I may say, that solving immigration right now is more serious than global warming." He unbuttons his collar, crosses his arms. Leans back toward me so the old couple a few stools over don't think he's wacko. "I can get passionate. I'm just saying there's got to be fairness involved. But we can't let every Tom, Dick, and Julio in. They're eating up entitlement programs. It's costing us. But still, there's got to be compassion. It's the moral dilemma of the age."

He shakes his head and polishes a glass.

"Next," I say.

"What do you mean, 'next'?"

"Let's stay out of politics."

"Immigration's not politics. It's people."

"How about something closer to the soul, something personal? How about music? Who are you listening to these days?"

He smiles. "Good topic. Motown and the Beatles. Those

sounds. My youth. A song can bring you back to when everything was a first. 'Norwegian Wood.'"

I get off the stool and take my scotch to the piano—a better upright than mine, but bruised and cracked and out of tune, jammed against the wall. I play "Norwegian Wood." Soft. Lenny leans at the corner of the bar. He likes it when I play, which is not often.

"First time I heard it," he says, "I was at a party, kissing a girl in a closet under a pile of coats. Julie Mason. I was in the sixth grade and I thought, 'Lord, just freeze me in this moment. Make my mom come late to pick me up. Let this song just go on and on, and keep that damn door closed.'" He laughs. "Did I ever tell you about Julie Mason? My first love. Brooklyn girl. Not the gentrified Brooklyn of today. The old Brooklyn. Her dad was a pipe fitter. Mean fucker. Anyway. We dated on and off through school and we kept in touch when I moved out here. We drifted apart, though. I hadn't talked to her in years. Then the strangest damn thing. When I got arrested, you know, for running the dope up the coast, she flew out for my hearing. She was married. Had two kids. I walked into the courtroom and there she was, sitting there. She blew me a kiss. Isn't that something? No words, no touch, just a blown kiss and then I was off in handcuffs. Never saw her again."

"That's bullshit."

"Hand to God, Sam. Hand to God."

"What happened to her?"

"I thought about calling her when I got out. Reconnecting, you know. But too much time had passed, and I thought even if I did see her again, nothing would be as perfect as that blown kiss."

I slide from "Norwegian Wood" to "Her Majesty," play it

slow, coil back through it, expand it a bit, and then pull it tight, letting the last note rise and hang. I close the lid. Lenny pours me another scotch.

"On the house. I like it when you play, Sam."

"Thanks, Lenny."

"You're a more classical guy, though, aren't you? All those symphonies you go to."

"I go a few times a season."

"Mmm, seems more often to me."

I take a sip and suddenly I'm happy. It's not the liquor, although that does play a part. It's being here in this place off Fifth Street, the way the light is soft, how the bottles are arranged, the swipe of Lenny's rag, the dull gleam of the bar, worn and smooth, the hush of it all, like a church at night. And Lenny's voice. A coaxing, pleasant thing, a sound you could build a conspiracy with. I don't see the dead in here, don't hear them calling. They're out there. Like Esmeralda's monsters. Gallagher. Jamieson. The others. But not here. It's just Lenny and his story of kissing a girl in a closet. That rushing, splendid moment. How do you make such a thing last? Lenny is saying something about our new president, but I'm still back in "Norwegian Wood."

The old couple at the bar, dressed like characters from a movie set, are playing cribbage and drinking lower-shelf cognac. "There's a shoot over on Spring," says Lenny, nodding toward the couple. "Some crime or mystery or Cold War thing. Espionage is dead, anyway. As a genre, I mean. I can't remember what they're filming. They're minor players. He told me he's got one line: 'I haven't seen Bill since Chicago.' Kind of cryptic, huh? We've been getting a lot of their kind. Ton of movies being shot down here. Casting director was in the other night, says, 'We can make LA look like any place in the goddamn world.' You know, Sam, these architect murders—that's a movie."

He winks at me, pours another shot. The door opens. Susan Chandler lets in a crack of night, takes a seat beside me.

"Jesus, Carver. Answer your phone much?"

"I've been busy, and I've got no comment. Don't you have other things to do? Isn't the *Times* interested in other stories?"

"You've got two dead architects and a freaking-out mayor. What other story is there? What are you drinking?"

"Scotch."

"Order me one."

Lenny pours, raises his eyebrows, smiles.

"Lenny," he says.

"Susan. How long have you known this guy?"

"We go back."

"Does he return your calls?"

Lenny doesn't answer. He drifts to the end of the bar, washes glasses.

"Naked guy, lipstick, no finger. How do you square that, Carver?"

"Let me relax, will you? I want to sit here with my drink. Don't you think the light is soft in here? Soothing. Let's enjoy it. See that old couple playing cards? Let's have a little quiet. Take in the atmosphere. It's feels old, doesn't it? From another time. Lenny just told me about his first kiss. Things are very nostalgic. That's what kind of night it is. A peaceful, quiet, remembering night."

"Whatever. You a little buzzed, Carver?"

Susan's a bit of art in the mirror behind the bar. Sharp face, blond hair falling, almost too Californian, tan and the air of beach and the freedom of knowing the power and limits of beauty.

Her hippie real-estate developer parents let her grow with little tending. Some children just know. I may have had too much to drink. I feel warm and a bit blurred. I like her in the mirror. She wrote a profile of me in the *Times* years ago. I was embarrassed by the publicity, but in two thousand words and a few pictures, she got me right, which is a hard thing to do with a man one superior described as a "reticent soul." A mischaracterization, but what are you going to do? She shadowed me across downtown, making me into urban myth, a detective who read Byron and had a boxer father. The department liked the story. "It humanizes us," said Ortiz, "although, Carver, you're one odd fuck." It's disquieting to read what's written about yourself, how another sees you in the world. A character. Like the old couple playing cribbage. Susan and I almost made love once. In my car in a Santa Monica beach parking lot at about two in the morning after we had drinks at a club, where we met to talk off the record about a case I was working. She sat on my lap and we kissed; I pushed my seat back, but then she said no, it would be unethical. "I can't sleep with you if I'm covering you. It's wrong." She slid off me and sat in the passenger seat. A long quiet passed. Then we laughed and cracked our windows and shared a cigarette until the sun came up behind us and turned the ocean bright.

She puts her phone on the bar. Sips. Takes a breath.

"It's the same doer, isn't it?"

"Very different MOs."

"Yeah," she says, "but you got a feeling, don't you? Two architects, friends, precise demises. Same doer."

"Are we off the record?"

"Listen, Carver, about that." She finishes her scotch, waves to Lenny for another pour. "Everything's off the record now. I'm leaving the *Times*. I took a job with the *Post*. I'm moving to DC in a few days. I want to write about politics, up close, in the capital. Trump's a great story. America is a great story. I can't write about murders in LA. It's draining me, you know, makes me feel sad for my species."

"That's pretty much how Trump will make you feel."

"But there'll be no chalk marks and blood stink."

I take a sip. "I wouldn't be too sure of that. And if you leave, you won't know."

"What?"

"How it ends."

"I'll read about it when you solve it."

"I think it's a woman."

"Me too."

"You're definitely not writing about this, right?"

"I quit the *Times* yesterday."

"I saw her on the surveillance video in Jamieson's building. She kept her face hidden. Smart, knew where the cameras were. A long coat and a fedora."

"Sexy."

"It was. In black and white."

"Any idea who she is?"

"No."

"Love triangle gone bad?"

"Maybe."

"Or she could be a hit woman for someone else."

"Possible."

"Maybe she's an architect. A fight over contracts. Taking out the competition. That seems far-fetched. I mean, we're talking architects, not mobs or union locals."

"I thought you were done with cop stuff," I say.

"Yeah, but the scenarios are endless. Always liked the guessing part. The woman, the kid, the strange little man you never figured. My ideas of who kills and why have changed."

"Never think you know, until you do."

"Is that your best existential detective wisdom?"

We catch each other's eyes in the mirror.

"How long have you been coming here, Carver?"

"A few years."

"It suits you. Disheveled, a touch of class, and dim light. Seductive in a gritty way."

"You coming on to me?"

"Thinking about it."

"Any ethical concerns?"

She smiles. "You want to dance?"

"Lenny can play us Sinatra," I say. "But I'm not much of a dancer."

"I figured that." She turns. "Hey, Lenny, can you put on some Frank?"

A piano and Sinatra's voice. She steps into my arms. I pull her close, feel her hair on my cheek, smell her soap and scotch, hear her breathing, feel the warmth through her denim jacket. We spin in a slow circle, merry-go-round glimpses in the mirror. Frank is singing, and the old cribbage players are dancing too. Lenny, arms crossed, is watching. I feel as if I were in a David Lynch movie, but it is truer than that. It is real. I feel her hips against mine, her shoes scraping mine. Slow, so slow we go; she kisses me on the neck, a finger in my hair. We spin. I kiss her lips. She tastes like me, and I close my eyes and the world falls away and I am warm and half numb, gliding on Frank and thinking I need this, that for too long I haven't had the simple thing of a woman in my arms—not just a woman, but Susan, sans notebooks and ethical equations, here before me like a character in a story of my making. It should be like this always. It won't be; it never is, but when it comes like now, I feel the way Lenny felt kissing Julie Mason under that pile of coats. That is what we get: moments laid into memory, pieces in time we look back on, making us think we were once close to that thing people talk about and Frank sings about, that thing with no words that's written about so often.

Susan stops and looks at me. She wipes away a tear. "It's ridiculous, isn't it? I've wanted to dance with you for a long time. I don't know why. I don't dance much, either. But it seemed like something we should do."

"I'm not very good."

"You're not so bad."

We laugh and turn to the bar. Lenny has poured new drinks. We down them and head out the door to Fifth Street, turn at Hill, and go past Esmeralda and across the street to my building. The night guard is in a half slumber. The building is still. I open the door to my apartment. Susan and I kiss down the hall into the living room. We hold each other in the darkness. She steps back and looks around. I turn on a lamp; she goes to the piano. "You play? Play something."

"Maybe later," I say.

She goes to my records. "I knew you were a vinyl guy." She puts on George Shearing and Nancy Wilson. "I love the crackle when the needle touches," she says.

"You want a drink?" I ask.

"No."

"A cigarette?"

"No. We both quit, I thought."

"Mostly."

"You're bad, Carver."

"I try."

"Is this your father?"

"It was taken before a fight in Providence."

"He looks like he could hurt someone."

"He did his share of damage." I put the picture back on the bookcase. "There's a hot tub on the roof."

"No, turn the lamp off and dance with me." She steps toward me. We kiss and slow-spin and I can see down Hill Street. Not a car moving. "Hey, Carver, take me to bed." I carry her down the hall. "You do it," she says. I undress her. Denim jacket, white blouse, jeans. "All of it." She lies naked on the bed and pulls me to her. "We don't speak until morning," she says. I sit up and undress and lie back with her. Her profile sharpens in the moonlight; everything is slow and warm and quiet, except for her breaths and the soft gasps she makes in the minutes before dawn. She slips under my arm and curls beside me. We sleep.

She comes down the hall yawning in her half-buttoned blouse and sky-blue underpants.

"What's this?"

"Breakfast."

"I never figured you for a cook."

"Omelets, toast, feta, melon, slightly fresh."

"You trying to impress? I'm not the marrying type."

"I feel good, you know. I wanted to make breakfast."

"Did you make coffee, too?"

"Oh, sorry. Here."

"Hey, Carver …"

"Yeah."

"Thanks."

"For what?"

"Being like I imagined. We don't get many of those."

"You too."

"I'm still going to Washington."

"I know."

"Maybe …"

"Let's just eat and drink coffee."

"And do it one more time."

She winks. I don't say a word.

"Play me something on that piano."

"When you come back from Washington for a visit, I'll play you a song."

"Okay, Carver, okay. Where'd you get this feta?"

"That Armenian market up near Western. You know it?"

"It's good. You look rested, Carver."

"It's been a long month."

"You like it, don't you? The endless hours. The work." She waves a hand across the room. "Nice place. These carpets, very tasteful. That picture. It's from Sudan, isn't it? Those colors and how tall the women are. Where's that icon from? Bulgaria, Romania? You get around, or did. But you know, Carver, it doesn't feel lived in. It feels like we're in a borrowed house. I only feel half your spirit here. You need to spend more time here, listening to your records, letting home grow into you. You'll never solve all the murders. Too many. Every one you put down, another one comes."

"Like newspaper stories."

"Yeah, a little, I guess. I can put them aside when I have to. I don't know if you can. You're indivisible with death. What would you do without a victim? You ever think of that? It's the ones you don't expect, right? The ones lying there that shouldn't be there, as if they stepped into the wrong scene. The others, the criminals, dealers, and pervs—they deserved it, right? There's a logic and a symmetry to it. But not the unexpected ones. What do you figure for these architects: deserving or victims?"

She reaches over and pours us coffee. Her hair falls across her open blouse.

"Somewhere between. I don't know enough to know what side they'll end up on. They were pricks, though. Very good at what they did. Full of hubris. You know what I like about this job? Going layer by layer. A guy on a street, right? He's a mystery. You pass him. Catch his eye. But he goes on and you may never see him again. Who is he? Every day I get a mystery guy or woman. I see what they never wanted seen. Even the innocent ones. They have something, some dark, hidden piece."

"That's life. Being human."

"Yes, but how different all those pieces are. My father was an unexpected one. He shouldn't have been. He couldn't dole out or absorb enough pain. It was like living with a beaten dog. How could it have ended any other way but violently? My aunt Maggie says that. Once he was gone, all the rooms in the house were different. His watch, his wallet, a ring, pictures, shoes, boxing gloves, his shirt draped over a chair. They were all there, but one by one, they disappeared, and the house held him but didn't."

She stands and holds me, my head to her breast, her hair around me, the scent of her. She takes off her blouse and sits on my lap, light as a bird's wing. She rests her head on my shoulder. We sit in silence. I remember a poem I read years ago about banked fires and the chronic aches of a house, the hurt inside those who live there. It is not like that now; the minutes bring a different poem, one I haven't read but feel inside. The eggs, plates, coffee cups, and melon are arranged like a still life in the sun. I feel her breath, her warmth. I rise and carry her down the hall in this borrowed home of my half-life. I smiled at the way she said that over breakfast. There was truth in it. She puts her lips to my ear, and we cross into the bedroom. "Hey, Carver," she says, "I have this fantasy."

She's gone when I get out of the shower. *"It was lovely. S."* I look at the note for a while, hold it to the window light, as if maybe a clue lingers between the letters. I pour coffee and feel, at least for a moment, that the day, a few clouds to the west but all else clear, is mine. I put on *Rubber Soul*, wash the dishes, sweep the place. The unsolved things can wait. I press Susan's words into James Salter's *A Sport and a Pastime*. I flip the record to the B side and feel the sudden joy I felt when I would take the train from Newport to New York with my mother and we'd speed silver along the coast, the great city rising. "A dream built by men," my mother would say. We'd go to a show, walk through Central Park, eat ice cream, and take the last train home. It was in the years after my father died.

My phone buzzes. Ortiz.

CHAPTER 17

I'm not angry.

No rant, no screed.

I marvel at my restraint. How I hold it together. *That bitch.* Oops. A slip. Sorry. I'll be good. But why, Sam? Why? Why the distraction? No, I didn't see what you did last night. But you wrote two lines about her in your laptop. "Susan and I danced. She calls me Carver." Cursory, yes, nothing explicit, but I can tell. Nobody *just* dances. I'm sure you'll write more when you have time. But there's no future there. I'm the one for you. I don't blame you, though. You don't know I exist. But, Sam (if she can call you Carver, I can call you Sam), you must feel an inkling of me. I am the one you seek. The doer, the perp. The woman in raincoat and fedora, your *fantasy.* Or so I thought.

I've been known to expect too much, to bore in. I know, it's annoying; I can be too focused. But, Sam, really, this girl, this child, this new-breed Martha Gellhorn. Is that what you want? A scribe? I understand, though, I do. She's been after you. I knew all along, and, in a way I don't like to admit, I admire her. A clever, patient one. Writing that story about you, pretending to have ethics, appearing saintlike. Clever designs, that girl. Men. Why do they fall so? I wish I had her, let's call it *charm*, the way she lingers after she's gone. *Susan*. The name floats alone on the screen. Susan. Five letters that carry the weight of a book. That, my detective, is dangerous. Write a poem and be done with it; smile for a few days; enjoy the post*dance* glow. But, Sam, really, let's get back to the game.

You're looking for Stephen Jensen. Where, oh, where could he be?

I know.

I am clever too. Cleverer than she. You'll see. But there's the question. What to do with Jensen? That has been the dilemma from the beginning. Gallagher and Jamieson. *No problemas*. Verdicts handed down, sentences carried out. But Jensen—he's the crooked line, the slanted portico. He's nudged us into the muted grays of moral quandary. Vengeance or forgiveness. Venom or antidote. Which is stronger? I had thought the tender part of me was gone, but it is there, deep, like a voice in a well. I've been reading about complicity. I'm quite the reader these days. Insatiable, looking for parables like mine. The Nazis and the Khmer Rouge thrived on those too pitiful to speak out or resist—all those Germans and Cambodians who looked the other way, went on, pretended not to see the stained horizon. Are the weak blameless? They took part. They went through the actions. Some froze, yes, but even inaction is a kind of terrorism. Can the spineless be absolved? What capacity for forgiveness must the injured possess toward the guilty?

A sin lasts long after its commission. It marks all that follows.

But it will fade if we let it. Should we? I don't think I'm being too grandiose to suggest these are the real questions for humankind. I'm only a fleck, I know. I'm not a country, a state, a people. I'm a footnote, an aggrieved asterisk. But does that make the injustice any less? I think not. You know this. I know what you write, how you think. I've been deep in your files. You believe in sanctity and forgiveness, but forgiveness can be granted only if sanctity is violated. Hello, paradox. You hold them both inside—strange Christian twins, I think, but you're not religious. Okay, maybe a few nostalgic cold, candlelit Sundays in a New England pew. Not a true believer. Not even after your father was killed and you, like me now, wanted vengeance. But then you didn't. Why? How did you soothe the seething fire? Maybe because you were still a boy. Children outgrow what adults cannot. Or perhaps it is something else, some gene I do not possess. It's what mystifies me about you. What I love about you. Did I say "love"? Yes.

What to do with Stephen Jensen? Forget about Montana or wherever his Ethiopian wife, an unknowing innocent, pointed you. Jensen is much closer. Oh, yes. In a safe place. While I decide. It's always about what I decide. That's what you need to know. You come to the place I've been and see what I've done. One step behind. Don't worry, you'll catch up.

I went to the Norton Simon Museum in Pasadena the other day, just to get out, you know, to see beautiful things from long ago. They hung so hushed and brilliant. We humans can be magnificent when we want to. I wandered past brocaded frames and through the scents of aftershave from security guards, buttoned and watchful in their blazers and shiny black shoes. *Squeak, squeak.* I found myself among the impressionists. Edgar Degas, to be specific. So watery, insubstantial; mists of ballerinas, really, nothing precise. But lovely. Like gauze puffs in pastel-colored rain. They made me want to dance. I did a pirouette.

"Miss," said a guard waving his finger. "No dancing."

"But don't they make you want to?"

"Miss," he said stepping toward me. "They are beautiful. I see them every day. But no dancing."

But I think he understood my burst of joy. The hall was quiet. Only Degas, the guard, and me. What would I have said to Degas? "*Très bien, monsieur.*" Perhaps I would have invited him for a glass of wine and showed him my designs, and he would have shown me his sketches. We would have sat in the courtyard amid flagstones and statues and talked of Gauguin, Paris, wars, Andy Warhol, punk rockers, the internet, and then gone our separate ways. As strangers do. When I stepped away from the ballerinas, my eyes drifted left. I gasped. No kidding, I did. There she was: *Actress in Her Dressing Room.* Painted around 1875 and reworked twenty years later. She stood facing a mirror. A gown unfurled around her like a scarlet sea. So slim, her waist; her dresser looking on in the gaslight. It was damp in the painting, a bit of makeup powder in the air, perhaps—you know, the dreary kind from the old theaters. But what took my breath was her face in the mirror. It did not fit the woman with her back to me. I expected refinement, an angular, aristocratic beauty. But no, the face in the mirror was scary, as if reflecting a jaded heart, a mind in disarray. Skin pale, incandescent almost, blunt line of lipstick, long nose, dark splotches for eyes. It was a face hanging in a black dream. Severe. So ready to bite, like a viper, a woman peering into a self no one but her sees. The world knows only her mask. But Degas gave us the terrifying and real inside.

I couldn't move, Sam. I stood staring into her face. It was me.

Degas had painted me in a garret. With no words, he understood. How did he know the inside of a creature not yet born? I know what you're thinking. Art speaks to our spirit, finds us, and gives us back ourselves. Yes. But still. That was me and the face no one sees. Jamieson may have glimpsed it before the end. The way he looked at me in that last second, as if he had finally met truth. I wept when the knife went in. I knelt before him and pushed it deep, and blood mixed with tears.

But still, what to do with Jensen?

CHAPTER 18

The mayor appears in front of City Hall before twenty or so reporters and bloggers. Ortiz and I are off to the side, behind the chief and the commissioners. Bursts of blue and silver. Lenses press in and microphones crowd the air. I look around, hoping to see Susan, but she's gone, maybe on her way to Washington. An aide whispers in the mayor's ear; the commissioners nod. The mayor unleashes brisk, clean sentences that dissolve without much substance. He says the killer or killers will be caught and that these "heinous" crimes will not stop the city's Renaissance. Rebirth. Revival. He sounds a bit messianic. He praises Gallagher and Jamieson and the architects and firms that are reimagining Los Angeles. "Our great city," he says, poking the air with his thumb the way they do, "is rising with splendor in a new century." A few print scribes roll their eyes, but the mayor—trim, perfect haircut, gleaming shoes, eyes afire—presses on with adjectives and references to Paris and Rome. He doesn't mention New York; the mayor never mentions New York.

"What the fuck," whispers Ortiz. "We got two dead guys and he's talking aesthetics."

"Diversion. Get the bodies out of the way. Focus on the dream. Stay on the dream."

Ortiz shoots me a sideways glance.

"You're chirpy today," he says. "Unlike yourself."

"I slept well."

"Make an arrest so we all can sleep well."

"Why we here?"

"Show of force. Calm the city. Mayor's on the case. Politics. There's talk the mayor might run for president. First Latino prez. How about that? He's a Jew and an Italian too. Covers a lot of bases. Don't look at me like that. It could happen. Look who's in there now. Anyway, the big money's watching," says Ortiz, checking his phone, craving a cigarette. "It's amazing how the world works. Shit going on we don't see. Cocktail party shit, Beverly Hills dinners. Malibu houses you never see, you know. Big tucked-away houses full of rich people. All kinds. The invisibles. *Tale of Two Cities* bullshit."

"Dickens is dense, though, don't you think?"

"Whatever. I'm just saying."

"Maybe the rich are thinking the Renaissance isn't in good hands."

"They're spooked for sure. Financial crimes are one thing. They don't bother the one percent. They're like tickets for speeding or watering your lawn during a drought. Put a check in the mail. But the rich don't like stiffs, especially their own." He cuts me another glance. "You grew up rich, though, right, kind of? Your dad's family, right? You don't look like you're rich now, but you have this thing that you once might have been. A trace of money."

I shoot him a glance. "Don't look at me like that. You know what I mean. Once, you had money, that's all I'm saying, so you know most likely how the rich might think. No sin in that. It's a plus knowing the arrangement of forks and what to do with a wine cork. Good survival skills."

"You're a font of insight and wisdom …"

He raises one eyebrow; the mayor drones on.

"You may not remember," says Ortiz. "You weren't here then, but O. J. freaked out the rich. Upset the Brentwood bubble. Blood on the poolside. A madman on the loose in a Bronco. What a roller-coaster day that was." He catches his voice getting loud and lowers it. "A thing like that gets the rich extrapolating. One thing leads to another, and pretty soon someone's coming through the window for the jewels. They spook, man. Easily. It's an equilibrium thing. All their bullshit master-of-the-universe talk, especially those Hollywood guys, but the rich are pussies. My opinion. You, I'm sure, would know better. Even Phil Spector, that crazy shit, freaked them out, running around with that wild hair and a gun. The list is long."

"So you're thinking …"

"Get me a perp I can parade in front of the cameras."

"Might be a woman."

"I don't give a shit if it's fucking Marge Simpson."

He nods to the chief, fingers his mustache. Sometimes when I look at Ortiz, I see him as he'll be twenty years from now, retired if he doesn't have a heart attack, sitting on Hermosa Beach with a cooler and a radio, listening to soccer games from South America. He'll be slimmer, grayer, calmer, holding hands with his wife in the sand, going to church during Lent, and making fun of the cop shows on Netflix and Hulu. If I'm still around, I might even drive down and visit him, eat hamburgers and smoke cigars and remember days like today, laughing at the crazy shit cops and mayors get into.

Ortiz collects old maps. He rolled one out to me once, of California in the early 1800s. He traced the lines slowly and methodically, mentioning this town and that, how this boundary would move and that one stay the same, how phantom gold was once to the north, and how water would come in from Colorado and other points east and funnel across the dryness into farms and cities and how, without it, the land could not provide. Ortiz likes the feel of the paper, yellow edges, mountains and deserts, the lay of roads, the outline of the ocean, a great empty space pressing against the coast.

"You ever notice?" I say.

"What?"

"Reporters and cops are a lot alike."

"How so? I hate the fuckers."

"Clothes, for one thing. Look at them and look at us. Check the shoes, the jackets. Different styles, maybe, but same quality."

"I think we dress better."

"And bitching."

"They bitch better. Like they're carrying around the world's sins."

He tamps his mustache.

"The public likes us more," he says.

"Debatable."

The mayor wraps up, takes a few questions, and disappears in an SUV. The chief calls on a few hands. Sharp, curt answers. The press hates that. The mikes go down and it's done as a guy on a bike, wearing no shirt and a Viking helmet, rides past, doing tricks and figure eights and singing "I Can't Get No Satisfaction." He stops and bows. A few coins and a dollar are thrown his way. He collects them and pedals toward Little Tokyo and skid row.

"LA," says Ortiz. "Land of loonies."

I look around.

"Where's that *Times* chick who's always bothering you? Thought this would be right up her alley."

"Don't know."

"Consider it a blessing. Where you off to?"

"Crime lab says they pulled some stuff from one of Jamieson's computers."

"Call me," Ortiz says, and we go our separate ways.

The lab's probably at lunch, so I walk down Spring for a coffee. A TV reporter approaches, but I wave him off and head past a dog park. A pit bull chases a tennis ball, and a guy off his meds— or on too many meds—is twirling on the grass and screaming about aliens. He's bearded, lean, and schizophrenic, two voices roaring inside, bursting out in different sounds. He claws at his skin and bangs his head. He wants them to stop, but they won't. They follow him, like the aliens, wherever he goes, and one voice screams at the other and no one goes to him, no one takes him by the hand. He is part of the scenery, someone's crazy unwashed cousin wandering the neighborhood, in the evening finding his way back to skid row, where other voices join his chorus, and eyes peek from tents, cardboard, and shopping carts. I get called to skid row for the occasional murder, a body under papers on a sidewalk or curled beneath an underpass. No Renaissance there. That word is becoming more annoying.

Ortiz was right, though. I was rich once—not grandly so, but enough. My mother took the million dollars my grandfather left to my father and put it in a bank. Suspicious of markets, she never invested, but interest rates were good back then, and the money grew for a while. After my father died, we lived on it and my mother's teaching salary, draining it little by little, paying for my college, trips, and unexpected things. There's a bit of it left, more than enough for my mother and Maggie. I send them money too. The rich days, whatever "rich days" means, ended when my father, boxer and family black sheep, received a much smaller inheritance than his siblings. "I knew the bastard hated me," my mother once quoted my father as saying of my grandfather, "but I thought he'd leave more. I guess they never do."

My mother used to take me by the old mansion. It had been sold and we'd stand outside in the dark and see people moving in lighted windows. "That was your father's room," she'd say. "It had eaves and angles. It was like a garret, but big. Everyone had a big room. I wonder who's in there now." She wondered too, about the initials my father had carved in the windowsill as a boy, and the picture of a face he drew in charcoal behind the hanging coats in his closet. She had hoped they were still there, but suspected they weren't, yet she believed that those old houses held past lives that slipped into the present and moved among the living.

A man appears beside me and keeps pace.

"You Detective Carver?"

"Yes."

"I saw you on TV. You live downtown, don't you?"

"What can I help you with?"

He's fat and sweaty, dressed in a snug blazer with too-long pants, worn loafers, and mirrored aviator sunglasses—the cheap kind from Rite Aid. He's smoking a cigarillo. He's swift, with a slight whistle in his sentences.

"I'm a barber."

"I don't need a haircut. I do, but I haven't got time."

I pick up the pace.

"I saw you with the mayor," he says. "He's a twerp. Good hair, but a twerp. You think you're going to catch the killer?"

"We'll get him."

"I think it's a her."

He pulls down his aviators and flashes a set of blue eyes that don't go with the rest of him.

"You've got my attention."

"Good, 'cause you walk too fast. Let's stop. Get a coffee and a sandwich and we'll talk."

"No time. I have to be somewhere. Let's talk here in the shade. What's your name?"

"Earle-with-an-*e*-at-the-end Reed. People often forget the last *e*." He takes a breath. "Everyone's in a rush—you notice that? Technology. All these screens. It's exasperating. The pleasantries of life have vanished. Rush, rush. We've become uncivilized, if I may say. These young guys wanting haircuts today. The skinny ones with the tight pants, beards, and those droopy earlobes. Who would do that to an ear? They want a haircut, but fast. They don't want to enjoy it, to sit back and feel it. A haircut is social. A ritual, like church. You don't rush church." He pauses and catches his breath. "Amazing how Spring Street has changed."

Why do they always drone on so? I need to hurry this guy along, grab a coffee, and get to the crime lab. I can't tell if he's one of those avid newspaper and crime blog readers, an interventionist with a police scanner and a vivid imagination. I open my notebook.

"Why a her?"

He takes off his aviators and cleans them with a handkerchief he's pulled from his breast pocket with all the flair of a Vegas magician. Job done, he slips it back in with the same flourish. He takes a breath and leans against a tree. Relights his cigarillo and exhales.

"The architect, the one up on Grand in that nice tower by the Broad. Paul Jamieson."

"Yes."

"I was up there—don't want to say why exactly, if you don't mind. Nothing unseemly, of course. I'm certainly not connected to the murder. Nooo. I run a side business; let's leave it at that." I shoot him a hard glance. "Okay, okay, I'm a bookie. I was up there seeing a guy—rich older guy. He wanted to lay some money on a few games. We had a drink. Now, there's a guy who can slow down and enjoy the pleasantries. A gentleman. Tailored, if you know what I mean. Good hair. Not good-looking, but suave. We sit and talk, let the night run. No harm, right? Two guys whiling a couple of hours away. Anyway, I take his money—always puts it in a crisp envelope, very old-school. So I ride the elevator down and step outside for a smoke. I love to light up in the dark and watch the smoke curl in the night. It's special, you know. A little bit of special. So I'm standing there a while, enjoying the stars. It was a cool night. A clean night."

He takes a drag on his cigarillo, exhales, enjoying his own voice.

"That's when, you know, I see her."

"Okay. What'd she look like?"

"That's the thing," he says. "She was wearing a hat, sort of in the Indiana Jones style, and a coat like a raincoat but not—a flimsy, pretty thing with a slit in the back. Blue, I think. A dark shade. She was tall too. Long legs. I turned toward her. She tilted her head and pulled the brim down. She turned right and went down the hill and around the corner."

"Why would you think she was a killer?"

"Can't say precisely. It was the way she moved, like something that was there and shouldn't have been. She was wanting to get away fast but not show she was getting away fast. Like a shoplifter. It's complicated, but you know what I mean. The next day, the old guy, my client, calls and tells me about a murder in an apartment two floors above. I turn on the news later that day. And I figure ..."

"You figure you were standing next to a killer."

"Gave me chills. You think it could have been her?"

"Any other description? Distinguishing features?"

"Just a hat and a chin. I didn't see her face. The collar on the coat was up so I couldn't see her hair. What color it was. I would have noticed the hair. A quick glimpse is all I had of her. Like I said, she was tall. Trim and tall. She looked like an actress. That's what I figured at first. She's up there making a movie. Nothing unusual, right? Shoot movies up on Grand all the time. That's what immediately came to mind. There was a thing about her, you know? I mean, it was just a second, but she had style. Isn't that funny how you can see something like that in a split second, not even see a face or anything else, but just know?"

I write down his name and number and hand him my card and tell him to stop by the station later to give a more detailed statement.

"We'll keep the bookie stuff between us, right? Harmless little side business."

"Only interested in what you saw."

"So you think she could be ..."

"We follow every lead."

"Yes, every lead. Whatever I can do to help."

He puffs his cigarillo, brushes ash from his blazer.

"You should stop by for a haircut. I'm down on Eighth. Earle's. You could use a trim."

Earle-with-an-*e*-at-the-end nods and strolls away.

He was right, she did have style. I saw it on the video. A quick grace. I call Stephen Jensen again. No answer. I phone Wanita. She hasn't heard from him. "But as I told you," she says, "this is not unusual. Stephen likes his solitude—how do you say in this country? To 'go off the grid,' yes?" Her voice is worried, though. Really worried. A face can trick you, but not a voice. Cracks in consonants, a broken vowel. They give you away even when you're thinking your face is the perfect mask. Suspects will keep talking in the interrogation box, go on for hours and hours, thinking they're playing us, thinking their mask can't be broken, not knowing that their voice is betraying them, and when the mask shatters, they look at you as if to say, *Why? I had this beat.* Self-delusion is the magic of survival. How does she survive? I can't stop seeing the surveillance video in my head. She was there but not there. The coat, the way she moved. Earle sensed it too. He exhaled to the stars, and she was gone.

I get a coffee at another new café on Spring. Organic. Four bucks. Christ. The Renaissance is getting expensive. I head toward the crime lab and think of that morning with Susan. Two people eating eggs, drinking coffee. Normal. Talking. Teasing. You can forget how it all can be, the good things, having an extra voice in your home, the scent of another. Susan had style, the way she spun down the hall in her half-buttoned shirt and stood naked in the bedroom, her arms reaching out for me.

I walk down the hall to room 502. Crime lab. Wires, tools, circuits, vials, tubes, and the insides of things spread out on tables.

A guy with tweezers is pulling something from a DVD player, and a woman in a hairnet is peeking into the back of an iPhone. Fingerprints and faces of perps float across computer screens, and two guys are watching surveillance video of a clerk in a market—must be Boyle Heights—getting whacked with two pops from a nine-millimeter. The thief's hand reaches into the cash drawer, pulls out a fistful, and disappears through the front door. But he doesn't really disappear. The outside camera catches him throwing the gun into a dumpster.

"What a dumb fuck," says Doug Watkins, holding up the gun with gloved hands. "Prints all over it. You ever wonder about the criminal mind, Carver? I mean, how fucked up it is, how unaware? Not thinking. Just doesn't think who's watching. Serious lack of planning. I mean, you whack a guy, right, you wear gloves, and you don't dump the gun at the scene. What do you figure he grabbed? That time of day. Afternoon. Maybe a few hundred bucks, tops. Now he's done. Life over. In jail eating up taxpayer money, playing checkers, watching *Judge Judy*, and getting it up the ass. You gotta wonder if we're all the same species."

"So you're having a good day."

"An amazing day. Who you looking for?"

"Whoever's got the laptops from the Jamieson house."

"Jamieson. Jamieson. Oh, the place up off Sunset. The architect with his pecker out and his finger gone."

"That's him."

Doug points.

"Tommy?" I say.

"Yup."

Doug smiles and returns his attention to the dumb fuck's gun. Tommy Yan is the lab's mad scientist, a scattered, wiry, jumpy-eyed strange syntax of a man. Thorough and unnervingly precise, he loves theories, the why and how of things, which is to be expected in forensics, but Yan bores down to the last molecule of dust, the millionth fiber. His nickname is "Mr. Airtight." Never loses a case. But it takes a while for him to get out a report. He is what Doug calls "one easily distractible motherfucker. Working on something like a monk and then, boom, something new comes through the door and Mr. Airtight comes peeking."

I knock. Yan looks up, his eyes floating like two Jupiters behind his magnifying goggles. He pulls the goggles off and slips on his regular glasses, holds up a finger, writes on a pad, whispers into an audio recorder, swivels in his chair, and looks at me as if I'm a cat that's wandered over from a neighbor's house.

"Ahhhhh, Carver, sorry. In the moment, you know. Odd case here. Guy kills his wife, doesn't know what to do with the body. Then, I guess, he gets the idea to make a puzzle out of her. Chops her up. Buries her in different parts of the yard. This is out near Beverly Hills, so, you know, the lawn is landscaped and big, so she's all over the place. Got all of her but the head. And the weapon. Can't find it. Trying to figure out what it was. The cuts are odd. Not a Walmart knife. I'm thinking it must be a sword or machete. Something foreign. Ancient, maybe. I'm matching metal fragments."

He catches himself, takes off his regular glasses, and puts on another pair.

"Sorry, man. They changed my prescription. Everything's blurry. They gave me the wrong glasses. Now I gotta go back. It's an imprecise world. Imprecise." He sighs like someone who has just lost a week's pay on a long-shot horse at Santa Anita. "Sorry, Carver, what can I do for you?"

"Jamieson. Paul Jamieson."

"You're working the Jamieson thing. Oh, yeah, it was downtown, your turf."

"Killed up on Grand."

Yan nods toward two laptops.

"These were pulled from his place off Sunset."

"That was his main house. He kept a small apartment on Grand."

Yan laughs. He swivels, rolls toward the laptops, pops open the screens.

"We swept them. Building designs, bank statements, investment stuff. Guy had some serious cash. Wasn't much of an internet surfer, though. Not many cookies. But he did like the Italian period from the late medieval through Caravaggio. Downloaded a lot of art and architecture from that era. Research papers. Was obsessed with that time. Lots of travel stories too." Tommy takes off his glasses, holds them to the light, puts them back on. "It's funny, you know, but you go through a guy's laptop and there he is, staring back at you. The whole of him. This guy was from another era. Didn't live in our world. The things he loved were gone, in the past."

"So you're a shrink now?"

"No. Just saying. This laptop tells me."

"What about this one?"

"New. Not much there. A few three-D diagrams of buildings he'd been working on. You look at them and then you look at the stuff on that computer and you see. He was trying to connect that old world with this one. In buildings. Pretty cool. But they don't seem right, you know. They don't really exist together." Yan runs his fingers over the keyboard. "Oh, yeah, I forgot. Once a month or so, he did visit a website for an escort service. Anna Bella. That's the name. Kind of chic sounding. You probably definitely want to check that out."

Yan swivels and rolls back toward me. He's got that look I know from past cases. I cross my arms and wait. He likes to draw out the drama, make a little play of it. He looks at me. I look at him. He holds up a flash drive.

"Now, this baby," he says, "is something you're going to want to see."

He plugs the drive into the second laptop, hits a key, leans back, and points to the screen.

CHAPTER 19

So now you know.

My secret.

What's it like to watch? I wonder. To come at it cold, see it pop up like that? Maybe you're used to it, but I think, knowing you, Sam, it hurts. I hope so. I hope it makes you understand. Do you like the mask they put on me? It's Venetian. From the Carnevale, fifteenth century. When I see it, I think of whispers on a floating city. That's me. The naked girl in the mask. Don't Gallagher and Jamieson look much younger? The pale creature off to the side, by the way, is Jensen, the reluctant one. What a strange sliver of a man. I don't know what they gave me. That still bothers me. They must have slipped a potion—a dark fairy-tale word—into my drink. We'd been in Los Angeles only a few months, new architects among the angels. We were introduced by a man I don't remember. An older man, I think. Quiet, tailored. He left shortly after, and Jamieson, Gallagher, and I went barhopping along Sunset. So cool that night. You know the kind: hard and black and ancient beyond the lights. Then, at some point, we ended up at Jamieson's. I should mention now that Jensen was not with us at the beginning of the night. He joined us later at Jamieson's, but by that time my mask was on. Jensen never saw my face. How curious for him, don't you think? I didn't know exactly what happened in the hours after. I woke up on the couch in my underpants and a T-shirt not mine. I assumed I had made the mistake of the young: too much drinking and fumbling sex with a handsome man. Jamieson is (was) handsome, as you can see. I won't deny him that.

I went into the kitchen, where Jamieson, shirtless and in pajama bottoms, was drinking coffee and thumbing through a picture book of gargoyles. Black-and-white and taken up close, teeth and wings and savage eyes, the demons of architecture. He closed the book and looked at me. I told him I was a bit blurry and, with a sheepish smile, asked him what had happened. He said we all partied and came to his place. Gallagher and Jensen stayed for a while, drinking martinis and eating prosciutto, and left a little before dawn. Jamieson blushed and gave me a look that said, *Well, you know what happened next.* He said we tried to make love, but it wasn't good. We were too drunk. He didn't say it with venom or judgment, or even insecurity about, maybe, his performance. It just didn't go well, like a bad day on the Nasdaq. That was the look in his eyes. But then, ever so briefly, he smiled—not a happy smile, but one of a boy caught in a bit of mischief. He didn't comfort me, didn't pull me to his lap and have a bashful laugh about us being half-dressed strangers in the uncomfortable light of morning. No. None of that. The whole time he was talking, I kept thinking that more had happened. Gallagher and Jensen appeared at the edges of my mind, foggy, like men underwater floating around me. Voices and laughter.

Weight pressing against flesh. Bodies at different angles, slanted and straight, contorted, grabbing. I remembered music that may have been opera. I couldn't be sure. I felt a soreness down there. A faint bloom of blood in my underpants. But nothing else. I asked Jamieson again what had happened. He said, "Nothing. Honestly, we were way wasted. We undressed, fooled around. You put my T-shirt on and went to the couch." He looked as though he wanted to get on with his day, as if I was keeping him from a great burst of architecture. He didn't seem like a rapist. An insufferable egotist, yes—I do remember, the night before, how he talked about his aesthetic, his concept of beauty—but not a rapist. I had, over the years, slept with one or two relative strangers after a night of drinking. It's human, is it not, to make mistakes and spot the soul with tiny infractions? No harm in a little after-hours sex. This is how I thought. Take a shower, towel dry, and be gone. It was different that night, though. Something more had happened. I felt it.

"No, no," Jamieson said. "Sit and have a coffee. You must be wiped out; I know I am. Would you like an aspirin? I've got a killer hangover. Do you like LA? I'm still adjusting. I'd love to see your work sometime. Would you like a croissant? I can make eggs."

"Are you sure there was nothing else?"

"Yes," he said, his voice sharpening. "Nothing happened." A rigid smile. "Sit for a minute and have something."

He didn't mean any of it. He was as empathetic as Scandinavian stone. I didn't know what to do. I had coffee, a croissant, and a few aspirin. I didn't flee. Why was that, Sam? Why didn't I run out of that place? A flaw in instinct, perhaps. Curiosity? I think I thought that if I stayed long enough, he'd confess to something. But as he kept talking, his version became mine. I hate that. The trick he played, the trick played on all women. The arrogance, the smugness of it. Yes, I still remember that smug face sipping coffee. I'm glad he's dead. I celebrate it. I do. But I don't like going back to that night. I feel smaller, less sure, a murky pool of things inside. You'll notice if (when) we meet. Jamieson and I talked a bit longer, and he asked me something I'll never forget.

"When did you know you were tall?"

"What do you mean?"

"The moment you realized you were different. Special."

"You mean, for a girl. They always said, 'You're tall for a girl.' I hated that growing up."

"You are tall for a girl. I don't mean that, though. I mean the first time you saw yourself and said, 'This is me.'"

"I don't know. One time, I caught myself in a store window I was walking past with friends. I saw how I stood out, towered over them. It's strange to see yourself like that. It doesn't seem you. For an instant, you're a stranger to yourself."

"Do you see yourself as an architect?"

"I am an architect."

"I wonder, because I don't think …"

His phone rang then. He answered it, spoke a few clipped words, and hung up. He turned back to me, and I asked him what he meant by his architect remark. He shook his head and said, "Nothing important." I wanted to press him, but he told me he had to hurry to an appointment. I put on my clothes from the night before. They had been neatly draped over a chair, but they had that air about them: wrinkles; scents of smoke, drink, and sweat—clothes to slink home in and wash a thousand times. He didn't offer to drive me home. Can you imagine? Not even an offer. I called a cab and was off.

Time passed. That phrase has always seemed romantic to me. Like something from a novel in another land, a piece of a life not your own anymore. Do you know what I mean? There was nothing romantic about it, though. Rage and depression filled the spaces once taken up by the truth I didn't know; they became my little demons. My gargoyles. I kept trying to piece that night together, to find shreds in my mind and sew them into a picture. I'd close my eyes and will myself back there, but only shadows—even less, just wisps and voices, indiscernible words in my ears. I had thought about going to the police, but it was too late. And besides, what did I know for sure? Nothing.

When I got home from Jamieson's that morning, I stripped and checked myself. A few red marks on my shoulder, but no bruising. A scratch on my thigh. Nothing on my breasts, my hips spotless, no blotches on my stomach, my bottom smooth, but a slight ache beneath. I reached into myself, felt the damp inner walls, but no trace of him—none my fingers could detect, anyway. I held a mirror between my legs. I cried when I did this, embarrassed at this naked person in a bathroom, a pathetic soul searching for clues to a sin she created. Isn't that what we've been taught? I was sore to the touch. But no stings of pain. It has been that way before, on occasion. Wouldn't it have hurt? Wouldn't there have been some obvious signs if what happened, happened? Mind and body could not agree on this.

I dressed the morning after—such an ominous phrase, a sobering quiet after a storm—and went to work. I had just started at John's firm and had a design of a boutique hotel I wanted to impress him with. I was young. I wanted no sidetracks, no rail leading me away from my sketches and where I saw myself destined. I folded it all into my work. Time passed. Oh, yes. In drips. Jamieson never called. I never called him or Gallagher or Jensen. I think I was scared to know, and as days went by, I pushed it all further from me. I'd see Jamieson and Gallagher at architecture events. Once, we passed on Manhattan Beach. I was running. They were tanned, carrying surfboards. Even with a tan and the sun on him, Gallagher was a beady man, but Jamieson was strong, as if shaped by the elements and the sea. That seems overstated, I know, but he was like a fine building. We spoke for a minute, about what, I don't know. I was too nervous. We said goodbye, and I sensed a snicker behind their lips. I looked back and saw Jamieson lean over and whisper in Gallagher's ear. They laughed. I remember thinking in that moment how you feel when you discover that back in elementary school, the other kids were making fun of your shoes behind your back, but you never knew until years later, and you feel embarrassed for the little unaware self you were. And you hate the ones who laughed while you weren't looking. I never saw Jensen with them. I'd heard they had drifted apart. I think it was because of that night with me, but I can't be sure. Jensen was the reluctant one. You can see it in the video. How he stands at the edges, naked, unsteady, drunk, Gallagher and Jamieson slapping him on the back, pulling him, urging him toward the woman in the mask. Me. If you look closely, slow the video down, you can see disgust and fear on Jensen's face—just for an instant, but it's there, a boy not wanting to do man things. I played that part over and over as if, in Jensen, there was a redeemable story from that night. But no.

The video. I discovered it a couple of years ago, the night before I took those pills and Isabella and John held me in my Victorian in Angelino Heights. What a comfort they were, sitting with me on the stripped floors, a single lamp in the window. They didn't know, but a few days earlier, I had decided to hack Gallagher's computer. It came quite logically when I think of it now, but back then I was never sure what to do. I knew that those men had done something. I had to know what. It was breaking me. You must understand, Sam, I'm not crazy. I'm not my sweet, demented mother. Part of her, yes, but the larger part, *they* brought.

Years went by, but it never left me. At least, that's how it felt, revisiting me at unexpected times, barging in like a rabid dog, even when I went to the shrink, took his pills, felt numbness spread from my fingertips to my heart. I had to act. The way it seethes, Sam, you wouldn't believe—this deep-down, bubbling thing you carry, trying to escape it, like running in from the rain, but the rain is inside you. The rain *is* you. Why Gallagher's computer? Good question. He was vain, more so than Jamieson, and that's saying something. He wrote a blog for his firm's website, filled it with his designs, pictures, architectural asides, random bullshit, as if everything he did should be enshrined. A man like that leaves a trail. He keeps things, an elaborate mosaic of self. Am I right? So I did what I do. It was a tough hack, much harder than yours, Sam—you really do need a better firewall—but after a few hours I was in like a jinni. I rummaged around. Bank accounts, investments, emails from mentors, love letters from Miranda, his wife. Also downloaded stories from architectural magazines and a diary, but one strictly about work: meeting times, design tweaks, cost overruns—quite detailed. Boring. In all that data, in all those megabytes, no self-reflection, no questions of afterlife and philosophies, no "What does it all mean?" Nothing deeper than artifice. That's why Gallagher would never have been great. He was too narrow a man.

I came to a folder marked "Contrapasso." I knew that word but couldn't place it. I plugged it into Google, and, yes, Sam, the meaning appeared: the condemned souls in Dante's *Inferno*, you know, the ones whose eternal punishment is never to escape their most grievous sin. Those guilty of lust, for instance, are blown about in the underworld by violent winds that never allow their flesh any repose. The flesh they indulged so much in life becomes their endless torment. A kind of poetic justice. Was Gallagher being clever? I stared at the folder and remembered a long-ago English class and reading of that guided journey through the nine circles of hell. You remember those English books, Sam, the ones with the sketches of pain? *Contrapasso.* Something in me stirred. *Click.* What Gallagher lacked in self-reflection, he made up for in porn. Files of it. All kinds. But mostly gross amateur pictures and videos filmed in cheap hotel rooms and apartments by fat men with inexpensive cameras. There were pictures of Miranda too. In the shower. I don't think she knew. Pretty, wet, ginger hair down her back, a scrim of mist. She had the gaze of the unaware. As if he had sneaked in on his own wife. I felt I was violating her just by looking. I clicked away from her and scrolled and scrolled until I spotted a file marked "Night at the Opera." I stared at those words for a long time. I thought, *Let it be; don't go behind there.*

I got up from the computer, walked around, made tea. But the words taunted and dared. Should one know the mystery, or let it go? My hand paused. But then it moved on its own. *Click.* My heart dropped. There I was. Naked on a couch, passed out, propped up, legs spread, head drooping, mussed hair, wearing a Venetian mask: red lips, ornate eyes, a face speckled with cheap jewels, as if you were at a long-ago palace ball. Inscrutable, erotic, a sly disguise. The mask is timeless, is it not? Looking at you, betraying nothing. You wonder. Who's behind the mask? You never find out. I am never unmasked in the video. I pretended it wasn't me. No face, no identity. It could have been anyone. That would be a lie, though. It was me. We know ourselves, don't we? Our markings, invisible or not, rise up like mirrors and expose us.

A disguise cannot hide our essence. I have learned this. But to anyone watching—like you, Sam—I am a mystery. My stripped body a thing of clues. Pink, red, areola. Yes, I am vulgar, but look, Sam, is there any other way to be? Look. Stare. See me. Splayed. The camera on me, stealing me bit by bit. I won't be vulgar if (when) we meet. I'll be a lady. I am refined, but not in what you see before you. No, they turned me into something else. Jamieson whispered in my ear, grabbed my breasts, and laughed. A cackle. Not human. Can you imagine seeing yourself like that? Looking back through time and there you are, alive in a man's laptop, like nothing, like a million other women, faceless, reduced to flesh. It's you, but it's not you. How can it be?

I sat stunned, watching. I cried. The tears wouldn't stop. I kept watching, drawn to it, thinking it a trick, an illusion. It was not. In a way, I was vindicated, all those years believing that something had happened. Something *did* happen. But my vindication became my disgrace. The opera my attackers were playing—Mozart's *Così fan tutte*, a story of deception, love, and heartbreak—grew louder. I can be indifferent to Mozart, but *Così* is tender and beautiful and did not go at all with what was happening to me. You saw. First, Jamieson picks me up, folds me over the couch. I am so lifeless as to be dead. Jamieson pushes, the music filling the room, Gallagher standing a breath away, watching, a sneer even in his strange pleasure. Jamieson finishes. Is that what we should call it? He and Gallagher lift me to a table, lay me on my back. My mask is fixed; through all of it, my expression is the same. Gallagher begins while Jamieson pulls my arms over my head and holds them. As if I were a spear or some sad, trapped marsh bird. Don't you think that's how it looks, Sam? The image. He laughs and kisses my mask. Jamieson slaps him on the shoulder, laughing too, but scolding: "Be careful. That's an antique."

I lie there. My skin reddens, or is that just the light? They sip wine and examine me. You can feel their eyes, can't you? The delight and hate in them. What makes eyes shine so? They call for Jensen. He's not in the picture but suddenly appears. They taunt and tease him. He says he doesn't want to, that he's had too much to drink—the sound of a voice looking for escape. Jamieson allows him none. That was startling, wasn't it? The way Jamieson changed, Gallagher too, grabbing Jensen …

I'm so embarrassed, Sam. All my hiding places gone. I am scoured in light. To be before you like that. Who I became is what they made, at least for a little longer. Do you understand? I have discovered the place of hate, somewhere inside me, with its own little heart. Why go on with the video? You've seen it all. I don't want to watch anymore. I'm tired. Still so much to do. I'm reading your diary now. You finished typing just moments ago. It's almost as if we were together. You mentioned me for the first time. I am words in your laptop. No name. "The girl in the mask." That's what you wrote. I can tell you care. I knew you would. I like this line best: "There was a beauty in her they didn't take." Thank you for seeing that. To watch the video and be able to write that, well, Sam, what can I say? You understand. There is a clue in the video. Very subtle. When we meet, perhaps I'll point it out, or maybe you'll see for yourself.

Oh, one more thing. Don't worry about Jensen. I know where he is. So close, I can touch him.

CHAPTER 20

Ortiz sits on a metal chair in Grand Central Market. It's a little after eight in the morning, and the place is stirring to life. His scowl is aimed and cocked. He lights a cigarette, daring someone to tell him to put it out, and watches lawyers, city workers, tourists from Denmark, and a bunch of squat, hunched men, a few in cowboy hats, a few in hard hats, eating noodles and drinking Budweiser at the China Café counter. The hipsters have yet to descend. A chill blows through the big, open doors where, years ago, trucks delivered produce from the north, driving past gangbangers and homeless and fleeing before sunset. It is not the same city it was then.

"Every time I come here, something's different," says Ortiz. "You know, when I was a kid, it was all Latino vendors. Cheap too, man. And there was this little guy, a Chilean if I recall, selling beer and whiskey over there in the far corner, near Broadway. It's gone, man. Look at it. Went fancy. Neon. Grass-fed hamburgers, eleven-dollar falafels—that's *chickpeas,* man. Eleven bucks for a pita full of chickpeas. Jesus. Look over there. Oysters on the half shell and white wine. What the fuck."

"It's the Ren—"

"Don't say it. I hate that word."

"How about 'rebirth,' then," I say, teasing him. "Rejuvenation. Reinvention. Renewal. Before it was a market, this was the Ville de Paris. Best department store in the city. No kidding. Back in the eighteen-hundreds. It's changing back to what it was. Like in the Bible, everything has a season." Ortiz looks at me, makes a fist, reels up his middle finger. "You look skeptical. Don't worry. You can still get a taco for three bucks."

"They'll push them out too. Just wait. Where did you come up with this Ville de whatever?"

"It's on the plaque outside."

He fidgets with his mustache, looks tired.

"That Salvadoran's joint's doing well," I say. "So is the nut seller by the watch-repair guy."

"Who wears a watch anymore? That guy won't last. Something new comes; something old's gotta die. I miss the grit and the lack of pretension. It's gone, and for what? Bitter coffee sold by some bearded wastrel calling it Ethiopian and charging you four bucks. Christ." He shakes his head, scratches his face. "You ever have one of those sandwiches from Egg Slut? You see the lines around that place? Bet it's a two-hour wait to get an egg-and-cheese sandwich. And they all stand there, iPhones out, taking selfies, making a show of it. Doesn't the world have important stuff to do? Who can stand that long in line for an egg sandwich? I'm lost."

"I like the beer over there," I say, nodding to the left.

"Never figured you for a craft guy."

"Every now and then, I like a hoppier taste. A bite."

"Jesus, you're just like them. I thought you hung out at the place over on Fifth."

"The Little Easy's my go-to."

"That looks sufficiently gritty. Used to be something else. I can't remember what. A dry cleaner's, maybe. Had a murder there way back when I was starting out."

"It's got a beat-up charm. Like Budapest."

"I like something a little beat-up and worn out. Real, you know. But *Budapest*? What's that got to do with it? I'm assuming you mean the city, right? It's not an apt analogy. Kind of off the wall. 'Cause 'Little Easy' would naturally make one think of New Orleans."

"First thing that came to mind."

"You're weird. You do that a lot, you know. Drop in off-the-wall references. I've noticed. You can be an opaque fucker."

"You mean hard to follow?"

"Pain in the ass, more like."

"I don't see myself that way."

"No. You see yourself as sensitive. Smart and aloof too. You have this smart thing going."

"Is that bad?"

"It's annoying."

Ortiz and I chat away about useless shit. We don't want to talk about what we're here to talk about. The video. I can't stop seeing it in my head. What they did to her. I've seen a lot of degradation over the years, but something about her, in that mask, her body, long, flimsy, dead to the world, hands on her, moving her like a puppet, setting her in positions, and the whole time, the mask not changing expression, showing neither fear nor pain, nor anything at all. It had a knowing look to it, as if it had glimpsed centuries and deciphered secrets. Her body, her nakedness, drew you to her. You wanted to cover her, but at the same time, you couldn't turn away. The strange loveliness of a victim. It happens from time to time. A victim of a sex crime can draw out your darker places, even as you weep for her. It makes you ashamed of what's inside you.

"This one bothers me," says Ortiz. "Young woman like that. It's not even that so much as the perverse staging of it. How old you think that tape is? Gallagher and Jamieson look young."

"Crime lab's working on it. Maybe eight, ten years."

"What was the opera in the background?"

"*Così fan tutte*, by Mozart."

"Not on my playlist," says Ortiz, no smile.

"Jamieson was a classics guy. Architecture, music. I told you about the paintings in his office and the statue by his pool."

"The rape of somebody by Zeus, right?"

"*Rape of Proserpina*. Pluto kidnaps a maiden to the underworld. Greek mythology. You ever get into it? I was addicted to it as a kid. Bernini did the statue in Rome."

"Whatever. You find anything on the escort service Jamieson used? He rough up a lot of girls? More videos?"

"That's the only one we've got."

"I can't stop thinking about that mask. Sick fucks. Sick rich guys thinking they run the world."

"Not anymore—at least two of them, anyway."

"But they knew they were gonna. You could see it. Brazen contempt. Looking right at the camera. Glad they got wasted." He fidgets with his mustache and sighs. "So what are you thinking?"

"The doer's that woman. Probably never knew what happened that night, could never be sure, and then somehow, sometime, she comes across the video. Maybe she's the one who hacked

Gallagher's computer a couple years ago. Remember, he threw it in the ocean. Jamieson's kept his files on a flash drive. She must have a copy too."

"She planned it?"

"Vengeance."

"Who is she? The mask never comes off."

"They never mention her name. No reference to her at all. We don't know who she is."

"Or even if she's the doer." Ortiz sighs. "They could have killed her. We don't know what happened after the video ended. Killer could be someone else—not likely, but I wouldn't completely rule out the possibility. Could be a boyfriend or husband who found out. Could be a bunch of people. Could still be some turf battle between architectural firms—again, not likely, I know, but a lot of money at stake in these contracts."

"But we have surveillance video of a woman in a fedora coming out of the Grand Street building the night Jamieson was killed. We know she went into his apartment. We have a witness who saw her on the sidewalk. Earle something, the barber-bookie I told you about."

"The guy who thought she was up there on a movie shoot?"

"Yes. And now we have the rape video."

"I don't know," says Ortiz, moving pieces in his mind. "How about this. Hear me out before you say anything. How about Jensen as the doer, or at least, he has a connection to the doer. He didn't want to be there that night. He didn't want to do it. Not really. He was young and drunk and scared. Jamieson and Gallagher are threatening him. Egging him on. Guy was scared of them. He didn't have a mask; you could see the disgust on his face."

"But he does it. He rapes her."

"I said let me finish. Yeah, he does. He's pretty aggressive too, once he gets going. I just think he broke. Snapped. He wanted it to be over fast, and he did it as hard as he could. He hated those guys. Didn't you say Jensen's wife …"

"Wanita."

"Didn't you say she and Jamieson's boss, that old architect, the guy with the tailored suits, told you about a falling-out between Jensen and the other two? Didn't you say Jamieson told you the same thing at Gallagher's funeral and was real cagey about it? Gallagher's wife also said something happened between them, right? Here's what I'm thinking. Jensen and this woman somehow come across the video. They reconcile and make a plan. The video's bad for both of them. They want to destroy the two who made it."

"That's a stretch. Why would she do that? He raped her."

"She's seen the video. She knows he didn't want to. Maybe he wants revenge too."

"I don't know, Ortiz. I don't buy it. Besides, he never saw her. Jensen got there and the mask was on. We saw him rush out of the house while Gallagher and Jamieson still had her naked."

"They told him who she was later. Could be."

"Doubt it. They didn't want him to know. It was Jamieson and Gallagher's schoolboy secret. Jensen was the weak one. They wanted to keep him guessing. Toy with him. They had him on video. He doesn't know her identity. He can't confess, contact her. They have him. He wasn't going to talk, but he breaks from them. And they say fine, screw him, and time goes by."

"Then, where is he?"

"Wife says Montana. He often goes off the grid."

"Pretty convenient, wouldn't you say?" says Ortiz, lighting another cigarette, yawning. "He's the doer. If not, he's dead and she, or whoever, has a trifecta."

"No body. We found the other two quick. Jensen disappeared days ago."

Ortiz runs a hand through his hair, leans back in his chair, uncomfortable, edgy.

"The shit that goes on inside people, huh?" he says. "The shit we do to one another."

"Who you telling about the video?"

"Nobody."

"Mayor's office?"

"Nope. Can't afford a leak. That video gets out, and boom, it's viral. You know what kind of shit comes with that. I'll tell the chief we've got a significant lead. Getting close."

"Are we?"

"Better be."

"This one's getting to me," I say, looking away a second and then back to Ortiz. "I feel a pull, you know. When I saw her on the surveillance video in that raincoat and hat, she's this woman disappearing into the night. The way she walked away and vanished. Then the sex tape. Is it the same person? What happened to her between then and now? How do you go on? How do you look at yourself and not think back? Where do you put that horrific experience? Every time someone touches you, a burn, a memory. You think that?"

"Jesus, Carver. You got a thing for this woman? Listen, man, we get over shit. No matter how bad. It's what people do. Get on. Put it in a box. How else you gonna make it? You got over your father; I got over stuff; we all do."

"This is a different kind of box. I don't know if this one did. You kill like that, you didn't get over much."

"Maybe this is how she gets over it. What do they say in yoga? A cleansing breath."

"Didn't know you did yoga."

"Tried it once. Didn't take," says Ortiz, standing and finishing his coffee.

A girl in cutoffs and black boots kisses a bearded guy wearing an earring. He hands her an iPad and tells her she's got to read an article on vacationing in the Galapagos Islands. She smiles and twirls and kisses him again. She holds up the screen and slides under his arm. They walk toward the neon and the steam rising from the Pupusa Stand, and a woman in a ponytail selling artisanal bread and sea salt.

"Hey," says Ortiz. "For the hell of it, let's try one of those egg sandwiches. The line's not too long. I'm buying."

CHAPTER 21

Sunday.

A hushed, pleasant ache.

Not yet dawn. Still and silent as a cat, I sit at the window with a coffee, looking out. A headlight, a bus. Latino voices gathering at the corner. A priest heads toward mass. The blue-black sky, a break of orange in the east. I am warm, serene. I don't know why. It's like a pause in a war, I guess. Guns go quiet and nothing moves. There must be those days in a war, momentary reprieves to remind you that you're human. You do terrible things, but you are human. Soldiers must feel that on the battlefield. I feel it now.

Sam is looking for me. The city wonders where I am. Who I am. This woman who leaves a man naked, takes his finger. Leaves another man on a sidewalk, a dark pool around his neck. Yes, they look. Here I am in this window in Angelino Heights. Sought but not seen. So much power in that, to stray through crowds, anonymous.

I sketched a small church last night, with a cross and overhead beams and circles of stained glass. Simple, the lines symmetrical and clean. My first church was built years ago in Chaparral out near Joshua Tree. This one is another in an evolution of small churches in unexpected places, like the one I saw with my father in New Mexico when I was a girl.

I like this coffee, this roast, this bean. It's just right. What shall I wear to meet Sam? I shouldn't think about that now, but with him I get ahead of myself. Don't rush. I am a rusher. The running, weights, punching bag—my muscles are tight, lean, like when I played tennis but more so. Sam will be impressed.

The water boils. I make new coffee—a wonderful phrase—and press it slow, and the scent rises, fills me. I reach into the cupboard for another mug. I pour. A bit of cream. I put on my mask and open the basement door. I descend. My feet creak on the steps. I hear him rustle, the sound of his chain.

I walk toward him in the dark. He scurries away, rattle, rattle. He's breathing hard, almost gasping. "Who are you? What do you want?" A sniffle, like a little boy. A whimpering dog. I set the coffee beside him and step back to a chair—his chain won't reach that far—and turn on a lamp. The light is soft and yellow. He squints toward it. I sit. Still as a statue. I feel my breath inside the mask, warm moisture on my face. I breathe. Calm. It is the moment I have waited years for. He turns and looks at me. His face contorts; a shiver runs through him. He pushes himself against the wall as if he might find a crack, an opening; then, after a few moments, his expression goes slack, a look of disbelief and dark wonder. Fear, sorrow, hurt, pity, and, yes, I would say terror, all at play on his face, as if an apparition deep within had arisen and appeared before him. Me. In my mask.

I stand and slip off my robe. Naked. I want him to see my

body, a bit aged but strong, tall and lean like before, when he first saw me. I turn and bend over. Slow. So he can see. Remember. I feel no shame. That is over. I am using my body to shame him. Let him study me, take me in. Let him be broken. I rise and turn. He looks away, closes his eyes. I slip on my robe and sit by the lamp. I wait. He turns toward me. I nod to the coffee. He doesn't reach for it, his face twisted and amazed. He leans against the wall. He feels his chain, rubs his eyes, and weeps. His chest heaves. A long time goes by. He quiets like the air at the end of a storm. He looks at me. He wants to climb through my mask eyes to see who I am. There is power in the mask. I feel it. Not the first time I wore it, but now … oh, yes. Note to self: it radiates.

"It's you," says Jensen. "From that night."

I am like a sphinx.

"I never saw your face," he says. "Only the …" He looks down, back to the mask. "I see it every day."

No words from me.

He pushes back tears, swallows.

"They never told me your name. Not in all that time. They kept you a mystery."

Silence from the mask.

"I'm sorry," he says. The words small, quiet; they hang for a bit. A new sentence begins but stops. I hear him breathe. "Sorry" is a nothing word. He must be thinking that. To say something so ridiculous. *Sorry*. A coward's word. "I should have stopped it," he says, shaking his head. "We were young and drunk." Another pathetic phrase. Does he know how he sounds to the girl from that night? I did feel like a girl. Young. Clever in many ways, unsuspecting in others. I saw so much before me then, the outline of a life I had imagined in a new city. "We were all just starting out. I admired their talents. I wanted to be in their circle," says Stephen Jensen. He doesn't know what to say, how to take all this in and find a starting point, a context for then and now, to squeeze history through a prism so the colors may speak. "They were terrible people," he says. "But I wanted their praise. That makes no sense, I know, but …" He trails off. His sentences have run out of air. He breathes in. "They sent me a video. To keep me quiet. I didn't remember much of what happened that night. I watched it and went to Jamieson. I asked if you were a prostitute or someone hired to act out what they wanted. He said no. He said, 'Don't be a fool. You weren't that drunk. You did it too, Stephen. Don't forget, you did it too.' I didn't know what to believe." He lowers his head. "They wanted to shame me. I realized that later. I was the weak one. I watched the video again and then I destroyed it. I saw myself doing a thing that was not me. But it was. I was that."

I cross my legs.

"I can't imagine—"

I jump up and kick him in the face. Twice. He doesn't turn from the blows. He accepts them. He bleeds from the lip. I sit. Heat runs through my skin; my eyes water. I breathe in. I need to calm. Focus. I look toward the stairs and around the unfinished basement. Beams and cobwebs and circuit breakers and washer and dryer and boxes of things, some too old to remember. I should go through them. I haven't decided what to do with the basement. No design has come to me. I think I'll leave it as it is. Raw, dark, the scent of the earth through the walls. Basements can't become something else. Not really. I turn back to Jensen. He pulls his legs up under him. He looks at the wrist clasp fastened to his chain. He doesn't pull on it or try to break away. He doesn't yell. He sits, transfixed by the mask. He doesn't curse me. He doesn't plead. He is my prisoner, my man on a leash. He came quite easily into my possession.

I knew he was going to Montana—the merits of computer hacking cannot be overstated—on one of his get-off-the-grid mind-cleansing trips. I parked down the street from his Santa Monica home. Dressed in black Lycra—the same style I wore to kill Gallagher—I knelt and waited beside the hedges along his driveway. He came out about four a.m., with a backpack. He opened the Range Rover door and tossed it in. He went back inside the house. I slipped into the well behind the driver's seat, tucked myself small, pulled down the visor of a ball cap to hide my face, and waited. He came out of the house with a coffee, and we were off. He turned on NPR, a Chopin sonata, faint and mournful. A bit of news. The scent of aftershave. When we were on the 10, I eased up behind him and put a gun, a 9mm bought at a Walmart in the Valley, to his neck. He nearly drove off the highway. He steadied. I told him to break off the rearview mirror. He did. We went down the highway in darkness. Fast and sleek. Barely a trickle of traffic as we merged onto the 110 toward the 101. I'd sit back for a couple of miles, then lean in and press the gun to his neck, then sit back. Kept him guessing. I led him to my house. He said nothing. The radio played. Beethoven, I think. And news about Trump and Putin and spies. I reached for the door opener in my pocket, and we pulled into my garage—everything planned, just like with Gallagher and Jamieson. He shut off the engine. I stayed behind him as he got out. I jammed the gun into his back. Tugged down the brim of my hat again. It was dark, the cover so cool and sweet. We slipped out the side garage door. No one saw. I walked him inside the house, down to the basement, pricked him with a needle. Not as strong a concoction as I used with Jamieson. He went down on his knees, then drooped. He never saw my face. I chained him to the wall. Gave him a pitcher of water and a bucket to pee in. If he chose.

"What will you do?" he says. "I have a wife."

The mask speaks: "Are you a good architect?"

The question startles him. He's quiet for a while.

"Not the one I wanted to be."

"What do you design?"

"Homes."

"For the rich?"

"Along the coast."

"Are they original?"

"A few."

"You're going to need to talk more. Two-word answers are boring, and if I'm bored … well, who knows what could happen."

"I try to make angles and curves fit the coast," he says. He's thin like jerky, hazel eyes—bullied as a child, I'm sure. He's taller up close. Long arms, winglike hands, pinched nose, hair brown and thinning. Not ugly, not beautiful—a bland, in-between man. A bit of blood runs from his mouth; a bruise rises beneath his eye. He's taken my warning and is talking as if we were out for coffee, imagining himself far from here. Strange. A way of coping, I suppose. I need him to talk. But really, how is one supposed to act when chained to a basement wall? "I want them to feel organic, you know, to be part of nature. It's hard to be both subtle and dramatic with the earth, if you understand what I mean."

"Nature is beautiful and unyielding."

"Yes," he says. "It won't conform. You have to conform to it."

"Like religion."

"I never thought of it—"

"What about Frank Lloyd Wright?" I say, cutting him off so we don't veer into the ecclesiastical. "He was one with nature. He designed houses."

"Well, yes, but I thought I would do bigger things. When I was younger, I saw cities in my head."

"Back when you first saw this mask."

"Yes, back then, and much before."

He turns away.

"What kind of cities?" says the mask.

"I don't see them anymore."

"You gave up." The mask shakes her head. "You're a pussy. This seems to be a recurring theme with you."

"I suppose, yes, in a way."

"'I suppose, yes, in a way.' What kind of answer is that? It's noncommittal. So weak. Jamieson and Gallagher were right about you. Have you always been this weak? I don't like men who give up," I say, gritting my teeth, snarling in a voice I have never heard before. "I don't like weak men. They're pathetic. Excruciatingly pathetic. What good are weak men? They should die, don't you think?"

Fear flashes across his face. It is only terror looking at the mask now. I say nothing more on this point. Let him wonder. Then I say—to myself, of course—let's ramp things up a bit. I go to the cabinet above the washing machine and pull a knife from a shelf. The same one I used for Jamieson: six inches, sturdy, balanced weight, silver gleam. I turn. Jensen tries to make himself smaller. He says nothing. He closes his eyes. No fight, no pleading, no tugging at the chain. I sit and lay the knife by the lamp. It becomes the center of his universe. I cross my legs and sigh. I am suddenly amused. "But," I say, "you must still see something in your head. Designs and the way you wanted buildings to be."

He looks at the knife. Then at the mask. I can see him calculating. How to stay alive? Must be thinking he's doomed, like a goat tied to a post during Ramadan, which I saw once in Cairo, knives flashing and blood filling alleys in praise to God. There's something about Jensen, though. It's as if he'd wanted this: to sit across from the mask, like a penitent slipping into a confessional and waiting for the priest's shadow. Does he want forgiveness? Does he want to die? Maybe both. He just sits, chained, almost intrigued, like a man whose sin is too heavy to bear. Look at the way he stares at the mask. Not blinking. Amazed, like a child playing make-believe in a closet. Frightened but inviting it. Oh, yes. Am I to be confessor and executioner? I hadn't anticipated this. Fascinating. Let's see how it plays out.

"When I was a child, my father took me to New York," he says, wiping away tears (Or is it sweat?), shaking a little, calming again. Spasms run through him. Maybe he doesn't know what he wants. I wait. I want to hear this story. I lean toward him, my mask hovering not like a priest but like a vengeful spirit. "We walked from Grand Central Station. It was just after dusk and drizzling. The sky was full of mist and going black. We passed the New York Library. Those big lions. Do you know them? We kept walking along Bryant Park. Everyone was rushing with umbrellas. Then I saw it: the American Radiator building. Do you know it?"

I nod that I do.

"It's beautiful, isn't it? Black stone dipped in gold. Like a castle. It seemed to float in the fog and rain. I had never seen anything like it. I stood and stared. My eyes climbed from floor to floor. The top was half hidden in the mist. I'd never experienced anything like it before or since. My father put his arm around me. We didn't budge."

"You wanted to build something like that?"

"Yes," he says, looking at the mask. "It's foolish. A boy's fantasy. Do you know architecture? You mentioned Frank Lloyd Wright."

I rise, smack him in the face. Again he accepts it. Rage burns, and my mind is back to that night. Yes, I am an architect. I have my own dreams and cities. You did not take them from me. You raped me and broke my body with the others, but you did not take my designs and imagination. They're alive inside me, not so easily surrendered. An architect? Yes, I am. I understand him, that feeling he had. Seeing that building. A magical building in a boy's life. It changed him. Just as that little mission church in New Mexico changed me when I was a girl. The things that come into us. Sharp and fast as arrows. Those realizations; nothing afterward is the same. We become newborn. I understand this about Jensen. Why, then, did he do what he did? Why did he dirty that little boy's dream?

"What did your father do?" says the mask.

"My parents were teachers. History and science."

"Did you love them?"

"Yes."

"Was either of them crazy in any way? Mental illness?" An odd question, but I have my reasons.

"No."

"A happy, normal family."

"My father drank. Never abusive. But often distant, away from us."

"Ah, the flaw. No family is immune."

"He smelled of bourbon and pipe tobacco. That's what I remember most. He died in a car accident. Hit a pole after a night at a bar."

"How cliché."

"It was. Yes. It didn't feel so then. It felt unique and sad." He pauses, swallows. "Your parents?"

"No, no, no. We don't talk about me. This is your trial. The trial of a weak little man."

Nice touch, that phrase. *Trial* has an ominous ring. He quiets, a slight scrape of chain.

"May I stand?"

The mask nods. He rises against the wall.

"How many days have I been here?"

"Does time matter?" I laugh like a ghoul, not intending to, but it just happens.

"I'm hungry. Can I use the bathroom?"

I nod to the bucket, which needs to be emptied.

"Please. A toilet."

Men. Fucking men. I walk upstairs, pull the 9mm out of the kitchen drawer, return to the basement, point the gun at him, hand him the key to unlock the clasp around his wrist, follow him upstairs, gun to his back, let him use the hallway powder room. I hear him washing his face, the pat of a towel. He steps out. We are so close. Face-to-mask. He looks into my eyes. I poke the gun into his side. I almost pull the trigger. I nod. He turns, and we go back to the basement. He chains himself to the wall, throws me the key. He looks at me and sits, rests his head on his knees. I return to the kitchen and make him a sandwich—What am I doing? Why is he still alive?—and bring it down with a bottle of water. I place the gun on the table by the knife. I sit and watch him eat, like at a zoo.

"Thank you. This is good. This is a Victorian house, isn't it? You're restoring it. There used to be so many of them in this city, up in Angelino Heights and over on Bunker Hill. The Bunker Hill ones are gone."

Ooh, a clever little shit. But still, it's not as if he were leaving.

"We don't talk about me. Or my house," I say. "Why did you go that night to Jamieson's place? Tell me everything. Every detail. I want to know every piece of what happened."

He swallows the last bit of sandwich, sips water.

"I was supposed to meet them earlier, at a bar. We had all just started new jobs and wanted to celebrate. We'd gone to college together. I had to work late and couldn't make it. They called later and told me to come to Jamieson's. They were drunk and acting strange when I got there. Like they were hiding something. They brought me in the back door and we sat in the kitchen. They kept sliding shots of tequila at me. Opera was playing. Jamieson loved opera. He blasted it all the time. I was getting tipsy." (Thought to self: strong men don't say "tipsy.") "It was fun. I felt like one of them," he says. "I was the less secure one, always worrying. I've been that way ever since I can remember. I don't know why. I always felt like the one trying harder than everybody else. I didn't feel that way that night, though. I liked not feeling that way. I wanted it to last. We kept drinking and talking. Gallagher said one day the three of us would start our own firm and redesign the city."

"Like gods."

"Gallagher's ego was that big. We were young and drunk. We talked about great architects. Wright, Piano, Foster, Nouvel. Of favorite buildings and styles. Art and public space." (Again, note to self: they were talking about this, my passion, while I was drugged and naked in another room.) "It was dreamer talk from men who had yet to do anything. Do you know what I mean?

We were showing off in front of one another." He sips his water, fingers his chain. "The conversation turned, though. It got mean." He takes a breath. "Gallagher and Jamieson started railing about women. How they shouldn't be architects. They lacked aesthetics, precision, and discipline. They saw the world differently than men and could not blend poetics and pragmatism. Jamieson used those exact words. Even drunk, he was a blowhard. At first, I thought they were kidding. I mentioned Zaha Hadid. I don't know if you know her, but she was revolutionary. Her buildings curve and seem to stretch as if she'd invented a new geometry. I brought up a few others too. I didn't know that many, to be honest. Architecture is a men's club. Jamieson waved me off. He was quite intense about it. Gallagher nodded in agreement. They kept going on and on. I'd never seen that in them before. Vanity and ego, yes, but not blatant misogyny. They let it pass and we moved on to other things. The opera got louder. Jamieson sang tenor and Gallagher pretended to be conducting an orchestra with a fork."

"Why didn't you defend women more? Why didn't you leave? Bringing up Hadid. Big whoop, she's the poster child. You should have done more. People who do nothing are as guilty as those who act. That's the first lesson of history, or religion. It sounded like a party of little Nazis with opera and architecture thrown in."

"I thought what they were saying was nonsense. But I didn't stop it."

The eyes in the mask glare. They water and glare.

"You're weak. Why should you live?"

I reach for the gun, retract my hand before I touch it. I prefer the knife. When the time comes. But let him wonder. Let him sit there and wonder whether that is the last sandwich he's going to eat. I didn't know that about Jamieson and Gallagher. I was selected and targeted. To be culled from the herd. It was hate and contempt, not your drunken frat-boy-variety rape. They wanted to damage me and prove their superiority, keep me as their little private joke. They had never seen my designs, didn't know my concept of math and beauty, of calculus and form, of the history and artifacts we pull from to shape the present and contemplate the future. They knew none of that about me. They never asked, weren't interested. I was a woman. Young and pretty and not scared of her opinion. I wonder what I sounded like before they drugged me. Was I eloquent? Did I speak of Gothic or Spanish Revival? Did they plan it, or did it just happen after martinis at a bar? I can't remember now whether it was arranged. The way I recall it—and my memory is blurred—was that new architects in the city went out for drinks to get to know one another. Other architects were there. Were they all men? I don't remember. Statistically, probably. Was I a real-life Architect Barbie, some toy Mattel put out to "inspire" little girls, like President Barbie and Veterinarian Barbie? Did we need a doll to make us matter? Was it a setup? Was I that naive? No. Yes. But I was a disruption, a flaw in their grand design. The how of my flaw doesn't really matter, though, does it? Not now. We know the price—oh, yes, the price. Naked and splayed, a tumble thing in a mask. Shamed. Never knowing exactly what happened, but left wondering, trying to piece together broken parts of a night. I never could until the video. That was their mistake. A record of their vanity and hate, like the ledgers kept at concentration camps, the pictures of Serbs raping Muslim girls. The list of crimes is endless, some of them well known, shocking the world. But most, like mine, remain deep, hidden slivers.

"What next?" I say.

"They told me they had a surprise," he says. His voice cracks. He's tired. Remembering is draining him. He's more humiliated than scared—a strange repentant, this Stephen Jensen. "We went to the living room, and a woman in a mask was slumped naked on a couch."

"*This* mask?"

"Yes."

He looks right at me. Doesn't turn away.

"You saw the video," he says. Ah! "You" means admission. We are in this together now. The woman in the mask has become a "you." How touching.

"Yes, I have seen it. Many times."

"You came after us," he whispers.

"One by one. Down to you. Rapist number three."

Pain covers his face, but it is a pain with repose in it, a pain of unburdening. Like a man justly at the gallows.

"The video tells everything," he says. "I don't want to say any more."

"Not everything. It doesn't tell me why you did it. Jamieson and Gallagher, I understand. I didn't before, but I do now. They wanted me gone. Get rid of the lady architect. She's beneath us. Jamieson attacked me with such rage. Why did you wince when I said that? That's what he did. That's what Gallagher did. That's what *you* did. But Jamieson and Gallagher did it with hate. Glee. It was obvious. I can see that now. Their expressions, the way they laughed. It was their own sick opera."

I stop. Play the video in my mind. The minutes pass. Faces from that night come back to me. Then I see them dead, pale, eyes closed. It's hot in this mask; it presses against my skin. I turn toward my prisoner.

"But you, the scared one at the edge. You finally appear, pulling off your clothes, standing behind me. Did you like how they draped me over the couch? I am not a man, but I wouldn't think that would be a turn-on. A passed-out girl folded over a sofa, with two other naked men standing around as if waiting for a bus. Is that erotic? Tell me, I want to know. Do men really like things like that? Did you really want to be third in line? Yes, you're right, the video tells much about you, Stephen Jensen. But it doesn't tell me why."

I scrape the knife blade against the table.

"I've thought about that every day," he says. "On my wedding day, when I sit to draw. That mask is there. In my mind. It follows me. Sometimes, when I haven't seen it in a few days, I think it's gone. But it comes back. It hovers just out of reach, like a light you can't blow out. I apologize to it. Isn't that strange? I apologize to an image in my head."

"It's before you now. Real. Want to touch?"

I rise, take a step toward him, bend closer. He doesn't move. I step back and sit down.

"It's in me. Inseparable as my breath," he says. "I did it because I was a young, misguided, screwed-up, drunk man. That's all the excuse I have. I've been through it every day. It is all I have. I was repulsed and attracted. Your vulnerability, helplessness."

"You're reducing it to the drunken primal? Can't you do better than that?"

He pauses, swallows.

"It gave me power, a power I'd never had," he says. "It's sick, I know. How could you understand? I'm being honest. That's what it was. That and wanting to please them. Sometimes, I hate myself as much for that as for what I did to you." He looks at the mask. It does not react. "The man I thought I was to become was gone. My better self, if I ever had one, disappeared. That's no justice for you, I know that. But it destroyed me. It got quieter and quieter through the years, but it was always there. Look at me. Not much of a prize. Not like Gallagher or Jamieson. I am sorry. That's all I have to give you. It is who I am. Is that selfish? I'm sure it is. What I—we—did to you …" He trails off, looks at the knife. He weeps but doesn't make a sound. I sit still. Tears pool at the bottom of my mask. I am crying over his words and the many years it took to hear them. My rapist is as ruined as I—two fools sacrificed long ago. Is that true? Can the two be one? No. I'm not giving him a pass. He is not a victim. That is sacrilege. He's trying to wheedle. But his end is near. Oh, yes. I like seeing the pieces of him before me. They're the toll. He didn't get away with it. The chain scrapes. He pushes back against the wall.

"I think I know who you are," he says. "I was walking on the beach about two years after that night. I saw you in a bathing suit. You were ahead of me. It was the way your shoulders moved, your legs. I followed but not too closely. You stopped and sat in the sand. You were alone. I knew I had seen you before. I remembered. I'd seen you at an architects' gathering. It all made sense then. That moment on the beach, I knew." He took a deep breath and again looked right at the mask. "But until you saw the video, you never knew who I was. Gallagher and Jamieson brought you to the house, through the back door. I came hours after you arrived with them. You were drugged and passed out by then. I was a mystery to you, just as you were to me until that day on the beach. I kept saying to myself after I saw you that it couldn't have been you. You seemed so free. I thought, *No, this is not a damaged girl.* But it was you. I wouldn't admit it. I let it pass. I let time pass."

He takes another breath.

"You're Dylan Cross," he says. "You did that beautiful, lonely church out near Joshua Tree."

I fly toward him with the knife.

CHAPTER 22

"How could that have been missed?"

"Typical stupid shit."

"Jesus, Ortiz."

"I know. I'm pissed."

"A nine-one-one call. A woman says she sees someone holding a gun to the head of a driver in a Range Rover ahead of her. She gives the license plate."

"Yeah, then she drives away. Scared. Who wouldn't be? Dark, just before dawn."

"Jensen's car?"

"Yup. Got off the 101 around Echo Park near Angelino Heights. A car responded right away. But after the caller stopped following, we never knew where the Rover went. Only a few minutes passed, but it's a big goddamn city."

"Any street cam video?"

"That's the thing too. The camera over by the freeway was broken. Nothing but black fuzz, really."

"Christ. So a doer and a vic vanish right before us. The mayor's going to love that."

"The mayor won't know about it. Understand me, Carver. The mayor won't know."

"Why did it take days before we found out it was Jensen's car?"

"You really asking that question? How long you been on the force? How much crap falls through the cracks? Get over it. We have something to go on. Jensen's not in Montana or Wyoming or wherever. He's here. Dead or a hostage, I'm thinking."

"No shit. Or maybe he escaped and is sitting in a Starbucks."

"Screw you, Carver."

Click. I throw the phone on the counter. Jensen's out there. I don't think he's dead. No body. No sign of his car. No bead on his phone. She's clever. What did she do with him? Gallagher's death was visceral and quick. Jamieson's was a spectacle. Jensen is different. He doesn't fit. He raped her, but not like the other two; there was no rabid pleasure in it. Jensen's not ready-made for revenge. He's her key to what happened. Or maybe I'm wrong and he's in a ditch with his heart cut out. So far, though, she's been smart, untraceable. But they begin to crack. They all do. No matter how well planned, killing takes parts of you and makes them something else, and the perfect crime starts to unravel— slowly at first, but then with unsettling speed.

Seven a.m. The city's moving. A guy in a Dr. Seuss hat is walking through traffic, flipping the bird and yelling bat-shit verse I can't hear. Esmeralda and her scarves and bags are gone from in front of the Clark. She must be eating breakfast at the Mission. I scroll through the news. North Korea's launched another test missile, the Arctic melts and shrinks, ISIS is battling in Mosul, and Princess Leia has died. I remember her, so young with her laser gun and funny doughnut-twisted hair, running through galaxies. You think you know the ones like her, the sly, clever ones who stay in your life like relatives; famous ones who don't seem to age until, one day, they're gray, troubled, and then gone. Even they can't last. I close the laptop, pour a new coffee, and sit by the window. I feel beaten. I play out the strands of the case, draw lines with a pencil. It's an old habit that makes me feel closer to things. I reopen the laptop and watch the video again. Who is she? So pretty and ruined in her mask. For a few seconds, she seems to look right at the camera—a glimmer of eyes, then gone. I click it off and call Wanita. No, he's not dead, I tell her. We haven't found him. No, he's not in Montana. Then I tell her flat.

"Your husband, Gallagher, and Jamieson raped a woman years ago, before you were married. We believe that the woman—we have no name—kidnapped him and may be holding him in the Los Angeles area."

I let it sink in. I can hear Wanita breathing.

"Stephen wouldn't rape anyone," she says, swallowing a sob.

"He did."

"He's too gentle. Are you sure?"

"Yes."

A gasp, a fissure of pain. Her whole world changed in a few sentences.

"My God, this is not what I know. Stephen? *My* Stephen? No. You would know if you knew him. How could this be? This is a mistake, Detective. I know him like I know the lines on my own hand. A man can't keep secrets. He can't be someone else. For years? No. It's impossible."

She trails off, following any thought that leads away from the truth. She quiets. I let time pass.

"Do you think he'll be killed?" she says.

"I don't know."

A longer silence hangs. It goes on for more than a minute. I wonder whether she's standing at the window, looking at the ocean. An intake of breath. Another. She tries to say something but can't. She hangs up.

I shower, pour a last coffee, and head out to the firms of Gallagher and Jamieson.

Gallagher's mentor, Arthur Kimmel, perched up in his office on the thirtieth floor, offers little and says less. Young architects dart around him.

"We have a contract deadline," he says, running a hand through his silver hair and glancing at me with kind impatience. He is no longer the man in mourning I saw days ago at the funeral. "I don't know anything about a video like that. I cannot believe Michael would be mixed up in such a thing. Three architects raping a woman. My God. As I told you before, Detective, Michael was an egotist, a narcissist." He leans over a desk and writes numbers on a blueprint. "Michael could have made his mark. He was consumed with work. I never suspected any tendencies like that. He was married. I told you about Miranda. Did you see her? She may know more. My God. A video like that." He pauses, steps closer, whispers. "You don't think this video would ever get, you know, made public. It could be quite damaging to the firm."

"With the Renaissance and all," I say.

He cuts me a smirk. "I hear that word a lot these days. I may have even used it myself. 'Renaissance,'" he says. "Let's hope so. I see a lack of uniformity, though. A lot of rushing, Detective.

Too much money, perhaps. Money and politics change aesthetics. Rome and Florence. They're beautiful, man's realization of his dreams. But what compromises were made? To politics, the Church, the money men. We'll never know." He steps back and moves toward the window. "I'm sorry. I'm rambling."

"Is there anything more you can think of about Gallagher? I don't believe a man could do something like that and not show some inkling. You follow me? A rape like that doesn't happen out of nowhere. Not in my experience. You ever suspect anything along those lines, something in his character? An offhand comment, any revelation? He saw a prostitute, you know."

"I read about that. In that awful hotel on Main."

Kimmel looks at me and walks to the window.

"If all our secrets were exposed, Detective, the world would slip its axis." He closes his eyes, feels the sun on his face, turns back to me. "But to answer your question, no. I never suspected anything like that about Michael. I didn't know about his prostitute. Michael knew how I admired Miranda. He would never have told me about that. I wonder if she knew. Perhaps that is what broke them up. He never told me why. Neither did she. When I think about it now, it must have been something ugly." He pauses, takes a moment to himself, turns back toward the window. I see only the back of him, a silhouette against the sky. "A couple can survive most things, but some are unfixable. Surely, you have some of those, Detective. I do. 'Dark vapors.' Didn't Shakespeare or Beckett or somebody call them that?"

I join him at the window and look out on the city.

"It's terrifying and beautiful at once," he says, "the unfinished."

I leave him. I walk amid sirens and the clatter of construction. Los Angeles is changing. Though it's not my city, I have adopted it.

And there are moments, especially at dusk, when the palms scratch against the last bits of sun, and a hard, clarifying coolness settles in and the winds gust from the canyons and the ocean, cleansing and quieting as night falls, when it leaves me spellbound. You can raise all the pretty buildings you want, but they will pale against what existed long before the first architect arrived. That is the sacred lie of LA: the belief that we can tame a cruel, unsparing paradise, a place not imagined for us but where we have nonetheless brought our strange, restless, unattainable dreams.

I call Ortiz. No answer. I arrive at McKinley, Jamieson, and Burns.

"Detective Carver, you sounded quite furtive on the phone," says Matthew McKinley, tamping down a billow of white hair and sliding a pen into the pocket of his ironed blue Oxford shirt. He is russet, well shaved. He points to a chair. "Please sit. Is there a development? An arrest? How may I help you?"

I tell him about the video.

"Oh, my," he says. "That's horrible, frightening." He blots his forehead with a handkerchief and reaches for the tumbler of water on his desk. "This is quite unnerving. How does one respond to such a thing? Paul Jamieson did this? You're sure?"

"Yes."

"With Gallagher. I told you when we first met, I never liked him. A schemer. Like a petulant little crow. Who was the other, Stephen Jensen? I don't know him well. What can I say, Detective? You work with a young, talented man. You try to instill something. Not just about architecture but about life. A little wisdom. Is that naive? Does that sound ridiculous? I hope not. I would hope there's some civility left. A sense of handing things down. But this is not Paul Jamieson. This subversion can't be his legacy."

"It happened at Jamieson's house, his old house. They raped her while opera played. *Così fan tutte*, as it happens."

"Why Mozart for such a thing?"

"We don't know."

"The woman was in a mask, you say?"

"Yes. A Venetian mask, the kind they wear at Carnevale."

"Poor thing. My God. And you think she may be doing this as revenge."

"There are other possibilities, but yes. This seems the most likely given what we know."

"Who is she?"

"No identity. The mask never came off." I pour myself some water. "Jamieson had started with you back then. He had been in LA only a short while. Is there anything you can remember about that time?"

"That was years ago, Detective. I can't recall. This is all so overwhelming."

"Jamieson used an escort service. The last time you and I spoke, you thought that was impossible."

"Why would he? He had women all the time. I can't understand any of this. This secret life. He didn't have that in here," says McKinley, waving a hand around the office. "He was pure in here. It was always the work—how to make it better, how to make function conform to beauty. That was his gift—not the other way around, the easy way. He loved the old Italians. I think I told you that. He could have been great, Detective. He had that potential. He was maturing." He stops and shakes his head. "And all the time, he had this other life. How? My wife—she died a few years ago of cancer—adored Paul. He often came to our house for dinner. Sometimes, he'd bring a date. Intelligent and beautiful like him. You can be a little envious of that when you get older, Detective. You're too young, but one day you'll know. The excellence of youth—that's what my wife called it."

"What about these women? Did he ever talk about them?"

"Nobody in particular. They came and went. I can't recall his ever going out with anyone too long. As I said, he brought a few to dinner, or we'd see him with someone at the symphony or the opera. One was in a dance company, I think. She ate like a bird. There was a lawyer, and an actress who had a part in one of those streaming things. She loved martinis."

The old man leans back, looks at the ceiling, down to his hands. A large black-and-white photograph of a desert hangs on the wall. Dunes like waves, the coming moon. I stand and walk to it. Let the old man think. I look at the other walls. All deserts. McKinley steps beside me. "They're magnificent, aren't they?" he says. "Scoured. Repositories of time. They make me wonder, Detective, about man's audacity in seeking to fill nature with his own images. I look at these photographs when I'm designing a new building. They remind me that the space we fill is sacred. Our buildings must reflect that in some way." He shakes his head, lifts a hand as if batting away a thought. "Just an old man talking."

"You're crying."

"Yes."

He wipes his eyes and sits back at his desk.

"This has all been too much."

He folds his handkerchief.

"Have you noticed there are no women in our office, Detective?"

"No, I hadn't."

"Not one. Paul wanted it that way. I fought him on it a few

times. We had very good women prospects over the years. But Paul always said no. He didn't think women made good architects. He never actually said that, but the subtext was clear enough. Once, when I pressed on the fact that we should hire one very qualified girl who could have complemented him—his designs, I mean—he cut me off. I saw rage in his eyes. Very brief, like a flash. I had never seen that in him before." He pulls his pen from his pocket and fidgets with it. "We're not the best profession for women. In that way, we're like the military. A boys' club. Only twenty percent of all architects are women, did you know that? Why would you? But it's true. They're paid much less than men. It's not remotely fair, I know, but it's the way of things." He rubs a hand across his mouth and says nothing for a long while. "You know, a few years back, they made an Architect Barbie. She had black-rimmed glasses, a hard hat, blueprints, and, of course, she was blond. There was a black one too, I think ... Or is it 'African American'? Terminologies change so often these days."

He leans forward and clasps his hands.

"I think women can be brilliant architects," he says. "I should have fought Paul on that, and we should have hired a few. I relented, though. I thought his talent was that great. I almost hired a woman about the same time I hired Paul, before I knew how he felt about such things. She was striking. Tall. Fit. She'd sent me her designs, and I liked them. She blended the classical and the modern. Unique. Sparse but with a flourish, here and there, of the Old World. Time frozen and time moving. She and Paul together would have been a wonderful team. As I said, she would have complemented him, and he her." McKinley narrows his eyes, puts a hand to his chin. "What was her name? It was a different name for a girl. Oh, yes. Dylan Cross. I hesitated, and she accepted another job. She's still around. Works for a small firm in the city."

"Did they know each other?"

"I don't think so. He never mentioned her. I haven't seen much of her work since. She did a lovely church out near Joshua Tree. It rises like magic off the high desert. Quite something. Classical, modern, organic. Hard to pull off, Detective. That was years ago. It was written up in a trade magazine. Not much else of hers comes to mind. That happens sometimes. Early brilliance often fades in this profession, for some reason or other. Like poets."

I write the name "Dylan Cross" in my notebook.

"Thank you, Mr. McKinley."

I stand.

"I'm afraid I haven't been much help," he says, wiping his eyes. "I feel betrayed. A fool, almost. Thinking you know somebody so well, and you don't know them at all."

"That's pretty common."

"Is it? That's a shame. But I guess you would know."

I turn to leave. McKinley sits at his desk, dazed and so much smaller than when we first met. I stop in a café and order an Americano. The place is nearly empty. I sit in the back and phone Miranda in New York.

"Yes, Detective. Of course I recall. It was my dead husband we talked about, after all."

I could sense the pot in her voice. Syllables floated.

"Did you know about the video?" I ask.

An audible inhalation.

"So you found the laptop. I thought he had thrown it in the ocean."

"We got it off Paul Jamieson's flash drive."

"Boys will be boys. Keeping their little souvenirs."

"Why didn't you say anything?"

"What to say, Detective? How to put that into words? I saw it and fled. It broke me. That's not too strong a term, believe me. I thought this man and I were having quite a life. We had problems, sure, but who doesn't? We had a house and a view and a pool and a maid and a mountain lion in the hills. I had no idea. I don't think I was tricking myself. I thought we were really good, maybe. I don't know; there were things. But they were put-the-toilet-seat-down tolerable things, like all relationships have. Then one day, he's frantic. He found that his laptop had been hacked. He had it on in his home office. He was enraged, looking in the screen like a madman. Scrolling and checking files. Cursing. He called Jamieson." Another inhalation. "I was in the kitchen and he walked to the pool so I wouldn't hear. I went into his office and hit a key on his laptop. The screen lit up. Usually, he clicks it off and closes it. But he didn't. He was that out of sorts. I saw only a minute or two of it. It was terrible. They were naked like animals, dogs around this woman in a mask. I kept listening for him to come back in. He had so many files." An inhalation and a long breath out. A crack in her voice. "One of me. Did you know that? Taking a shower. Was that on Jamieson's flash drive? My husband, the Peeping Tom. On his own wife. What kind of man does that? It's an overused word these days, but I felt violated, Detective. *In my own shower.* I wanted to see more, but I heard him coming back in and I hurried out."

Another breath in.

"I confronted him later that night. It was a terrible fight. I was so angry I couldn't cry. He told me the video of the girl in the mask was from before we married. He said it was an escort they hired.

A woman to play a part. I asked why. What kind of perversion was this? That really set him off. 'Perversion.' The word really got to him. He came at me but stopped. I saw for the first time who he was. In full. I hadn't seen enough of the video to know if it was a play as he said, or an honest-to-God rape. I didn't know. Was she acting? I hadn't seen enough of it. Or maybe I didn't want to. But I had to get out. He stormed out of the house and went and threw the laptop in the ocean. He called Jamieson again when he got back. We slept in separate rooms that night. At dawn, I stood in his doorway and asked why he filmed me in the shower. He said people are the most beautiful when they don't know they're being watched. I told him he was sick."

Another sharp breath in and a long one out. A sip of something. Crying.

"I moved into a hotel. A few weeks later, I got a job and moved here. Never went back. When he was killed, when you came to visit, I suspected it might have had something to do with the laptop. I couldn't be sure. I didn't see everything that was there. Who knows how many incriminating, lurid things he kept? How much did you see?"

"Only the video of the girl in the mask. More than an hour of it."

"I saw only a few minutes."

"It wasn't a play. They raped her."

"God. He and Jamieson?"

"And Stephen Jensen."

"I didn't see him. Who was the girl? They didn't kill her, I hope."

"We don't know who she is. The mask stays on her the whole time."

"I'm glad they're dead."

Silence.

"Jensen's missing," I say. "We think it's the woman. Going after them one by one. She may have been the one who hacked your husband's computer."

"I'm sorry. I should have come forward immediately. I'm a lawyer. But I didn't know, and I didn't want that part of me out there. Naked in the shower. I used to check YouTube and a few of those amateur porn sites every day when I first moved here, to see if he posted it. He could be vindictive like that. But I guess he wanted it to go away too. He thought throwing it in the ocean would wipe it clean."

"Any idea who the woman might …"

"I have no idea who that woman was. I admire whoever she is if she's the one doing this. Don't be alarmed. There's no conspiracy. No assassin hired by me. But I'd like to talk to her about that night and what it did. We were compressed into the same folder, she and I."

Miranda's sobs grow louder. I can imagine her small, lean body shaking in her loft, tears on her pale face, standing at her window with her ginger hair and muslin shirt, looking into the street. I hang up and call Ortiz.

"We've got something," he says. "A jogger saw Jamieson's Rover pass him that morning. He says he saw someone sitting in the back—a woman, leaning in real close to the driver's head. He thought it was probably someone just giving directions to the driver. He didn't see a gun. The car went up Edgeware and he kept jogging down the hill. Didn't see where it went. I sent a couple cars up to prowl around Angelino Heights and Echo Park. Likely nothing, but you never know."

I fill him in on Kimmel, McKinley, and Miranda.

"Jesus, that poor ex-wife," he says. "Bad karma follows ex-wives. No shit. You ever notice? Gallagher really filmed her in the shower? Christ. Listen, though, you don't think she's an accomplice covering up?"

"She was too damaged. She just fled him. I need you to run a name for me. It's a hunch, but McKinley mentioned a woman architect he almost hired around the time he hired Jamieson."

"So?"

"Might be a lead."

"Name."

"Dylan Cross."

"Isn't Dylan a guy's name?"

"It goes both ways."

"Story of the world, huh? I'll run it and get back to you."

"McKinley told me where she worked. I'm heading over there now."

"Not a lot to go on. Does she have a connection to these guys?"

"Not that McKinley was aware of. Other than that, they're all architects. But we don't have anything else."

Ortiz sighs and hangs up. I slip into a small courtyard behind the Biltmore, near the library. I had never noticed it before, a little cove of light and shadows; the sounds of the city fall away. I walk past a fountain of goldfish and into the firm of John Hillerman. Small foyer and a few rooms in the Spanish style, mustard walls, exposed wood, soft yellow lights. The receptionist's desk is empty. A tall man with flowing blond hair, wearing jeans and a T-shirt, approaches. He moves like one of those British actors in a Merchant Ivory production—delicate with a bit of disheveled flair. He shakes my hand.

"John Hillerman. How may I help you?"

"I'm Detective Sam Carver."

A shade of worry passes over his face. "Is everything okay?"

"I'm looking for Dylan Cross."

I show him my shield.

"Dylan's out in the high desert for a couple of days. She has a project out there. Perhaps I could be of help. She and I have worked together for a long time. Is this serious? Has something happened to her?"

"Did she know Michael Gallagher and Paul Jamieson?"

Hillerman is startled. He waves me down the hall into his office.

"Please, sit," he says. "It's awful what's happened to them. It's on the TV all the time. It's shaken us all. The architect community is not that big. Do you have any leads? There's a lot of concern. People looking over their shoulders. I didn't know them very well. They were with bigger firms, as I'm sure you know. Gifted men, in their way. We never had any dealings with them. I saw them every now and then at industry functions."

"Did Dylan know them?"

"About the same as me, I guess. She never mentioned them. Of course, we talked about them when we saw what happened. It's made me sick. I tend to worry too much about things. Where society is headed. It can be very distressing. I'm sure I don't have to tell you."

I take out my notebook.

"Do you want me to call Dylan?"

He's dialing before I can answer. I can hear her phone ring, and an automated message voice.

"Dylan, it's John. Please call when you get this."

He looks at me.

"The signal's not always the best in the desert. Would you like her number?"

I tell him yes and jot it down.

"It's really nothing serious," I say. "We're just trying to talk to whoever might have known them. Matthew McKinley told me that years ago, he almost hired Dylan about the same time he hired Jamieson. Two young architects on the rise, and I thought, well, maybe they knew each other. Crossed paths."

"Yes, that's when I hired Dylan. She was talking to a number of firms back then. She's quite talented. Artistically she's impeccable. Her drawings are works of art in themselves. Would you like to see?"

He leads me into another office and turns on a desk lamp.

"This is hers," he says. "We're not a big firm. Just the two of us and a few assistants."

He turns on another lamp and unrolls a sketch. The lines are dark, fine, slender and arcing. It looks like a sketch an artist makes before she paints, or a sculptor's drawing of the form she sees within the marble. It's meticulous, mathematical, but there's a spirit in it, a beauty that doesn't conform to grids and numbers. It seems alive, fluid on the page as if mind and hand had summoned a miniature world, a place of escape. I could see myself walking through her rooms, standing at her windows. Hillerman is staring at me.

"You see it, don't you?" he says. "Not many architects can do that. It's for a library in Carmel. On the ocean. Imagine it in the mist and sun, taking in all hues of light. Transparency. Knowledge. See this," he says, moving a finger over the page. "A touch of the Greek, a faint allusion to the past. Where it all started, you know? The history of thought."

He steps back, blushing.

"I'm sorry. I tend to go on. I'm very fond of her. Not in the way you might think. I'm happily married. But Dylan and I are kindred spirits." He smooths the edge of the page. "It speaks to something inside, though. Don't you think?"

"A capacity to wonder."

"Exactly. Dylan sees things differently. Scales, dimensions. This is the best design she's done in years. She's been working furiously on it. To get it on paper so it wouldn't disappear. I asked her the other day where the inspiration came from, and she said, 'It is the calm in chaos.' She's been quite busy lately, and sometimes that kind of stress produces great work. She's always in the need to finish. My wife and I took her to dinner not long ago and told her she had to relax. She's been on edge. I'm sorry, Detective. I rave on. These days have been disconcerting, to say the least. Two dead men close to home."

"You said she's been on edge. What's been bothering her?"

"Dylan goes through periods from time to time, the way artists do."

"What kind of periods."

"Oh, you know, she's a perfectionist. Those kinds of periods."

He starts to say more but stops. I give the moment some air. We stand looking at the sketch, not saying anything. I don't ask about Jensen.

"Here's my card," I say. "If Dylan calls, have her phone me. I'll try her number later. Thank you."

I turn to leave and glimpse a picture on the desk. A close-up of a young woman hitting a two-handed backhand, the ball rising to the racket a split second before impact. Her arms are taut, long muscled, her lips pressed tight, eyes blue and fierce. Her skin is tanned, her black hair tied back. In that fury, though, as with all gifted athletes, is grace, the simplicity of movement. I wonder how the point ended. If she hit a winner. I think so. That's why she keeps the picture on her desk. It's who she wants to be—a captured moment of near perfection. The drawing of the library too. I pick up the photograph and hold it closer, studying the wild focus of the eyes, the shoulders, the lines of her body. I seem to know them.

"She was quite the player at Stanford," says Hillerman. "I think she still plays a little. We played once and, well, I don't think it was much fun for her, chasing my errant balls."

"Looks determined."

"Very."

I shake hands and say goodbye. The courtyard is filled with shadows, the last streams of light creeping up a brick wall. I step onto the sidewalk and head east, the picture still in my mind. An Escalade drops a family off at the Biltmore. Mother, father, two boys, hurrying toward the glass doors and into the lobby. The traffic light changes. Secretaries, accountants, and actuaries flee Bunker Hill. A bus rattles past, and to the west, the sky seeps with orange and distant purple. So pure, it looks fake. I take it in. Feel the dying warmth of the day on my face, the heat being drawn back to the ocean to turn into mist, linger a few seconds, and burn away. I call Ortiz.

"Hey, that woman you wanted checked, Dylan Cross. She lives up in Angelino Heights, off Edgeware."

Ortiz lets the sentence float.

"A bit of a coincidence," I say.

"Interesting, but that's all it is for now. You get anything from her?"

"She's out of town in the high desert. She's got a building

project out there. Her business partner, John Hillerman, didn't think she knew Gallagher or Jamieson. Not well, anyway."

"What about Jensen?"

"I didn't ask about him. No one except us and his wife knows he's disappeared. We should keep it that way."

"What are you thinking?"

"I've got a feeling," I say.

"Oh, shit."

"It could be her, Ortiz. She was coming up just as those guys were. Young, talented, good-looking, and a woman. Jamieson hated the idea of women architects. McKinley told me he never wanted one in their firm. Intense about it. Even more so with one who could have competed with him. That's motive. You following me? The woman in the mask is tall, in shape. Dylan Cross played tennis at Stanford. I saw a picture. An athlete's body. It could be her. Something about the girl in the mask and the girl playing tennis. They seem the same."

"'Seem.' That's a squishy word."

"I'm being honest. Plus, Hillerman said she's been edgy lately."

"Can't get a warrant with 'seems' and 'edgy.' You know what I mean? No judge is going for that. Hell, no. Can't take that to a judge, not even a sympathetic one—who, might I remind you, are getting scarce these days. Why do criminals have so many rights? You ever think about that?" He exhales and I can imagine him fidgeting with his mustache. "Take a run by her house. Knock. Nose around. Her car is registered as a midnight-blue Beemer. A few speeding tickets. No record."

I head along First, catching the back end of Disney Hall and down the hill and rising again. I cut over to Edgeware, slide over the 101, and climb into Angelino Heights. Barred windows, broken sidewalks, and couches on porches, until I get to the top, where the restored Victorians on Carroll Avenue float at the rim of the city. Dylan Cross' house is the third one in: honey colored with forest-green shutters, a turret, an arch of stained glass over the front door, a single rocker on the porch. A magnolia in the front yard. I park, walk up the steps, and knock. No answer. No lights. I peek in but can't see much: stairs, a hallway leading to the kitchen. I walk around back. A worn hammock, an untended garden, a shovel in the dirt, a pair of ripped work gloves. I bend and touch them, grab a handful of soil. Dry and cool. The air is fresh. I imagine her lolling in the hammock with pencil and sketchbook. An architect would like it up here, staring into the city, studying reflections, watching the light, thinking of the things she would build. No car in the driveway. The garage has no windows, no crack in the door. I can't see what's inside. I stand and listen to the end-of-the-day sounds and turn back to the house.

CHAPTER 23

Hello.

I'm up here.

Third floor, corner window. Peeking between shutter slats. I like you in my yard, Sam, doing your detective thing. What a prowler you are. There's nothing in the garage. I moved Jensen's Rover to a safe place. I don't like those things—too big and bulky for me. It'll never be found, though. You can talk to my neighbors, but they don't know much. I move at different hours. I'm a mystery in my neighborhood, I think. I'd love to knock on the window and wave and invite you in. I am too bold. But wouldn't that be something? We could play husband and wife, sitting in the kitchen, cutting vegetables, drinking wine, talking about work— little things that fill so much space over time. I could show you all I want to do with the house.

Would you like that, Sam? To know me? Not the me you came for. But the real me. I called John. He said you stopped by. I don't know where you got my name. I'm a bit angry about that, but it's not your fault. You're doing your job. It's changed the game, though. We were to meet as strangers in your Little Easy bar. I was to walk in and you'd buy me a drink, and then another. Lenny would tell us stories, and I would seduce you and walk you through the city night pointing out the architecture, frozen faces and gargoyles in the dark. I like you in my yard, Sam. Did I say that? I've been agitated, you know. So many things running together—the whole Jensen affair. The wimpiest of the three, but still a chore. A sad little broken man. John said you saw my library sketches. Aren't they lovely? It will be brilliant. It's been a long time since I designed anything like that. I'm getting back to myself, I guess—who I was before, you know. Maybe the doing away with them has brought me back, although I was here all along. Going through the motions, perhaps. No more than that. I can't explain. But I do feel the stirring of resurrection. A big word, I know. Some things are big. We can feel them. Like the city, I suppose. Ravaged things come back. How about that tennis picture? If you could have seen me then! So fast and strong. Oh, Sam, I could cover a court. I loved the singularity of it and of being alone between those painted lines, battling. I still play in Griffith Park. Not as much as I'd like to, though. I'd love to play tennis with you. Wouldn't that be normal, like couples do? What are you looking at down there? Studying my house. Thinking of me. On the video. In the picture. You have the face now, Sam. You know the face behind the mask. I am complete.

But where am I? The high desert? No. I'm here, Sam, but you can't see. You're moving now, through my grass. It needs to be cut; the boy comes next week. You're on the side of the house now, walking to the front. I'm racing across the hall to my bedroom window. Calm. I must be calm. Breathe. It's dark now. Night has fallen. I peek under a slat. You turn and give my house one last look. You walk to your car. Ragged old Porsche. It's you, Sam. That car is you. But still, fix the muffler. Jeez. Headlights on. Is that Sibelius I hear? Oh, I do love the symphony. It doesn't seem that long ago, the night Gallagher took his last breath—a slightly melodramatic way to put it, but hey, I was there. What a gasp, the final one. It was just a few hours after the concert at Disney Hall. Remember? Dudamel and Mahler. I walked past you and smelled your witch hazel and scotch. You were in your Macy's blazer, my little detective dressed up for the night with one of your four season tickets. You didn't see me. Just like now. That has to change, doesn't it? You have to see me. In the flesh. Soon. I'm reworking the plan. We will get together before I leave. I'm going on a trip. I feel I must, given the circumstances (ha-ha) I find myself in. I'm traveling to a place I've always wanted to go. Maybe I'll tell you about it, but if I do, you know what that means. The game is changing. Your pretty red taillights leave my street.

It's so quiet in my house.

CHAPTER 24

"How is she?"

"Good, Sam."

"Still drawing sparrows?"

"And waiting for your father."

"I miss you guys. Is it cold in Boston?"

"Not too. But your mother insists on wearing that thick sweater of hers."

"Is she eating?"

"About the same."

"How are you?"

"About the same."

"You sound tired, Maggie."

"I'm fine. I hate to see her mind go so. Lose a piece of her every day. A tiny thing we'll never get back. She keeps on about your father. I tell her he's dead; she won't believe it. A couple of days ago, I put her in the car and drove to Newport. To the cemetery. I showed her his grave. 'There he is,' I said. She knelt down and traced the letters. But on the way back, she leaned over to me and said, 'We better get home. He might be there.'"

"Should I come?" "You were just here."

I can imagine Maggie in the kitchen, sitting at the table, late, with a beer. My mother sleeping upstairs. Does she dream? I wonder. Do the demented dream?

"How's the case coming?" says Maggie.

"I think I've found her."

"The girl."

"The one in the mask."

"Oh, my. That poor soul. From what you told me—and I'm sure you didn't tell me all. What a thing to happen."

It's quiet in the Last Bookstore. I'm sitting in a worn chair in the memoir aisle. Blaze Foley is playing soft, a homeless guy is thumbing through a Johnny Cash biography, and two hipsters are kissing in the classics near bins of vinyl. The scents of old books and records, like deep inside a closet, take you back. I come here sometimes before I head to the Little Easy. To think. To let the day fall away while I read passages from favorite books: the last page of *The Great Gatsby*, the last two pages of Joyce's *The Dead*, poems by Neruda. I remember the first time I read them, place and time, the words inscribed on an invisible space inside me. I drift back and forth among pages and eras. I once spent three months reading only Jane Austen and the Brontë sisters—all three. Joan Didion and Charles Bukowski led me to the Los Angeles section, where naturally one encounters riffs on wildfires and the Santa Ana winds. Writers have a thing for the winds—their dry magic and how they blow across the land and incite the mind. Raymond Chandler did it best. I like the chair I'm in. It's ancient and soft, and I think I could sleep here with Cicero folded over my knee and Mary Shelley scrunched beside me.

"Is she the killer, the girl in the mask?"

"Don't know yet, Maggie. Circumstantial so far. You still reading that Hammett book?"

"No. I'm on to P. D. James. Devious little woman. What a plotter! Although it seems cleaner than what you do, real but not real. A romantic air to it. I'm sure it's not like that in real life. You sound tired, Sam. You need to rest. Whatever happened with that girl you liked, the reporter? Susan. Did she end up moving?"

"She's in Washington."

"You don't have the luck, do you, Sam?"

"One day."

"I'm sure. Well, I better go. I need to check on your mom one last time. It's after midnight here."

"Give her a kiss for me. I love you, Maggie."

"I love you too, Sam."

The bookstore is closing. No time for Winterson or a verse from Akhmatova, nothing to take into the dark. The late-nighters shuffle to the cashier with cheap books from the stacks upstairs. Blaze Foley is silent, lights are clicking off, the guy at the front who checks your bags yawns, and I wonder what this old bank building was like when the marquees shone over on Broadway and films were black-and-white and clever. I love classic movies. Not musicals so much, although I did have a thing for Cyd Charisse, who my father motioned to one night as we sat on our couch in Newport, both of us unable to sleep. My father, with a mischievous wink, looked to Cyd Charisse in the silver light as if to say, I love your mother, but *there* is a woman. Innocent in the way he did it, as if we'd both noticed the same splendid sunset.

My father knew a lot about movies. They gave him a place to put his restlessness; that's what my mother said. She'd start off watching with him but drift to bed around eleven, leaving him on the couch, whispers running through our house. I'd awaken many nights and think my father was conspiring with someone he dragged home from a tavern. But mostly it was Brando or Tracy or Frankenstein. I still remember the monster and the little girl and the flowers floating in the water, torches against castle walls. "You know, Sam," my father said one night, "the monster didn't ask to be brought into this world." He'd make eggs and bring the skillet into the living room, with two forks, a beer for him, and juice for me. I'd usually fall asleep on the couch, and in the morning, I would awake in my bed, thinking how magical that was. My father would be gone, out running and punching the air. "Training," my mother would say, and she and I would sit at the kitchen table and she'd ask what part of the movie I fell asleep at and then fill in the blanks. She would act out parts. She did a great Tippi Hedren in *The Birds*, a movie my father didn't like but tolerated because he admired Hitchcock overall. We'd go to theaters and see new movies, but I liked the old ones best, sitting in my house, my mother sleeping, the silhouette of my father, the night quiet all the way to the ocean.

I leave the Last Bookstore and walk across the street toward the winged-lion gargoyle standing stained and gritty above the Little Easy.

"There he is."

"Lenny."

"You've got that look, Sam."

"What look?"

"Your close-to-something look."

"What?"

"Kind of an aura. I can always tell when you're getting close."

"Scotch." I nod toward four men in zoot suits at the end of the bar.

"Who are they?"

"Another movie. Period piece." Lenny slides me the drink. "Seems like every night," he says, "they're filming a movie or series. Like Halloween, all these costumes. It's Netflix and Hulu. Streaming stuff, you know. You need a lot of content. It's a good moment for TV."

"Jesus, Lenny, you've been reading too much *Variety*."

"Fuck the trades. I'm just noticing things. You gotta be up on this stuff. Cultural shifts and all."

I sip. Lenny heads toward the zoot-suiters, wiping the bar along the way. I pull out my notebook and pencil. Images into words help me see. Her house, lawn, garden, hammock, windows. Stained glass and new paint on a quiet, tended street of wealth— not overbearing money, but the kind that allows indulgences and a bit of risk. It was fresh up there in the dusk: cool grass beneath my feet, the 101 hushed, the white stone of City Hall rising above Our Lady of Angels Cathedral and the federal buildings, which, when you slide down Temple Street toward Broadway, make you think of New York or Philadelphia. I write her name. Dylan Cross. Strong, a touch of the sacred, a boy's name but not entirely. Perhaps a family name or a sound pulled from a poem. "Do Not Go Gentle into That Good Night." I draw her mask. I stare into its blank, pale eyes. I'm not much of a sketcher. I don't try to draw her tennis picture, which floats with the mask, like tarot cards in my mind. Lenny's right. I'm close. She's smart, though. May have disappeared already. Talked to John Hillerman and vanished. If it is her. It must be. But there's no evidence linking her to either murder. No prints, no hair; only a filament of fiber, which, on the

Gallagher kill, is not surprising. Gloves and a mask, most likely. Quick and done. Jamieson took time. The makeup, bow, wine— the whole scene. She was in there a while. But forensics and the crime lab lifted nothing. The underpants she left were never worn. A tease. The surveillance video does not betray her, either. A shadow through the foyer and into the street. She upped it a tick with Jensen's kidnapping. I think she wanted him on her turf, a place she could control. Where? Would she have taken him into the high desert? I don't believe so. She's not working—at least, not on architecture. I close the notebook, set the pencil aside. I need a warrant to get into her house. I flag Lenny. Another pour.

"Got it figured out?"

"Maybe."

"Draining, huh? Fitting it all together."

"Yes."

"Someone's gotta do it."

Lenny smiles. Dusty Springfield is playing low, and the zoot-suit guys are practicing lines and holding fake guns.

"My mother's not doing well," I say. "Her mind's going."

"It's been a few years."

"It started slow, but not anymore."

"What are you going to do?"

"My aunt says she's okay taking care of her. It's getting to be too much, though. I can hear it in her voice. She never complains. Maggie's a strong woman."

"She loves her sister."

I shake my head and sip.

"Hey, Sam, you remember that guy who used to come in here with the trombone a while ago?"

"The little black guy."

"Yeah, the crazy one. Always wore a turtleneck. Big glasses, Afro."

"Hard to forget."

"He just made a record."

"No shit."

"He came in the other night. I almost called you. Had his horn and a woman with him. They had a few drinks and we're catching up, and he's telling me that for a long time he couldn't see himself in the world, where he belonged, why he mattered. Real existential shit. He's saying all this, and the woman's soft-kissing him on the ear, and he's kinda like pushing her away but gentle because he's really into what he's telling me. He said he thought he was nuts and couldn't figure it out and what to do with it. He lived on the streets for a while, then in a room at the Barclay. Shame what happened to that place. You ever see the tiles in there? Back in the day, that was the place to stay in LA. Now it's all low-income. Anyway, that's when he first started coming in here. One day, he said, he woke up and it was gone, like all the bad shit had cleared out. Hauled away in the night. He said he picked up his trombone and just started playing. Music was inside him. Just kept playing and writing thoughts down and somehow got it to a record company."

"He still have that Afro?"

"Looks the same. Little heavier, maybe. Better teeth."

Lenny pours, takes a small one for himself.

"You believe people can change like that, Sam?"

"Not often, but yes. When I was a kid, I thought my father might change. Wake up one day and be somebody else. The old self gone for a better self. You know? Sometimes, I thought I saw it, peeking through in the early mornings. There was peace in him then. He'd sit in the kitchen as the sun came through the window. He'd point himself toward it. Like a man thawing. It never lasted. My mother learned never to get too excited about those moments. They were tricks. She taught me to learn that too."

"Well, this trombone guy—Isaac Stapleton's his name—found something." Lenny wipes the bar. "He's going to play here next week."

"Here?"

"Nothing wrong with here," says Lenny, all of a sudden proud of the place. "Maybe you could sit in on piano. Hey, what happened with the blond you danced to Frank with? The reporter one? I liked her."

"Moved to Washington."

"You ever notice, Sam, how your timing sucks with women? What was her name?"

"Susan." I think of her, the way her hair fell down, like a curtain.

The zoot-suit guys are laughing and calling for Lenny to bring them another bottle.

"I'd hate to be on set with them tonight," Lenny says, walking toward them with a fifth of Jack.

The door opens, and a man hurries in wearing khakis and a frayed button-down that doesn't match his too-big muted-checkered blazer. His black hair is patted down and combed to the side. He slips his glasses into a pocket and tosses a folder on the counter. He's restless, looking around, heading toward me. He waves. Tommy Yan hops on the seat next to me. He takes in the place.

"There's a homeless guy pissing outside on the wall," he says. "Ortiz told me I'd find you here. Charming."

"Want a drink?"

"I gotta drive back to the Valley. Ah, what the hell, yeah. What are you drinking?"

"Scotch."

Lenny appears and pours.

"I've never seen you out of the crime lab before," I say. "I didn't recognize you without the white coat and tweezers. What's up, Tommy?"

"This Jamieson case. We've got nothing. Zilch. How could she have been in that apartment so long and left no trace. They always leave a trace. I sent a team back to scour it again. I keep studying surveillance video from Jamieson's building, and the rape tape. Nothing. I went through the Gallagher evidence too. Nothing. She's like air, man. Mist. All we have are the images. Nothing to stick a fork in. She's a ghost."

He takes off his blazer and drapes it over the chair. He sucks on a vape and says, "Ortiz says you may have something."

I look up and nod Lenny away. He walks slowly down the bar, hoping to catch a few words.

"Didn't figure you for a smoker," I say.

"Nerves," says Tommy.

I lean toward him.

"I think she's an architect. She's got an office over by the Biltmore. She's disappeared. Her boss says she's in the desert. We—I—think she's kidnapped the third man in the video. Stephen Jensen. He's missing. Last seen in a car getting off the 101. She lives up in Angelino Heights. I went up there, but it was quiet. No one around."

"Warrant?"

"Working on it."

Yan takes a long sip and catches himself in the mirror. He runs a hand through his hair.

"You can't blame her, can you?"

"What do you mean?"

"For taking some justice."

I feel the same way but don't say it. A cop should never say it. It's a line you don't cross.

"What's in the folder?"

"Stills I pulled from the video," says Tommy. "I'm going to go home and take a shower and then I'm going to put them under a light and a magnifying glass. Study every inch of her skin. There's got to be a mark, something, you know. We all have something. I didn't know what way to go with her. Thought she might be dead. Killed the night of the video. Now you say she could be the doer. Damn. Makes sense, though."

He pulls a picture from the folder and slides it toward me. The mask looks out, her skin frozen—a different sensation than in the video, as if the image were permanent like a statue or an icon on a church wall. The Venetian mask, the lighting, makes a strange art. I don't like thinking that, but there's a terrible beauty in it. Yan leans in and traces a pencil on the outline of her body, then the mask and the dark slits for eyes.

"The body," he says, "is like a country. We travel across it, we'll find something." He finishes his drink and slips the picture back into the folder. "I won't sleep tonight," he says. "Won't sleep until it's done." He puts on his blazer and stands to go. "What do men like us talk about, Carver? Away from work. I don't get out much."

"Married?"

"With three kids. It's work and home. I love my job, you

know, cases like this. I should get out more, though. Like now, having a drink in the night. Like this. Be somebody else. You ever want to do that? Be somebody else. Not forever. Just for a while. It's what we do, you know; it grinds. The mysteries and the solving. The bodies. Amazing what our species can do to a body. Am I right? I like the how. It's like a long equation. I was good in math. I'm empirically minded. My father was too."

"Some of the guys in the lab say you're anal with a short attention span."

"I've heard that. Not true. I just think faster than they do."

He laughs. His eyes drift to the zoot-suiters.

"Movie," I say.

"How'd you find this place?"

"I live around the corner."

"Why?"

"I like a city."

"LA's not a city. It's a collection of orphan neighborhoods."

"Downtown's a city. You don't think this is a city down here?"

"Maybe. But it feels more like a borderland. Not one thing or another. A kind of in-between place, half apocalypse, half unsure what it wants to be. I love the old theaters on Broadway, though. Makes you think of another time. But they ruined it."

"Haven't you heard about our Renaissance?"

"I see a lot of cranes. Lot of holes."

"There you go. A new Rome rising."

"Cut this man off," says Tommy, winking at Lenny.

"You live in the Valley."

"True. I shouldn't talk."

"It's dry out there."

"Bone."

We both go quiet and look into our glasses.

"If she's the doer, I hope you don't find her," says Yan.

"You're Mr. Airtight. Never lose a case. Always the best evidence. You'd be okay with one getting away?"

"Her, yes. Think I would."

He reaches into his pocket.

"I'll get this," I say.

"Thanks, Carver."

He's out the door, letting in cool air.

"Jumpy guy," says Lenny.

"Famous for it."

"Bet he's good, though, huh? Like a bird dog. You want another?"

"I better get home."

CHAPTER 25

I wait in darkness for the click.

How long have I been here?

An hour, maybe more. My legs are tired; the gun hangs heavy. I dare not move. This is not the way I had imagined things going, but circumstance has forced improvisation. How much longer? I look down the hall and out the windows. No one on the sidewalks, lights aglow in the jewelry district. So quiet. The city. This time of night. I feel the carpet beneath my feet, the pictures on the walls I know but cannot see in the dark: the monk, the weaver, the orange man with the big hands playing guitar under a Van Gogh moon. I was here not long ago, when Sam was in Boston. I walked through his rooms, sniffed his shaving cream, touched his razor, lay on his half-made bed, flipped through his magazines, ate a cookie, ran my fingers over his piano. I'm back.

I need to pee. But I dare not move. No. I wait. I wait for the click. I'm wearing my short black Herve and heels. I want him to know me in full. The length of me. A siren passes. Quiet. Note to self: my game is almost over. Gallagher, Jamieson, Jensen. All ended up as they should, and now it is only me, the final piece—and, of course, Sam. I am calling him Sam. He used to be "my detective," then "you," but now he's Sam. We have an intimacy. Not in the way most lovers do—ours is stronger, deeper, and we've never met. Ah, but the things between us! Not like some bored couple going to dinner and a movie, talking about the news, and pretending to give a damn about the new show at LACMA. No. Sam and I are far more interesting. We have this thing. I can't explain it, but it's in me like a soul. Not a separate soul floating inside us, but something more suffused, woven throughout and animating every speck and bone. I wait. How much longer? I didn't anticipate McKinley leading Sam to me. An unforeseen flaw in my plan, which makes me more alluring. A flaw offers entry. McKinley, I remember now, introduced me to Jamieson on that night way back when. I liked McKinley. He had a suave, disheveled charm. Old-school. He almost hired me. A lot of firms almost hired me then. A woman so close, so many times, but turned away. One has to wonder, how much longer? I don't want to keep chasing stray thoughts. The coral reefs are dying, new stars have been discovered, driverless cars are here, a Brahms symphony has been found beneath floorboards in Vienna, Chuck Berry has died, and …

Click.

Can it be? Is this happening?

Breathe. Turn. Gun up. Step. Barrel to head.

"Hi, Sam."

A pause, stillness.

"Dylan."

"Yes, Sam. It's me."

I take a step back.

"Don't move. No, no, Sam, don't turn. Hands up. Slow. Like the movies. Pretend like the movies. Good. Down the hall. Slow. Good. You're a little wobbly, Sam. You drink too much sometimes. Okay, good. Now sit. Sam, I will use this. Don't fuck around. I will kill you, Sam. I don't want to, but I will. Hands behind your back. I brought my own handcuffs. Might be a little tight. There. That's good. I hate to do this, but I have to. It shouldn't hurt too much."

Sam's out. I didn't want to hit him. But, again, circumstances. I was quite menacing. *Don't fuck around.* I scared myself with that one. I close the blinds, light a candle. I reach into my bag. Duct tape and a bandanna. I go to work, taping his legs and trunk to the chair. I unlock the cuffs and tape his arms to the arms of the chair. I tie the bandanna around his mouth. No, I won't need that. Sam won't yell. I wet a towel and pat the back of his head. A little blood. I struck him too hard. But the gash is not deep. He'll forgive me. I wet the towel again and pat his face. So close I am. So close I have wanted to be to this man. I kiss his forehead, kiss his still lips. Taste the scotch, run a hand through his hair, study his face, nose, brow, the way he comes together around the eyes, like a painting. I kneel in front of him. There's much to do. I light a cigarette, open a merlot I've brought, set out two glasses, and wait for him to wake. I flip through his vinyl collection and put on the Beatles' *White Album*, smoke another cigarette, dance with my wine to "Dear Prudence." The Beatles will go on forever, like Beethoven and the Pantheon. I haven't listened to them in years. My father was a big fan. The Beatles filled our house on weekend mornings while my mother brooded in some room and my father and I made plans over coffee and juice, the way normal people do. He's gone, my father. My last year at Stanford. Heart attack. A statistically normal death. But I loved him beyond numbers.

I have his ashes in my bag. I haven't been able to scatter them. How does one know the perfect place? I am an orphan and haven't learned such things. Sam's been out a while. I flip the LP. "Sexy Sadie." I keep it low. I peek out the blinds. Esmeralda. I see you in your tarps and rags, your suitcases stacked against the abandoned Hotel Clark, another century's architectural ghost. But once, Esmeralda, presidents slept there. It's what Sam sees when he looks down. You. This street. He should move out of the city. I don't think he will. He likes it here. I sit in his leather chair, the worn one. Here we are, Sam. Home. Like two lovers in the black of night, with your Afghan carpets and pictures of Sudan. Or is it South Sudan now? I read about it. Hacked limbs, women tied to trees, fires on grazing lands.

A breath.

"I didn't think you were in the high desert."

Ah, Sam's awake. His voice. As I expected. Deep, but not too. You could float on it. His eyes open and close. Focus.

"You were sleeping."

"My head hurts."

"Sorry about that."

He looks at my tape job.

"Is this necessary?"

"I thought you might go ballistic. A girl never knows." I wink at him. "But you expected me, didn't you? I can tell."

"I'm not surprised you're here. Now, cut me out of this so we can talk."

"Oh, Sam, you're so funny and cute. No."

I push the leather chair by the window toward him. An inlaid box, the kind you might buy in a souk, lies exposed on the floor. I know what it is. I've read about it in his diaries. It's his box of the dead's possessions. I look at it. He looks at me. I don't open it. I'll leave him those secrets. I place it on the table and nudge the chair closer to him and sit.

"I didn't want it to be this way. I wanted us to meet at the Little Easy. I had it all planned. I'd come in the hour before last call and sit two stools from you. I'd turn and say something clever and you'd laugh and I'd move closer and you'd buy me a drink and we'd talk to Lenny. I would have been wearing this." I stand and twirl in my black dress and heels. "We would have kissed. It would have been the best kiss. We would have finished our drinks and I would have walked you down Broadway—you know, before it was Broadway it was Eternity Street—and pointed out all the architecture. The little flourishes and hidden things people don't see when they rush past. I would have shown you what was in the architect's mind. You would have understood the city better. The beauty of details. We would have danced on the sidewalk, both a little drunk but not too, and you would have brought me back here and played me something on the piano, or you would have put on records and poured me wine. Like you did with her."

"Who?"

"Susan from the *Times*. Your little girlfriend. You really should watch who you fall for, Sam. She's not good for you."

"She's moved to Washington."

"I know. Thank God, right? I know everything about you, Sam."

"Omniscient."

"You have no idea."

"Have you been spying?"

I wink and step toward him.

"Have a sip of wine."

I lift the glass to his lips.

"Dylan Cross."

"Suspect?"

"A person of interest."

"You've been spying on me too," I say.

He's quite calm. Maybe it's the whiskey from earlier, or something they teach you in detective school when you're in a compromised position.

"I saw the tennis picture in your office. John showed me."

"My sport."

"You looked like you were good. It's the kind of picture people keep so they can remember."

"Remember what?"

"Those moments when we see our best self."

"Do you think that?"

"Yes."

"Where is your moment?"

"I'm still waiting for that picture to be taken."

Is he seducing me?

"Late bloomer," I say.

"Maybe."

"I could take one now."

"Please don't."

"I'm teasing, Sam. Don't be so serious. It's a trait of yours. I've noticed. When you get to know me better, you'll know when I'm teasing. I outgrew tennis, by the way."

"You have other hobbies."

"Ah, Sam. It's our first date. Don't go for the prize right away."

I give him another taste of wine. A sip of water.

"How did you get in?"

"When you visited your mother. How is she, anyway? It's hard when they live in that imaginary world, going bit by bit." I stop and look right into his eyes so he knows I care. "I met with an efficient, happy man in the leasing office downstairs. I told him I was looking for an apartment. He showed me a few. Let's not go into the whole leasing process thing, but I swiped one of the master keys. And, voilà, here I am. This was plan B. I told you I wanted to meet in the Little Easy. Circumstances, Sam. Circumstances."

"You're resourceful."

"Thank you."

"You hacked my laptop, didn't you? Like you did Gallagher's. That's how you know."

"You're quite the diarist, Sam. All those files. Particularly on your father. Your father is my mother. The ones we couldn't save. We thought we could. Children think a lot of things, don't they? One of your parents beaten to death. One of mine set the house on fire. She was nuts, my mother. All over the place. Bipolar and other things. There's never just one thing. My father called her 'the butterfly.' Perfect euphemism for a child to understand the crazy mind. She fluttered. I don't want to talk about her. She's gone. Your father's gone. Mine too. Your mother's going. Soon, it'll be just us. Or maybe just one of us."

That last sentence was maybe a little mean. But it is still a game. My game.

"So, we're alike?" he says.

"In some ways, very much. Do you feel violated?"

"Of course I feel violated. What do you think? I've been hit in the head and taped to a chair. My diary read."

"Yes. But I think I'm more of an expert on violation, wouldn't you say?"

He takes the bait.

"The vid—"

"Let's not go there yet. More wine? It's from a small vineyard outside Los Robles. I discovered it when I moved here. I liked Los Angeles right away. Did you? The theaters on Broadway. French baroque, Spanish Gothic, art deco. It's changing, though, isn't it? All the new buildings. The schizophrenic new mixed with the old ghosts. I wonder if they can pull it off. I have my doubts about men. They're mostly men, you know, with money and designs. All cities have ghosts, don't they Sam? But here they're scattered. I know by reading your files you like downtown. The ruin, the promise. That's sort of the story of you, Sam. Am I overstating? Being too melodramatic? All your little thoughts on neighborhoods and crime. You're an expert on ghosts. The bodies you've seen. All the trinkets you keep in that box." I turn and look to the box on the table. I guess I didn't leave him that secret after all. "But you like it still. That's what I admire about you, Sam: your capacity to adapt. Oh, yes. You believe in the world despite the things it gives you. Am I talking too much? I feel like I might be. I'm a little nervous. I have lived for this moment for so long."

"LA's home now."

"Yes, home." I cross my legs and smile. The wine is quite good. "Confession. I saw you on my lawn. I was on the third floor, peeking through a shutter. I pretended we were married and you had just gotten home from work and went to the backyard to see the day end, like you'd done a thousand times before. We had dinner and we danced. Just you and me in my big Victorian. Do you like what I've done with it? It's my labor of love, my endless weekend project, though I suppose it may be ending now, given, well, you know, what has … What's that word? *Transpired.*"

I shoot him a devil's grin. I rise and walk around him so he can see, take me in, wonder what it would be like to have me. To live in my house. I come up behind him and wrap my arms around his chest, kiss his neck, whisper in his ear.

"Welcome home, honey. Wouldn't that be something? I couldn't decide if we had children. I just saw us. What do you think?"

He looks at me. He has such tender, curious eyes. For a man who's seen so much, how can his eyes be so gentle? Not naive—no, Sam is not that—but knowing. I realized it from the moment I read about him in the story that bitch (Susan—she lingers, I can tell) wrote, and that picture of him near the Bradbury. I want to cut the tape away and dance with him, put on Coltrane and dance the way they did in those old movies he likes: round and round, slow. But I can't.

"You're crying," he says.

I reach up. I am. How unexpected.

"A little."

"I can't imagine," he says.

I wipe a tear away, sip my wine.

"What?"

"That night."

It's natural, of course, that he'd keep edging toward there. He's a detective.

"You saw," I say. "You know."

"I'm sorry."

I don't want his pity. Understanding, yes. But not pity. It cheapens me. You can't love someone you pity. It becomes something else. Silence. We look at one another for a long time. Killer and cop. That's what we are if anyone bursts in now. That's all we would leave the world. A story half told. But nobody's coming.

"Where's Jensen?"

"You know what was the hardest, Sam? The not knowing for so long. To have it inside, creeping around, whispering in my head, giving me this feeling of something. But I never knew. When I saw the video, I pretended it was someone else. But your own body, even in a mask, cannot deceive you. It was me. Not like the tennis picture. Not a beautiful moment, as you say. And they were out there, you know, having their lives and sketching their designs, talking their shit. They probably never thought about me. I disappeared into their files. A nothing along the way. I couldn't have that. Not once I knew. And so …"

"You acted."

"Yes. I like that. I acted."

"Gallagher."

He's clever, isn't he? Steering me with his short little sentences. He so much doesn't mind the empty space. Practically forces you to fill it. I'll indulge for a while.

"Easy. That's why he was first. A vile creature. You heard his laugh. That cackle. It was easy to end that sound. You found him. You know. I still remember the mint and gin on his breath after he came down from his whore. Smelled of a soap too. An after-the-fuck shower, I guess. Excuse my French." I stand and hold my arms out, shoulders back, the tautness of me, rising. "Look at me, Sam. That runt was no match. I surprised him. I'm not confessing, by the way. I'm just telling you what happened. Hypothetically."

I wink.

"Oh, Sam, don't you love this game?"

"It was a perfect cut."

"I practiced on meat. Rump roasts. Don't you love Ralphs? I like it better than Whole Foods. I'll bet you don't know this. I took martial arts classes in Westwood. You'd be surprised. A lot of rich women out there are super tough. I clung to Gallagher like a cat." I run a finger across my throat for dramatic effect. "Slice."

"Most people can practice it, play it in the mind, but not do it."

"There's nothing *most* about me, Sam. Please say you know that. You must at least know that. A little more wine. There, that's good. Let me cool your face. There."

I kiss him on the forehead. I am so bold. But I must be. Time is ticking. I step back and sit down.

"Jamieson."

"I was thinking theatrical. He loved opera, after all." Wink, wink. "I couldn't ambush him like puny Gallagher. He was big and in shape. Normally not a bad combination." I smile so Sam sees my humorous side. "He used an escort service, as you probably know. What is it about some men? Gallagher had a wife. Jamieson certainly didn't have to pay. I think it's naughtiness. I think some boys never grow out of their little-boy naughtiness. It perverts them. They like things hidden. Dangerous dirty, hidden things."

I lean back, go quiet, so we can ponder this. Sam says nothing.

"I hacked the escort service website. It's amazing how much hacking has been part of my game. Hypothetically, of course. I admit to nothing. If I did admit, well, I hacked him, intercepted his desire, and, presto, I am a hooker for the night. You know they charge *fifteen hundred dollars*? Before tip. You know the rub, though, right? I'm still me. He knows me. Well, we hadn't seen each other in years, and I never registered, anyway. Just flesh he once fucked. Pardon my expression. Jamieson makes me foulmouthed. I needed a disguise. I went shopping. It's quite devious to shop for killer clothes. Ha, ha. I am funny, Sam. I can be quite funny. Bought a blond wig, changed my skin hues, as they say at the makeup counter, to a lighter shade. A trans at Nordstrom's taught me how. I looked like me but not. Enough to trick him. You saw the surveillance video. Long, breezy coat. Fedora. I was quite the Ingrid Bergman." I sigh. He likes Bergman, but I don't mention his prepubescent celluloid crush. "Oh, Sam, do we have to keep talking about this? It's getting late."

"The surveillance video doesn't show what happened inside the apartment."

"You found him. I'm sure you can guess. Knife under the rib cage, up to the heart."

"The room had the feel of a ceremony. A ritual."

"Like the Mayans. Do you know Frank Lloyd Wright designed a house in Los Feliz that looks like a Mayan temple?"

"The blue bow, the mascara. Why was he naked? How did you do it? We know you shot him with a mix of ketamine and neuromuscular blockers. But when? How did you sneak up on him?"

"It's a delicate science, paralyzing someone. All those little molecules. I read for days. Billions of chemical compositions out there. Quite the questioner, aren't we, Sam?"

"My job."

"Of all the jobs in all the world, you had to pick that one …"

He gets the allusion. Touché for me.

I walk to a window, open the blinds a peek, and stand over the street, like … maybe an angel. Yes, an angel in a black dress, looking down. I know Sam's watching me. His eyes over me, legs, back, shoulders, the way my hair falls, shines. I am tall, and men have to take me in parts, in pieces. Like a slender building rising unexpectedly on a street. I see it in their eyes, the way they look at me. Sam too. But not like the others.

"How long have you known her?" I say.

"Who?"

"Esmeralda."

"She's there?"

"Same spot."

"She's getting weaker. She can't pull all her bags and things like she used to. I've known her for five years. I bring her tea and scotch. A five or a ten every now and then."

"She'll die. Right there, probably. Under her tarps."

"She's resilient. Must be close to seventy. Maybe younger. Her skin is so weathered, it's hard to tell. She keeps asking me why people want to put her in a shelter. Walls frighten her. She told me once that being inside was like being buried. She thinks there's monsters in this building."

I turn and give Sam a wink. I mean, how could I resist?

"Psychotic?"

"Sometimes, two or three voices inside. All yelling to be heard."

Voices. Whispers. Voices. And back again.

"What do they do with them when they die?"

"There's a cemetery outside town."

"Have you been?"

"Yes."

"Of course you have."

I turn from the window and sit down, reach into my bag for another cigarette.

"It's a smoke-free building."

"Arrest me."

The smoke—I love how it fills me. He strains at his tape, stills.

"Jamieson wasn't so hard. He didn't recognize me. I thought for a second he might have. He'd been drinking—not a lot, but he was relaxed. Didn't your toxicology find a bit of Valium? He opened a bottle of wine. We talked for a while. Such a braggart. About the city, the buildings he imagined. So pretentious. He said, 'I have buildings inside me.' What an ass. I must admit, though, he was a good architect. He was, Sam. He had art inside him. More than Gallagher and Jensen. He and I would have been a good team, architecturally speaking. He would have drawn out my sparser tendencies. I would have reined in his romanticism. I've always been good at understanding the strengths of my enemy. Tennis, I guess." I lean forward and brush the hair from Sam's forehead. "We drank, and he asked me to dance. Slow. To dance and strip. He undressed and sat in the chair. I sat in his lap and kissed him, tasting his wine. His skin so warm. He was a handsome man, as you've seen. I let him believe that, the way working girls do. I started dancing around him. Someone was singing arias. He closed his eyes and listened, kept telling me to dance. I had spiked his wine, so he was pretty numb by then. Words all slurry. My bag was behind his chair. I pulled the needle from it and jabbed it right to the neck. He slapped his skin like swatting a bee. He didn't know what it was. He was confused. He turned and tried to get up. But …"

A long drag. A sip of wine.

"I did my little makeup job on him. The bow, I got from Nordstrom's one day. Just walking through the aisle, it caught my eye."

"You wanted to humiliate him."

"Before I pushed the knife in—hypothetically, of course—I told him who I was. What he had done to me. I pulled off my wig. That woke him up. Recognition came over his face. Then I put on the mask. It was shattering. It shattered him, Sam. He saw the knife. Couldn't move. I let him think about it. We listened to arias. They went quiet after a while. His blurry eyes got terrified. It was strange. They were the only thing of him that moved, as if all his energy were in his eyes. They were wild. Like a horse's eyes in a stable fire. I worried the drugs might wear off. But he still couldn't move. I told him he would never build the buildings inside him. I laughed. A witch's laugh. I told him he would be forgotten before he was known. I sat back and watched the blood come."

"The finger?"

"I still can't figure that. Oh, dear, Sam. Sometimes, we just do things."

I stub out the cigarette and light another.

"I bet you don't know this, my inquisitive little detective. I taped it. Well, I pretended to. I held my cell phone up to Jamieson and started filming. He thought I was, anyway. He so much wanted to squirm. To hide his nakedness. I whispered to him, 'How does it feel?'"

"How did it feel?"

"Righteous. Like an evangelical. Power. The power to take. I saw the world like an animal. A lioness on the savanna. Is that too rich? It was that real, though. Instinctive. My heart beat so fast while he was dying. My mind raced. As I pushed the knife in—and I pushed it in ever so slowly—a calmness came. A serenity almost. I felt him leave this world. Not a gasp, really, the final breath. More like a soft whoosh. So much had gone into it, you know. The planning. Like the stuff you do for a party. You want it to be perfect. Ah. I see you disapprove. Don't look at me like that, Sam. Like I'm crazy. I'm not crazy." The smoke fills me; I exhale. We sit for a minute in silence. "I'm sorry. I shouldn't have yelled. But I was clearheaded. No doubts in what I did. No crazy lady's dream."

"And now?"

"I'm here with you."

"Why me? Like this?"

"Surely, you must know, Sam. I love you. There, I said it. Am I blushing? I feel I am. It just came out." I stare into him. "'Love' is maybe too strong. We just met. But I know you. I read everything on your laptop. I saw into you. Every crevice. That can be done. Even between strangers. But you are not a stranger. I suppose I am one to you, but not really, right? You have been after me. I know what you wrote after you saw the video. You said there was a grace—Was it grace or beauty? I don't remember—in me that they couldn't take away. Did you believe that, or was that what you hoped? There was something else too, wasn't there? You had lust, Sam. Deep down. A helpless woman naked. A rape. That's primal. The dark, deep place. It's natural. Your lust was fleeting, though. You were ashamed of it. That's what you wrote. But it was unconscious, Sam, that reaction. You pushed it aside and wanted to do good instead. That is what makes you, Sam. The need for good. You didn't see my face, but you saw something, something inside. My spirit. You saw it. Like you saw your father's. I know you were a boy then, but the way you wrote about him years later. A flawed, wild, beaten, broken man. Your father. You saw a beauty in him too, Sam. It is your nature. I believe this."

I stand, put his face in my hands, and kiss his forehead. I am crying tears stored for years. For this moment. My strange confession to murder and love. An ideal, maybe. Yes, perhaps Sam is just an ideal, a cop I once read about in a newspaper, his picture in front of the Bradbury Building. His eyes. A girl's infatuation. No. It is more. Way more.

"How can you pretend to know me?"

Ouch. I don't pretend. Does he think I pretend?

"Let me go," he says. "You're breaking. All your tough words about Gallagher and Jamieson—they're not you. They're part of this thing you created, but not really you. Let me go. It's gone too far, Dylan."

"You said, 'pretend to know me.' I do know you, Sam. Don't be difficult. I understand you might feel robbed of your secrets. But you know what? I still love you. Yes. Why not? I have no tough words for you. I see you in full. How often do we get that? To be seen as everything we are, and still be wanted. The dark and the light. Husbands and wives don't have that. Children and mothers don't have that. But we do. I had to tape you to the chair. I didn't want to. I told you, circumstance. Now you're mad at me. But you're no good mad. It's not you. I can be mad. I'm quite good at it. But not you. Talk to me."

"What do you expect me to say?"

"Use some of your cop psychology—you know, getting into the killer's mind."

"Into your mind?"

"Yes, the water's fine." I laugh. "My mother used to say that from the shore on summer days. 'Go on in, Dylan, the water's fine.'"

He almost smiles. I think. No. Maybe, I'm pretending.

"You wanted revenge," he says. "You took it. You killed three people. Very clever, Dylan."

Ooh, the way he says my name. A bit of annoyance in his voice. But still … the tingle.

"I understand why you did what you did," he says. "What they did to you. But you let them win. They won't design or build anymore. They took from you and you took from them. It took years, but you did it. Your rage became a colder thing. I've seen it with others, Dylan. You didn't know where to go. Who to tell.

Where to put the shame. I get that. No one can pretend to know what you felt. I've tried since I saw the video, but I can't. I hated them too. Their conceits. What I found out about them." He stops talking. He looks around the room. The bookcase, the record player that long ago went silent. The pictures, the rugs. His eyes find me again. They hold me, like hands. "You won't design anymore, either, Dylan. Your church in the desert and a few other buildings are all you'll have. Nothing splendid out there." He nods toward the window. "Where do you have to go now? It's done. Cut me loose and we'll talk some more. I'll make coffee. It's almost dawn."

I step to the window. He's right. The night is leaving the sky.

"What would you have done, Sam?"

"You're crying again."

"What would you have done?"

I'm tired. I hear the cracks in my voice. But so much to do.

"I don't know," he says. "You could have gone to the police. You could have come to me. But it's over now."

"No, Sam, it's not. The police? Please. Can't you just hear them? So, you're just finding this video now. Hmmm. How did you get it? Why didn't you report it right after that night? Drugged? You must have felt something had happened. So much time has passed. What were you doing in a house with three men drinking? Is it really you behind that mask? More degradation. My career. It was my drawings and designs that saved me. I drew places I wanted to go. To vanish in. No, Sam, I played the cop scenario out. Trials never end well in cases like mine. You know that. So don't give me that shit about justice and going to the police. Don't belittle it."

I stand and walk around him. Let him think. I reach into my bag and pull out the mask. I sit back in front of him and put it on.

"What do you think? Isn't she lovely? She's my little hiding place. Her expression never changes. So inscrutable she is. I think she has the face of eternity, don't you? A sly knowingness that the ages will pass and all will come to be. She's watching you, indifferent to what happens to you. It's all the same to her. I've become quite intimate with her. We have an understanding. She's my confidante."

"Dylan, you need to …"

"Don't patronize me. You don't know. You know nothing. I thought you did. I thought you would be my confidant too. But no, not Sam. Not Mr. By-the-Book Detective. But look at her, Sam. So old. From Venice. But she looks new. She is a survivor."

"I want to—"

"No."

"Do you know why?"

"Why what?"

"Why they did it."

"Is this finally a bit of detective psychology? Why they did it? They hated the idea of women architects. I know this. They wanted a fuck. They had mommy-complex issues. Poorly potty trained. We could go on and on."

"Jamieson thought women architects were beneath him. That women lacked the art and pragmatism needed. Or some crap like that. He kept quiet about it except to certain people. McKinley told me. The old man. He was going to hire you. McKinley loved your drawings. He thought you had great promise. His exact words. But Jamieson told him no. McKinley didn't resist. He regrets that. I could tell. Did you know anything about this?"

I step toward Sam. I stand for a moment. I push up my mask. Straddle him. We sit face-to-face, nose touching nose. I breathe in the hours of him: wine, whiskey, sweat, but still sweet. I kiss him. A slight reply. Or am I pretending? I am crying. My tears on both our faces. I want to be held. Just for a moment. To feel him around me. I cannot cut him free. No. I know that now. Perhaps one day. Maybe on Eternity Street. Isn't that funny? Broadway was once Eternity. I hold him, whisper in his ear.

"Yes, Sam, I knew that. I'm omniscient, after all. It's to be expected, though, don't you think?"

That's all I'll give him. A few lines of response. Why say more? Why fake surprise? Isn't history full of Jamiesons?

I stand and step back. The gray-speckled light of dawn is entering. The room sharpens. I put my mask in the bag, zip it shut. Sam watches. I wet the towel under the faucet and cool his head. There, there. We should have met another way, years ago, before all this. I would have liked that. I straighten my dress, pick up my bag.

"I'm going now, Sam."

"Let's talk some more."

"I'm tired of talking."

"Where are you going?"

"Oh, Sam, please. You are funny."

"Let me go."

"Someone will come."

"I'll find you."

"Says the man taped to a chair. I don't think you will. Maybe you'll get lucky, though. If it makes you feel better, tell me I'm under arrest."

"Where's Jensen?"

"Oh, yes, Jensen. Almost forgot about him. Easily forgettable type. A moth of a man. A real weeper." I sigh for effect. "He's in my basement. He's starting to ripen."

Sam's eyes, for the first time, show disappointment.

"You thought he was innocent?" I say.

"No, but he's not like the other two."

He nods to the water; I give him a sip.

"All that work on your house and you can't go back to it," he says.

"I'm on the lam, Sam. That rhymes." I laugh. "You should live in it. Wouldn't that be something?"

I walk to the table and put my key and tennis picture on his inlaid box for the dead. I gaze at him one more time. He looks at me. For the briefest moment, we are one. I pass him and brush my hand across his cheek. So many lives we could have led; so many truths that now slip past, unknown. I turn and step back and lean down and kiss him, pressing hard but then softening, no space between us, just a breath. He lets me hang there before him, our lips still but touching the way I had imagined. Why can't I have this man? I rise and walk down the hall on his long Afghan carpet, past the picture of the monk, resolute and serene in a faraway place. I would have loved to live in this apartment, sitting by the window with him, watching the city change, whispering to him about shape and form and how buildings have souls. He would have learned. He would have understood. I breathe. The door clicks. Cool air whirls in. A new day has begun.

"Bye, Sam."

CHAPTER 26

I wrap my mother tight in her scarf. She is balanced between Maggie and me, pointing to the mansions on the cliff, trying to make her mind remember what it was like in those days with the man she loved. It's cold. Winds are blowing off the ocean, and the weather lady says it will snow in the inlands beyond Newport. We came to visit my father's grave. My mother still insists she sees him, walking down the street, a face in the window, a man on church steps. Maggie and I put her in the car and drove up from Boston this morning. I haven't been here in years, and like my mother, I think I see him, punching the air, running in the mist. No. They are memories, and memories are ghosts. The ocean hits the rocks, and the spray rises toward a gray sky.

"Let's go swimming," my mother says.

"I think it's too cold."

"No. It's summer."

"It's not summer, Mom. You have a coat on."

"Someone put this thing on me. It's summer. Where's my

bathing suit? He's down there on the beach. He's waiting for me. We have picnics."

"He's not there."

"I think he is."

"Let's turn around," says Maggie. "It looks like rain."

"It rains in summer," says my mother. She looks at Maggie and lowers her voice. "Do you think this man with us will take us down to the beach?"

"That's Sam, your son. He lives in Los Angeles."

She looks at me. Steps closer. Puts a gloved hand on my face.

"Is it summer there?" she says.

The rain comes hard. We drive back to Boston. My mother sleeps the whole way. Maggie and I talk and listen to Simon and Garfunkel and Aretha Franklin. Maggie thinks it's funny that I like the same music as she. "You always were an old soul," she says, singing "Scarborough Fair" and wiping fog from the windshield. We eat sandwiches and soup for dinner in Maggie's kitchen. The radio plays low. We walk my mother upstairs to her bedroom. She sits by the window; her reflection floats in the night. She stands and presses her face against the glass.

"Maybe he'll come tomorrow."

"Let's get you to bed," says Maggie.

My mother slides like a small curled bird beneath the covers. I kiss her on the forehead and remember the scent of lemons. When I was a child, she would cut them in half and rub them over her face. She said it made her skin soft and cleaned better than soap. Our house was full of lemons, and my father used to joke that we lived in a garden. My mother looks at me, and for a second, I think she knows me. It passes, and she turns toward the window and the rooftops beyond.

"We're losing her, aren't we, Maggie?"

"Yes. It's good you took some time off and came back."

"She doesn't know who I am."

"She might remember. I show her your picture every day and tell her."

Maggie slides two glasses across the table, pulls two beers from the fridge.

"I like your kitchen," I say.

"It's getting a little shabby, but it has a character. It's my room, you know that."

We sip our beers and listen to the wind and the rain falling in the alley.

"Where do you suppose she vanished to, Sam?"

"Mom?"

"No. Dylan Cross."

"I don't know. No trace."

"She's smart."

"Very."

Maggie fidgets with a bottle cap.

"I know I shouldn't say this, and don't get mad, but I'm glad she got away."

She looks at me. I pour the last of my bottle into the glass. I sip and say nothing.

"Why do you think she let Jensen live?"

"He wasn't like the other two," I say. "He was weaker. That night destroyed a lot of him. She saw that. When we went down into the basement, he was sitting chained to the wall. Unshaven, dirty. He looked like a prisoner in an old Communist country. The knife she killed Jamieson with was lying just beyond his reach. He said she came at him with it. She flashed it in his face. He said he closed his eyes. He thought he was going to die. He felt the blade on his neck. He didn't fight or strain. He said he waited. For a long while, it was there. He could hear her breathing. He thought she whispered something, but couldn't make out what it was. He felt the blade lift away, and he opened his eyes. She was standing over him. She dropped the knife and stepped back. He said she stood there in her mask for what seemed an hour. Motionless. Staring at him. He told me, 'She didn't want me to forget. But I never did. I see that mask every day.' He said he wanted to be arrested for that night. He looked right at me and said, 'Detective, I want some record of guilt beyond my own.'"

"You didn't arrest him."

"We might later. We have no victim. Three men on a tape, and an unknown woman."

"It was a rape. You know who the woman is."

"We don't have her. We have no case."

"Did you believe what Jensen told you, about wanting to be arrested?"

"Yes."

"It doesn't absolve him, Sam."

"No, it doesn't. But it would free him. I've seen it with others. They end up not being able to live with it. Remember the case I told you about years ago. The guy who killed his family. We knew he did it, but we couldn't prove it. Couldn't get enough evidence. He went on with his life. Lived alone, went to work, bought new furniture, started dating. Then one day, I'm sitting at a coffee shop downtown and he comes in, sits beside me, and confesses. Just like that."

"I'd like to know Dylan Cross' mind. I went online and saw that church she designed in the desert. It's so elegant and simple.

If you were passing, you'd have to stop and look inside. Maybe she's somewhere in the desert, Sam, thinking of another building."

"You should be a detective, Maggie."

She laughs.

"I might have liked that in another life."

She gets up and puts two more beers on the table.

"I thought you stopped at one," I say.

"It's a special night."

The lamp glows. The rain is still falling. The kitchen is clean but old. It holds parts of my childhood: the pantry, the curved silver faucet, the crucifix above the sink.

"Tell me one thing, Sam. When you talk about her, she's different from anyone else. It's in your voice."

"She got away. She's unsolved."

"Yes, but something more. I hear it in you."

"I'll find her."

"What will you say to her?"

We drink our beers. A long quiet passes.

"Okay, Sam, I won't talk about it anymore."

"I'll catch her."

"I hope so, but then I hope not."

Maggie looks into her glass.

"She's beautiful," she says.

"Yes, she is."

Maggie gets up and goes to a drawer. She holds up a Baggie and smiles.

"Let's get high."

"I'll arrest you."

"Out of your jurisdiction, Detective."

"I thought you quit."

"Some things from the old days stay with you."

She opens the back door to the small porch facing the alley. We step out. Rain is falling, but not as hard as before. Maggie lights up. We pass the joint back and forth. We laugh. I tell her about Ortiz, how jumpy and frenetic he is. His endless phone calls and texts and worries about the mayor. I show her a text: "What the fuck, Sam? Vacation? We gotta find her. Can't have some broad with a mask running around loose killing architects." Followed by, "No. Stay on vacay. You need a break. But if we get a tip on her, your ass is on the next flight back." Maggie likes stories about Ortiz. She believes he's a good man and that he understands me. Maggie never liked my father, but she has a favorite story about him.

Late one night, after he won a fight, she thinks it was in Providence, he and my mother—it was before I was born—came up this same alley while Maggie was sitting on the porch. It was summer, getting close to autumn, and the air was cool. She heard them laughing, and when they got to the porch, she saw that my father was carrying a crate of Chinese takeout. "We ordered the whole goddamn menu, Maggie," he said. "We didn't know what you'd be in the mood for." They came inside and unloaded the crate on the table—boxes and boxes of food, like a banquet. Maggie thought it was frivolous and wonderful, and she looked at my father, who was excited and drinking a beer. She studied his bruises, cut eyes, and swollen hands, and she believed, for a moment, that he was magnificent.

Maggie goes quiet. Me too. When the joint's done, she tamps it out, squeezes my hand, and kisses me on the cheek. "Good night, Sam." She opens the door and disappears into the house.

I sit alone on the porch, listening to the rain and not minding the cold. After an hour or so, I go inside and lock up, shut the lights off, and walk upstairs. I peek into my mother's room, trace her outlines in the dark, and think of her as Maggie saw her on that night with the Chinese food and the fighter she loved. What must it all have seemed to my mother then? The rough man and his hidden tenderness and the way his voice echoed down the alley. His strength and unpredictability. The way he bled. I close her door and go down the hall to my room. It's almost dawn. I climb into bed and see Dylan Cross, like Maggie said, sitting in her church in the high desert, candles all around, her mask beside her on the pew, a man singing hymns.

CHAPTER 27

Impressive firewall, Sam.

It took me an extra thirty seconds to get in.

You're not writing as much, my little diarist. I understand, but I hope you get back to it. It's how I know you. It's important that you write. I've been following our story in the *Times*. Jensen unchained. Killer vanished. My house looks great on YouTube; so does my church in the desert. So many architects talking about me as if they knew me. Poor McKinley. Such a sad old man. I feel worse for John and Isabella having so many questions thrown at them. I've told them not to worry, that it will end soon. People get bored and move on. It's amazing, though, isn't it? The story of me told by everyone except me. I guess I've become a cutout to fill in and color. My own little noir shadow. No, that's not true. I am more than that. You know that, don't you? You would like where I'm living now. I meditate every day. I draw.

You said I would never have buildings again. I think you were angry; you didn't mean that. I will have buildings, Sam.

Somewhere. The world is vast and hard. It needs pretty things. I was thinking of the La Brea Tar Pits off Wilshire the other day. Millions of years old and holding the bones of animals we never knew, extinct long before a building, spire, cathedral, museum, prison was ever imagined. But they came, didn't they, Sam? The things we build, the things that say this is who we are, the bones, glass, and stone of our imagination. Our angles and arches, the way we reach into the sky. My pencil moves, and white space becomes a dream. Maybe not in Los Angeles, but someplace new.

I suppose I'll be a nomad for a while. A butterfly. Like my mother, fluttering about. I thought of her the other night, standing in her nightgown and twirling sparklers in the air. It must have been the Fourth of July. Of course, with my mother, it could have been any night. It's funny what comes to you. The thoughts, I mean, spilling out and staying alive. Even the uninvited ones. Hushed voices from the deep. The air is clear here. I've found a good, small place with a garden and a view and a table outside under the eaves, where I eat dinner and drink wine in the dusk. You would like it. There are ruins in a nearby village. I go and listen to the stones. They speak of ancient architects, and when the light dims, their warmth recedes deep into their cores. Stones have souls. I believe this.

I was out walking the other day and passed a tennis court. Two boys were playing. One of them—I don't know why—handed me his racket. I felt the grip, the weight of it, like a wing. The ball came, and, Sam, I was that girl in the picture again. The one you like so much, the one I left you. You're right about that: there are moments we carry that stay the best of us. If only we had more of them. Why can't we have more? I deleted the video. I hope you will too, but I know you can't. Open case, right? Evidence, and all that. But remember me most as the girl in the tennis picture.

That's who I am, Sam. The real me. Not this thing they created. I've come to believe certain things about what happened. What I wanted from it all. Or what I thought I did. Hypothetically, of course. This is no confession.

I touched vengeance, Sam. I felt hate. Let it melt through me. It felt good, I must say. But it didn't last. It did not bind the broken place, soothe the violated flesh. I carry it still—not vengeance, but memory. Of what was done to me. I have learned. We are supposed to learn from experience, become wiser. Vengeance does not heal. It leaves a hole. I am happy Gallagher and Jamieson are dead, but that is part of the hole—a happiness that, when I think of it, is not happiness at all, but loss. Their loss. My loss. Nobody won. The moment the mask went on, there were no winners. I don't know that I would do it again, but there was a reclaiming of self—perhaps a different self, but still, that's something. A small victory. I don't think the self before ever comes back. It is an angel on a distant rooftop, looking down. This is what I believe. She doesn't fly closer; she doesn't fly away. She is there until we are no more. I forgave, though, didn't I? Pathetic Jensen lives. I couldn't do it. Couldn't kill him. It ruined him too, in a way. That night. He is not the victim. No. That is my sole right. But I spared him. Somewhere in me, there is compassion. I like to think that. Makes me no saint, I know. But it is something. I am killer. I am redeemer. I wish I could draw all this in a building. Make people see all these things I feel, unexplainable but real. Inside me. Inside us. That would be some building. A renaissance. I will try. I am gone now, Sam. Gone like the air, a speck of dream. Maybe, just maybe, one day you'll come find me.

ACKNOWLEDGMENTS

I'm often struck by how people have come into my life, some many years ago, others newly arrived. They have shaped the stories I tell. This book is a culmination of those voices. I am indebted to Lindsay Maracotta for her wisdom in seeing things that needed to be pointed out. I thank my agent Jill Marr at the Sandra Dijkstra Literary Agency, my editor Michael Carr, and everyone at Blackstone Publishing. Special thanks to architects Miriam Mulder and John Rock who offered invaluable insights into their world.

I am fortunate for the writers, reporters, editors, and friends who, in their inimitable ways, have left a mark: Tom Lowry, Bianca Lopez, Amy Kaufman, Daniel Miller, Rich Nordwind, Tom Hundley, David Lynch, Scott Higham, Peter Finn, Karl Stark, Jonathan Neumann, Dan Reichl, Barbara Demick, David Erdman, Tim Darragh, C. J. Chivers, Scott Kraft, David Zucchino, Raja Abdulrahim, Rami Khouri, Bob Williams, Randi Danforth, Matt Bose, Louise Steinman, Smitty, and the Slattery and Aigner families.

I am grateful for my parents, and my brothers and their spouses, David, Avi, Greg, Michelle, Peter, Jo-Ann, Mark, Eve, and my sister, Lisa. I am thankful for my children, Aaron and Hannah, enduring sources of wonder and pride. And for my wife, Clare, whose quiet grace is stronger than anything I know.